WHO IS SHE?

Ben Cheetham

Visit the author's website at www.bencheetham.com

Printed in the United Kingdom

First Printing: Sept 2018

ISBN-13 978-1-7238039-0-1

Chapter 1

Her eyes popped open like someone surfacing from the worst nightmare of their life. A thousand bells seemed to be clanging in her ears. There was something in her mouth. A tasteless, gritty substance coated her tongue and clogged her throat. She spat it out and sucked in huge, ragged gasps of air. Her vision wobbled into focus. Shreds of pale light glimmered through a shivering canopy of darkness. Moonlight? Her fingers clutched spasmodically at something damp and cloying. Soil? Where was she? How did she get here? There was a strange, terrible smell. Both sweet and bitter. Like burnt meat. Oh shit, oh shit. What was going on? Why did her head feel as if it was made of cement? There was no pain, but her senses screamed that something was very, very wrong. Was she hurt? Was she dying?

She squinted as a bright light flashed into her eyes. Flames? Had she been in some kind of accident? She tried to cry for help, but somewhere between her brain and mouth the words were scrambled into, "Heeefff gggppt!"

The light swept over her body. Her gaze automatically followed it, taking in a filthy multicoloured blouse and slender hands that looked as if they'd been scrabbling at dirt. The dome of a potbelly hid her legs. The light strayed to one side, picking out the angles of a deep, rectangular hole. Twisting roots protruded through the hole's walls. Its rim was fringed with grass, yellow-brown leaves and piles of what looked to be freshly dug soil. A word went off like an alarm in her bewildered brain – *Grave!*

What if it wasn't an accident? What if someone had deliberately hurt her? What if they were about to bury her? Another word came at her, thundering over and over – *No! No! No!* It gave her the strength to turn her head, look beyond the light and try to identify its source. She made out a hand holding a torch. The hand was dirty like hers, but with fingers as thick as Cumberland sausages. It appeared to be attached to a human shaped bush.

She blinked. Her vision cleared a little more. The thing wasn't a walking bush. It was a bulky figure draped in camouflage netting, their face lost within a deep hood. She opened her mouth. *Who are you? What have you done to me?* Her short-circuited brain translated the questions into, "Wwwfffll ffgggoo? Wwgg yyyyeee?"

The figure stood as motionless as the surrounding trees. What was their game? Were they waiting for her to die? Again that word boomed in her head – *No*! She wasn't going to lie there and die like a wounded dumb animal.

Move, she silently yelled at herself. *Move!* She focused all her strength, all her will, all her fear on obeying. Tremors ran through her, building like steam in a kettle. She planted her palms against the earth and pushed. A pair of heavy-duty black boots came into view beyond her potbelly. Bare skinny legs criss-crossed with scratches. Thighs caked with gluey-looking soil.

Move, move...

Shaking all over, she fought her way to her feet. There was an itch between her thighs. She half-expected the camouflaged figure to pounce on her and wrestle her back to the ground. It wouldn't have taken much effort. She felt as if the slightest breeze would knock her off her feet. But the only movement the figure made was to direct the torch at her feet like a spotlight on a stage. Did the bastard want her to dance? Well they would be waiting a long time!

Keep moving.

She turned away from the figure, reeled forwards a few steps, stumbled to her knees. The ground seemed to be rocking like a boat in a stormy sea. She used a tree trunk to drag herself back to her feet. The itch between her thighs was intensifying. Something was running into her eyes. She swiped it away. It wasn't sweat. It looked as black as oil. *Why is there oil on my head?*

she wondered. *It isn't oil,* replied some other more lucid part of her mind. Whatever it was, it didn't matter right now. All that mattered was that she kept putting one foot in front of the other. With each faltering step, her boots sank into a soft carpet of leaves.

Then she was beyond the reach of the torch's beam. She risked a glance over her shoulder. The figure stepped forwards so that the light touched her again. Jerking back around so hard that she almost overbalanced, she staggered onwards. The ground began to slope away from her with increasing steepness. Her footsteps gathered momentum until she was running wildly, arms flailing. Branches whipped and clawed at her. Tree trunks tried to buffet her off her feet. But somehow, through a mixture of sheer determination and luck, she managed to remain upright.

Her lungs felt as if they were on fire. So did the space between her legs. It was as if someone had recently rammed a hot poker inside her. Had she been raped? Oh god. Was that it? Had some sicko knocked her out and stuck his filthy cock in her? What if he was diseased? What if he had hepatitis or HIV?

Something smacked her hard across the chest, clothes-lining her onto her back. She lay winded, tears misting her vision. She wiped her eyes. A branch vibrated above her. There was no sign of her rapist – if that's what the camouflaged figure was. Her hand trembled down to her vagina. It felt torn and shapeless. She looked at her hand. More oil. *No, not oil,* that other part of her mind cried out again. *You're mutilated. Ruined!*

For a moment her strength deserted her. She was too exhausted even to cry as the question came to her, *Why not just lie here and die?* It would be easier. A three-quarter moon glowed through the trees. She could see its pocked surface with almost painful clarity. Her gaze fixed on a cluster of dark patches. *That light bulb's dirty,* she thought. *It needs cleaning.* She lifted a hand as if to touch the moon. *Clean... Clean moon light... Light clean bulb... No clean... No... No! You will not die here. You will keep moving and live.*

She wrenched her gaze back to the woods. Still no sign of the camouflaged figure. She attempted to sit up, gritting her teeth, straining every muscle. She succeeded in lifting herself a few centimetres before collapsing backwards. It was no good. She didn't have the strength to stand. *Then crawl,* she commanded herself.

She rolled onto her belly. Waves of fiery pain radiated from it. *I can't do it. Yes you can! Fuck the pain. Fuck whoever did this to you. Just crawl!*

Digging her fingers into the mulchy ground, she clawed her way forwards. She was no longer fearful. She couldn't afford to be. She needed every last scrap of energy to keep worming a path through the undergrowth. The oil was in her eyes again. *It's not oil. It's– Oh for fuck's sake, it doesn't matter what it is. Just keep moving. Movement is life. Keep moving and your heart will keep beating. Pull with your hands, push with your feet, pull with your hands...*

Over and over, she mechanically repeated the process. Centimetre by centimetre, she advanced. Time dissolved away. How long had she been doing this for? Minutes? Hours? Her entire life? Perhaps this was all she'd ever done. Why was she crawling? She couldn't remember. All she knew was that she *had* to crawl. Crawling was her life's purpose. Nothing else mattered. Where was she going? Where had she been? She didn't know. Like a worm on a hook, she knew how to do only one thing – move. *Move, crawl, push, pull, push, move, forwards, onwards...*

Then she saw it. Up ahead through the trees. A light! A bright, shining speck that brought her mind flooding back. She remembered the figure. The walking bush. This light wasn't a torch. It was too bright. Too high off the ground. A window? She headed towards it. Her limbs were doing strange things. She couldn't seem to coordinate them to function in unison. It was as if each arm and leg had a mind of its own. She had to consciously tell them what to do. *Right hand grab that root. Now pull. Left leg bend at the knee. Push off that tree. Good. Now left hand it's your turn.*

The light was getting close. It was attached to a tall thin post and cast its white glow over a black surface with a broken white line running along its centre. It took her a few seconds to put names to the things she was seeing. *Lamppost... Road... Road! Roads mean vehicles. Vehicles mean people. All you have to do is get to it. Get to it and you'll survive.* Even as she thought it, one car sped by, then another and another.

The road was only a few metres away, but she might as well have been trying to climb Everest's final ridge without oxygen. Every movement was an agony of concentration and effort. *You're not going to make it. Good try, but no dice. Was that the saying? Or was it, no cigar?* Cigars. God, she loved the smell of cigars. Or did she? For that matter, what did cigars even smell like?

A movement in the shadows of a nearby tree yanked her back into the moment. The camouflaged figure stepped into view. *The fucker's playing with you like a cat.* A sob tried to force its way up her throat, but she held it in. *Don't give them the satisfaction. Right hand lift up. Middle finger do your thing. Come on you piece of shit finger. Do it!* Her middle finger reluctantly unfurled. It trembled in the air for a second before dropping to the ground. The figure showed no reaction to the defiant gesture.

She summoned up one last Herculean effort. Her fingers clawed at the earth. *Pull, push...* She knew it wasn't going to be enough, but that didn't stop her from trying. Then the ground was falling away again and she was slithering down a grassy bank. The bank spat her onto the road. She used the momentum to crawl into the path of oncoming headlights. She feebly raised a hand to alert the driver. The vehicle didn't slow down. She saw her death in its lights. *Please let it be over quickly,* she thought. There was a screech of brakes. A car swerved sharply, narrowly avoiding ploughing into the embankment. Its front doors flew open. Two lads sprang out and ran towards her. They looked to be in their late teens or early twenties. Their horrified expressions told her all she needed to know about the state she was in.

"Oh shit, Kyle, look at her head," gasped one of them. She could just barely hear him over the ringing in her ears.

"What happened to you?" the other asked shakily.

She pointed to the woods. *We need to get the fuck out of here!* "Wnnnfffg tthhhhrrr!"

The one called Kyle seemed to get the gist of what she was trying to say. "Let's get her into the car," he said.

"We need to call the police."

Kyle nervously eyed the darkness beneath the trees. "I'm not waiting around here for the police. Just get hold of her will you."

He took hold of her arms. The other boy grabbed her legs. His face twisted as if he was about to puke. "Oh my god, she's messed up bad down there."

"Don't look. Come on. Get your arse in gear, will you?"

Her body sagged between them, bare buttocks scraping the tarmac. Her limbs flopped about awkwardly as they manoeuvred her onto the backseat. The seat's fabric felt soft against her skin. So incredibly soft. They propped her up and fastened a seatbelt around her.

"We're taking you to hospital," Kyle told her.

"She's getting blood everywhere," said his friend. "My dad's gonna kill me."

"Shut up and get in the car."

Both boys started to turn, but stopped dead. She saw what had captured their attention. Her hulking, camouflaged tormentor was standing at the top of the bank. For an instant the boys seemed to be mesmerised by the sight. Then Kyle thrust his friend towards the front passenger door. He sprinted around to the driver side, barely avoiding being clipped by a passing car.

"You're not insured," yelled his friend.

Ignoring him, Kyle rammed the car into gear and floored the accelerator. The car bunny-hopped and the engine cut out. "Shit!" cried Kyle.

"Go, go, go!"

"I'm fucking trying."

The engine flared back into life. This time it stayed that way as they accelerated sharply. The woman twisted to look at her tormentor. The figure made no move to pursue the car. She unfurled her middle finger again. A high-pitched sound found its way through the ringing in her ears. She realised that she was laughing frenziedly. The laughter stopped as the car jerked leftwards. Her head flopped in the opposite direction. Turning, she glimpsed herself in the rearview mirror.

Bloodshot brown eyes bulged from a mask of grime and blood. A tangle of matted auburn hair hung around her shoulders. She looked like some kind of fairy-tale creature that had been abandoned in the woods as a baby and raised by wild animals. There was a circular hole in her forehead just below her hairline. The hole was big enough to poke her little finger into. Its edges were blackened. Burnt looking. Blood trickled from it, dripping off her left eyebrow.

"That was one scary looking... I dunno what," said Kyle.

The other boy twisted towards the backseat. "Hey, what's your name?"

She didn't answer. She couldn't. She was unconscious.

Chapter 2

Brrring, brrring, brrring. Jack's hand groped out from under the duvet towards his mobile phone. He squinted at its screen – 'Steve Platts'. Clearing his throat, he put the phone to his ear. "What's up, Steve?"

"We've got a bad one. Unidentified woman. Late twenties or early thirties. Gunshot wound to the head. Signs of sexual assault."

Jack glanced at the alarm clock – 2:34 am. "Dead?"

"Nope. They're working on her at North Manchester General. From the sounds of it, I don't much rate her chances."

"What else do we know?"

"Not much. Two lads driving home from a night out nearly ran her over. They took her to the hospital."

"What time?"

There was the rustle of a notepad being consulted. "They picked her up at approximately one fifteen and arrived at the hospital at twenty five to two."

"You said they almost ran her over. Does that mean she was on her feet?"

"It means someone put a bullet in her head and instead of dropping dead she legged it. Imagine that."

Jack didn't particularly want to imagine that. "Where do you want me?"

"M61 southbound slip road. Junction 2. Worsley Braided Interchange."

Jack jotted down the destination. "Got it. See you soon." He hung up and phoned Laura. "Sorry to do this to you, sis, but–"

"Yeah, I know," she broke in, her voice thick with sleep. "I'll be there in ten."

He put down the phone and reached for the socks he'd dumped on the carpet earlier that night. He dragged on jeans and a sweatshirt. Detective

Chief Inspector Paul Gunn liked his team to dress professional – shirt, tie, suit – but to hell with that. It was early November. It had been a cold day. The night would be even colder. He headed for the bathroom, splashed water over his face and short brown hair. He ran a hand over his stubble. He could do with a shave, but there was no time. He padded to a half-open door. Beyond it was a bedroom whose sky-blue walls were papered with posters of pop stars. Toys, pens and books were neatly arranged on a desk and bookshelves. Clothes lay folded on a chair. Unlike Jack, Naomi kept her room tidy.

His gaze rested on his daughter's sleeping face. She was cuddling her favourite stuffed toy – a bear with a broken heart held together by a plaster on its chest. She'd kicked off her duvet. A black-and-white cat was curled up on her feet. Her pyjama bottoms were several inches too short. She'd grown so much recently. Her limbs were becoming gawkily long. Like a foal's. She wasn't far off ten-years-old. It wouldn't be all that many years before puberty kicked in and her thoughts turned from teddy bears to boys. That didn't overly bother him. He knew how to handle boys. He'd been one himself. What he didn't know how to handle was the other stuff that girls went through – periods, hormones. Laura would be there to help out, but it wasn't an aunt that Naomi needed. What she needed was a...

Jack's gaze strayed from Naomi to a framed photo on her bedside table. In the photo, Naomi was snuggled up to a woman. Both of them were smiling. Both of them were heartbreakingly beautiful with coal black hair and piercing blue eyes. He felt a sharp twinge in his chest. Would he ever be able to look at Rebecca without feeling that sensation? He doubted it. There were some wounds time couldn't heal.

He went down to the kitchen and made two mugs of tea. There was a knock at the front door. He answered it and Laura bustled into the house, shivering. "It's freezing out there."

She hung up her coat and kicked off her shoes. Jack handed her a mug. "Thanks," she said, cupping her hands around its warmth.

They took their drinks into a living-room that was comfortably furnished if lacking in feminine touches. There were no ornaments on the shelves and mantelpiece, no pictures on the walls. The room had a clean, functional feel.

Yawning, Laura stretched out on the sofa. Her eyes were still puffy from sleep. "Yeah, I know, I've got a face like a smacked arse," she said, noticing Jack looking at her. "You would too if you'd just come off a fortnight of night shifts."

"Sorry," Jack said again.

"Stop apologising. I'm happy to do this." Her lips crooked into a half-smile. "And anyway, who needs sleep?"

"Not us apparently." Jack glanced at his watch. "I've got to go."

"How long do you think you'll be?"

"No idea. The spare bed's made up. If I don't get back in time for breakfast–"

"I know the routine. Shower, cereal, school run."

Laura wafted Jack out of the door. Taking a final swig of tea, he headed for his car. He typed his destination into the sat nav – Chorlton to M61 Junction 2, 10 miles, 16 mins. The journey took him south of the city centre, then north along the M60. At this time of night the roads would be quiet, mostly populated by lorries, taxis, emergency service vehicles and delivery vans. Of course, there would be other people on the roads too – night shift workers like Laura, holidaymakers heading to or from the airport, dads trying to lull crying babies to sleep, burglars, rapists, murderers...

Beyond the urban sprawl of Stretford, came the anonymity of the motorway. Concrete bridges, pylons, scrubby embankments, occasional tower blocks looming bleakly into the night sky. Jack cruised along with the radio turned down low. He didn't think about what he was driving into – the whirlwind of pain and ruined lives that inevitably swirled around such cases. He thought about what was most important to him – Naomi. Was there enough milk for her cereal and bread for her sandwiches? Was there a clean school uniform in her wardrobe? Had she finished last night's homework? Was parents' evening today? Or was it tomorrow? Pyjamas. She needed new pyjamas.

Before he knew it, he was at the tangle of slip roads and overpass bridges that locals called spaghetti junction. A police car was parked where the M61 slip road merged with the M60. He pulled onto the hard shoulder, got out and showed his ID to a constable who pointed him to the north end of the slip road. Jack's breath misted the air as he made his way along the hard shoulder. The road was hemmed in by grass embankments whose tops were lined with bushes and trees. A hundred and fifty metres or so up ahead, at roughly the mid-point of the slip road, was a cluster of police vehicles illuminated by halogen spotlights. Forensic, uniformed and plainclothes officers were doing their thing – taking photos, laying down evidence markers, removing evidence bags, rooting around with long sticks in the undergrowth.

Something crunched underfoot. Dropping to his haunches, Jack inspected the tarmac. It was scattered with particles of glass as if from a smashed window or headlight. He straightened and continued to the scene. He spotted Steve Platts chatting to Gary Crawley. Steve was pinching his mustachioed upper lip. A sure sign that something had got him puzzled. Gary was wearing the baggy-eyed, vacant expression of a man whose wife had recently given birth to twins.

Taking in Jack's jeans and trainers, Steve gave a smiling shake of his head. "The DCI's going to love that."

Jack made a dismissive gesture. He couldn't have cared less what Paul thought about his choice of outfit or pretty much anything else for that matter. "How are the twins?" he asked a yawning Gary.

"Noisy," said Gary.

Steve gave a throaty smoker's chuckle. "You do the crime, you serve the time."

"It'll get easier," said Jack. "In about three years."

"Three years," groaned Gary. "I'm not sure I can survive three more months of sleepless nights and shitty nappies. My brain's turning to mush."

"Well here's a job that doesn't require any thought. I stepped on broken glass back there." Jack pointed to the spot. "Get someone to check it out."

As Gary slouched off to collar a forensic officer, Steve said, "You've got to feel sorry for him."

Jack didn't feel sorry for Gary. The young DS was knackered. But so what? Rather that than climb into bed every night with nothing to keep you company but memories. No, not only memories. There was also the nagging fear that you might never fall in love again. There was a time when Jack hadn't been able to bear the thought of being with anyone other than Rebecca. But that time had passed. It was almost two years since she'd died. Increasingly, he found his thoughts turning to the future. He wasn't ready to resign himself to a life of sleeping alone. He ached for the feel of skin on skin, the smell of hair laced with shampoo and sweat, the soft sound of someone breathing beside him. But more than anything, he wanted to feel that sense of being at peace with the world that waking up with Rebecca had once given him.

"Mind you, I wouldn't mind a bit of what he's got," Steve added in a tone that suggested he too wasn't particularly enjoying the single life. He was staring down the barrel of his fifties with a failed marriage and a couple of kids he rarely saw. His career had stalled at DI, whilst younger officers like Paul leapfrogged over him.

A trace of concern entered Jack's expression. On first impressions, Steve came across as a sexist, misogynistic dinosaur. It was an image he seemed happy to cultivate. But Jack had seen another side to him. Once you won his trust, there was no one more loyal. And loyalty was hard to come by these days. "Aren't you getting a bit long in the tooth to be a dad again?"

"Christ yes. I'd rather pull my teeth out with pliers than have more kids," Steve replied with a shudder. "I was talking about Gary's wife. Have you seen her?" He cupped his hands in front of his chest. "Tits to die for."

Jack shook his head. "You had me worried for a second there."

"Why? Did you think I was going soft or something?"

"Or something. Right, shall we get down to business?"

"The DCI wants us to head over to Clifton. Knock on doors. Find out if anyone knows who the injured woman is."

"Have we got a photo?"

"Nope. They took her straight into surgery. We haven't even got a proper description. Apparently she was so covered in blood and dirt that the lads who picked her up could only see her eyes."

"So what have we got?"

Steve consulted his notepad. "White. We think. Shoulder length reddish hair. Brown eyes. Five four or so. 160 to 170 pounds. Twenty to forty-years-old."

"So she's overweight."

"Yes... No..." Steve pulled at his moustache again. "We'll get to that in a bit. First I'll give you the grand tour. So these two young lads are driving back from a night out in Bolton and they see a woman lying in the road." He pointed to a pair of skid marks that swerved towards the hard shoulder. "They pull over sharpish and go to her aid. The woman's in a bad way. She's naked from the waist down. Bleeding from the head and between her legs. They carry her to the car. Then they see a figure up there." He pointed to the tree-lined top of the embankment.

"Description?"

Steve shook his head. "It was too dark. All I've got is that the figure looked big."

"So most likely a man."

"Yeah, but these lads were scared shitless. You know how the mind inflates things. The DCI's with them. We should have more to go on soon. Anyway, the lads drive our mystery woman to North Manchester General and that's the end of their part in the story."

"As long as their alibi checks out."

"Can't see why it wouldn't. They're hardly likely to have shot her in the head then taken her to hospital."

Jack spread his hands. "Stranger things have happened. Where are the nearest traffic cameras?"

Steve pointed to where the slip road curved away from the M61's southbound carriageway. "About two hundred metres away. We're in a blind spot. Fifty metres back and we'd have it all on camera."

"Why doesn't that surprise me?" Jack commented wryly.

He followed Steve to the embankment. Their route was punctuated by numbered little yellow cones. Beside each cone were splotches of blood and other less easily identified substances. Beyond the edge of the road, an approach path of metal stepping-stone plates led up the embankment. There were more cones nestled amongst the grass and weeds. "From the blood and the flattening of the grass, we think she was crawling towards the road at this point," said Steve, turning on a torch. There was a short space of level ground, then another wooded slope. The cones abruptly became much more spread out.

"This must have been where her legs gave out," said Steve.

The slope plateaued again. They made their way through another fifty or so metres of trees before emerging into a small floodlit clearing cordoned off by plastic tape. Forensic officers were painstakingly sifting through the carpet of leaves and placing anything of interest on white sheets, ready to be logged and bagged. One officer was standing in a waist-deep hole with piles of soil and turves scattered around it. The steel plates led to its edge. A couple of metres from the hole there was a cluster of plastic cones. The leaves and grass thereabouts were discoloured with blood and a thick, congealing rusty-brown slime.

"Someone lost a lot of blood here," observed Jack. "Looks like there's some kind of discharge mixed in with it."

"Oh yeah, there's definitely something mixed in with it." Steve's eyes slide across to the hole. Once more his hand went to his moustache.

Whatever the 'something' was it had clearly bothered Steve. And nothing much bothered Steve. Jack steeled himself for an unpleasant sight as they approached the hole. The white-suited figure in it turned to them. Jack recognised the ever-serious eyes of senior pathologist Kim Leven.

He gave her a smile and a nod. The smile disappeared as he saw what lurked in the bottom of the hole. It looked like an alien lifeform – a wrinkled, translucent grey membrane encased a pillow of red meat. A yellowish tube, spiralled like pasta, was attached to the centre of the... thing. "What is *that*?"

"A placenta," said Kim, pulling down her dust-mask.

Jack's eyebrows lifted in realisation. "The victim gave birth here?"

"It certainly appears that way."

"So was she sexually assaulted?"

"We thought so at first," put in Steve. "But then we found that thing. I'm surprised you didn't know what it is. When my ex-wife gave birth to our first, the afterbirth came out hot on Dillon's heels." He wrinkled his nose. "Things were never quite the same in the bedroom department after that."

"I was too busy looking at Naomi to see what came out after her." Jack's reply led him to the obvious question. "Where's the baby?"

Steve shrugged. "Poor little bugger. What a way to come into the world."

"These were beside the placenta," said Kim, pointing to an evidence bag containing a bundle of dirty multicoloured material. "They're loose-fitting trousers. The sort of thing a pregnant woman might wear."

Jack stooped for a closer look at the trousers. "They look like tie-dye."

"That's because they are."

"Anything else?"

Kim pointed to more cones alongside the hole. "We've found several footprints. They appear to have been made by two pairs of shoes. Size five – we think those are the victim's – and size twelve."

"Size twelve. That backs up what the lads said about seeing a big figure." Jack's gaze circumnavigated the clearing. "So the woman gives birth, then someone – possibly this big figure – shoots her in the head and dumps her in this… I think we can safely call it a grave. Any idea when the grave was dug?"

"Some of the soil overlays the blood stains," said Kim.

"So it was dug after the shooting," said Jack. "Which means whoever did this probably hadn't planned it."

"But they did have a spade." Kim ran a hand down the sheer, cleanly sliced walls of the grave.

"OK, so they anticipated that they'd need to dig a grave, but not necessarily at this spot. I mean, you don't shoot someone in the head then hang around to dig a grave – unless you're inexperienced."

"How many people have experience of delivering babies *and* shooting new mums in the head?" Steve asked dryly. "It's sort of impressive when you think about it. It would take a very special type of scumbag to combine those skills."

The pathologist raised a not-entirely approving eyebrow at the darkly humorous observation. Jack merely nodded. He knew Steve's obnoxiousness was just a self-defence mechanism. Everyone had their own way of dealing with the shit the job flung at them. More than a few found solace in a bottle. Others kept their work and home life strictly separate. Steve dealt with it by acting like an arsehole.

Jack frowned. "Something about this doesn't make sense. Let's assume it went down like I said. She gives birth. She's shot. She lies unconscious while the big figure digs the grave. She's dumped into the grave along with her trousers and the placenta. Then what? She regains consciousness, climbs out of the grave, runs away, collapses and crawls to the road. Why didn't the big figure catch up with her? For that matter, why didn't they just smack her on the head when she came around? She's just given birth. She's lost a ton of blood. She's most likely brain-damaged. And yet she's able to escape. And then there's what happened on the road. The big figure just stands there watching. He or she doesn't try to stop the lads from driving away with the victim." Jack glanced enquiringly at Kim. "Have you recovered a bullet?"

"We've dug around," she replied. "So far nothing."

"So she could have been shot elsewhere?"

"Yes, but I don't think that was the case. Not considering the volume of blood. It's more likely the bullet is lodged in her skull."

"Is that possible if she was shot at close range?"

"It's unlikely, but possible. It depends on the calibre and velocity of the bullet, the angle at which she was shot, whether the bullet struck something else first and ricocheted into her skull. Etc, etc."

"Why didn't the big figure use the gun to at least scare the lads?" queried Jack. "And why was the woman so dirty?"

"Maybe the big figure starts burying her and that's what brings her around," offered Steve.

"She was so dirty the lads could only see her eyes. You don't get like that from a few spadefuls of soil."

"You do if you're already soaked with sweat, blood and Christ knows what else."

Jack made an unconvinced sound. "There's something else to consider. Where was the baby when all this was going on? The big figure didn't have it at the road. A newborn would have been bawling its lungs out."

The three of them were silent for an extended moment. Jack could see in his colleagues' eyes that they were thinking the same thing as him – *Unless it was dead.*

A drop of rain hit Jack's face. Kim looked skyward, muttering, "Bloody hell. The forecast didn't mention rain." She gestured to her white-suited colleagues. "We need a tent. Rapido!"

To the north of the clearing, a grassy bank sloped up into densely clustered trees. "Can I borrow your torch?" asked Jack. Steve passed it to him. They ducked under the plastic tape and Jack slowly swept the torch beam over the ground as they ascended the slope. Rain was pattering on the golden autumnal canopy.

"What's over this way?" asked Jack.

"The place we're heading after this – Clifton."

"A suburb of Manchester?"

"Salford. Don't confuse Salford and Manchester. People can get funny about that."

Near the top of the slope, Jack stopped and turned. A narrow channel through the trees gave a view of the clearing. A movement in the treetops halfway down the slope caught his eye. "Look at that," he whispered, pointing. A small bird with a short flat head and plump body was shuffling along a branch. The bird had greyish brown feathers mottled with white. White lines angled down over big yellow eyes, giving it a frowning expression. "I think it's some kind of owl."

"A Little Owl," Steve said as the bird stretched out its wings in the rain. "It's taking a shower. I've seen one doing it before. I used to do a bit of birdwatching when the kids were little."

Jack cocked an eyebrow. "You were a birder?"

"Yeah well you know how it is. You get home from a shift absolutely bolloxed. The kids are fighting. The house is a tip. The wife's pissed off at you for some reason or other. So you find yourself looking for any excuse to get away from it all – birding, the pub, the footy. And then before even know what's what, your wife's not your wife anymore and you can do your own thing every night of the week." Steve faded off into a sigh. He quickly followed up with a forced-sounding chuckle. "These days the only birdwatching I do is in the city centre. You should come out with me and the lads one Saturday. We'll take you around the meat markets. All the MILFs will be creaming themselves over you."

"Thanks but no thanks."

"Take it from me, mate, you need to get back on the horse, start enjoying life. That is unless you're planning on becoming a monk."

"That might not be such a bad idea," Jack said humourlessly. He started back down the slope before Steve could reply. The conversation was heading into uncomfortable territory. Time to knock on some doors.

Chapter 3

Junction 16 of the M60 led into Clifton along a road of semi-detached houses and low-rise blocks of flats. Jack and Steve started with the side of town closest to the crime scene. Under their direction, constables fanned out across an estate of bland modern detached houses. It was a little past four in the morning. No hint of light showed in the starless November sky. People were slow to wake and even slower to open their doors. This wasn't a particularly affluent area, but it was far from poor. Houses without alarms were a rarity. The place had a small community feel. The people Jack spoke to were friendly enough, but wary. As one man said after making Jack slide his ID through the letterbox, "Scallies don't usually knock on doors, but you never know around here."

After an hour or so, the officers regrouped. Most had nothing to report. A few had come up with potential matches, but that was to be expected. *Caucasian, shoulder length reddish hair, brown eyes, five four or so, 160ish pounds.* There must have been dozens of women within a mile of where they were who fitted that description. The key was to find a woman who fitted that description *and* was missing. No luck so far on that score. Steve and the majority of the constables moved on to a neighbouring estate. Jack took four officers with him to check out a scattering of houses at the end of a narrow, pitch-dark lane. Strings of potholes exposed worn cobblestones through the lane's tarmacked surface. To its right was a grassy field. To its left was a patchwork fence of green-streaked wood and rusty corrugated panels.

Jack shone his torch over the fence. Horse stables, allotments and chicken coops were mixed in with yards cluttered with caravans, vans, cars, porta-cabins and sheds. A little oasis of businesses operating in the grey economy.

The light set a dog off barking. A sign warned that 'Security Patrol And Protect These Premises'. Beyond the last allotment was a short terrace of two-up, two-down houses. The lane continued past the houses towards what Google Maps indicated to be a farm. Jack sent a couple of constables on to the farm whilst he and a constable worked through the houses, starting at opposite ends of the terrace.

The rain was coming down hard. Jack scurried across a small front yard and rapped at a door. A light came on in the upstairs window. Half a minute passed. A minute. He hunched his shoulders. Water was seeping through his coat. *They're either slow on their feet or they're not answering,* he thought.

A tremulous old woman's voice came through the door. "Who is it?"

"Detective Inspector Jack Anderson of Greater Manchester Police."

"Who?"

Jack repeated himself more loudly, adding, "I'm sorry for the disturbance, but I need to ask you some questions."

"Why? What's happened?"

"A woman has been hurt. We're–" Jack broke off as the door opened, revealing a short barrel of a lady somewhere in her late seventies or early eighties. A hairnet protected her permed white hair. A quilted pink dressing-gown insulated her from the chill air. She eyed Jack uneasily through milk-bottle glasses. He displayed his ID and her unease turned to sympathy.

"It's raining like the devil," she said. "Come in."

Smiling gratefully, Jack stepped into a little hallway that smelled of cigarettes and fried food. A jumble of coats, woolly hats and scarves occupied pegs to the left of the door. Underneath were brollies, wellies and fur-lined boots. The dark carpet and yellowed wallpaper looked almost as old as the house.

"Would you like a cup of tea?" asked the old lady.

"No thanks," replied Jack, but the woman didn't seem to hear. She was already shuffling towards a cramped kitchen at the back of the house.

Jack followed, glancing through a half-open door into a living-room. Embers glowed invitingly in a stone hearth, casting their orange light on a threadbare rug, an armchair with an ashtray precariously balanced on its arm and shelves overcrowded with a lifetime's worth of ceramic figurines, Toby jugs, bits and bobs of brass and silver and other ornaments. Magazines and books were scattered across a table – 'Where To Watch Birds In Britain', 'Birdwatching In Lancashire', 'Britain's Birds'...

"Are you a birdwatcher?" asked Jack.

The old lady's wrinkled features were starkly illuminated as she took milk from a fridge. "No. My husband Bill was the birdwatcher." She added matter-of-factly, "He's been dead almost ten years."

"Can I ask your name please?"

"Doreen Salter. I like to look at Bill's books. They remind me of him."

Jack jotted down her name and kept the conversation on track. "So about this woman."

"What woman?"

Jack had dealt with a thousand old dears like this one back when he was in uniform. There was no point trying to hurry them. They did things in their own time. He described the woman. Doreen frowned in thought then shook her head.

"No love. Doesn't ring any bells. What's her name?"

"That's what we're trying to find out. Have there been any disturbances tonight? Unusual noises or lights in the lane?"

"No."

"OK. Well thanks for your time, Mrs Salter. I'll let you get back to bed."

"What about your tea?"

Jack smiled ruefully. He would have liked to sit by the embers with a hot drink, but time was of the essence. There was a newborn baby out there somewhere. Alive or dead, it had to be found as fast as possible. "Sorry, but duty calls."

He closed the door on his way out and moved on to the neighbouring house. Twenty minutes later he and the constable met in the middle of the terrace.

"Anything?" asked Jack.

"No sir," replied the constable.

The other constables returned from the farm with the same answer. The four of them headed back to Manchester Road and re-joined the main group. Jack found Steve puffing irritably on a wet, drooping cigarette. "Sometimes I wonder why I bother with this job," muttered Steve, grumpy as an old dog. "I might as well be a parking warden for all the thanks I get."

"It's not all bad. A nice old lady just invited me in for a cuppa."

Steve humphed. "Lucky you. Did she offer you anything else while she was at it? I've always had a thing for older women."

Jack didn't reply to the crude remark. "Where to now?"

Steve's phone rang. "The DCI," he told Jack before answering it. "Hello sir... We've done about half the houses south of Manchester Road... Nothing so far... OK, I'll tell him." He hung up and said to Jack, "In answer to your question, you're off to North Manchester General. The victim's out of surgery. The DCI wants a photo of her."

Jack frowned. "Do I look like a photographer? And why can't the prick tell me directly what he wants me to do?"

Steve spread his hands. "I dunno what's going on between you two and frankly I don't want to know, but I've had a gutful of being your go-between." As Jack turned to head for his car, Steve called after him, "Sort it out."

Chapter 4

North Manchester General Hospital was a sprawling assortment of buildings a couple of miles north of the city centre. Jack parked near the main entrance and made his way through a labyrinthine series of corridors to the Intensive Care Unit. A bored-looking constable stationed outside the unit pointed Jack to a ward sister. At Jack's request, the nurse phoned the surgeon who'd operated on the victim. A few minutes later a man with sharp grey eyes and the long delicate fingers of a concert pianist approached and introduced himself as Doctor Medland.

"How is she?" Jack asked in a voice that matched the funereal hush of the ward.

Doctor Medland pointed at his forehead above his left eye. "The bullet penetrated the frontal bone and travelled downwards, grazing the frontal and temporal lobes and lodging itself about here." He drew a line from his forehead to behind his left ear. "We attempted to remove it, but there's too much swelling."

"So she's going to need more surgery."

"It's likely, but I can't say for certain until things settle down and we get a clearer picture of what's going on in there."

"How do you rate her chances?"

"Penetrating brain injuries are difficult to predict. If the brain continues to swell or if the bullet moves even a few millimetres, the effect could be catastrophic. The best I can say right now is she has a chance."

"Can I see her?"

"Yes, but I must insist on absolute silence."

Doctor Medland led Jack to a room filled with the hum of monitoring devices. The woman was almost lost amidst a bewildering array of medical equipment. Her head and neck were immobilised by a brace. A ventilator tube was taped to her mouth. Another thinner tube snaked up her nose. Her chest was a forest of electrodes. The skin surrounding her left eye was swollen and purple. A thick gauze pad covered the entry wound. The left half of her long auburn hair had been shaved off. She'd been cleaned up, but there was ingrained dirt under her nubby fingernails. Scratches that might have been defensive wounds crisscrossed her arms. But what really caught Jack's attention was the tattoo that flared outwards like a wing from her right eye, covering part of her forehead, cheek and temple. Concentric circles of white, then black, then white ringed her eye. Beyond them, the 'wing' was rusty red, except for a thin line of brown along its ragged outer edge.

Jack photographed her from different angles with his phone. He studied her for a moment, listening to the gentle whoosh of the ventilator. Even with all the swelling, it was apparent that she was good looking. He wondered why she – why anyone – would want to tattoo their face. He'd seen ex-cons – mainly men, but also women – with spider webs, knives, guns, tears and the like inked on their faces. Such tattoos were like stripes on a soldier's uniform. They commanded respect and fear. Had this woman been in prison? Or maybe she was simply into tattoos. When he was growing up, tattoos had been taboo, something that marked out criminals and drug addicts. Today they were mainstream. Fresh-faced middle-class kids paraded around flaunting their ink. Still, facial tattoos were rare. You had to be either extremely confident or stupid to think someone would employ you with a big red wing on your face, unless you worked in the tattoo industry or some other niche business where tattoos might boost your credibility.

"Does she have any other tattoos or birthmarks?" asked Jack.

Doctor Medland sharply shushed him and ushered him from the room. "No."

"Are there any drugs or alcohol in her system?"

"No."

"Was she wearing jewellery?"

"Not that I'm aware of."

"Is there anything else you can tell me?"

"According to the two men who brought her here she couldn't speak properly, which may indicate damage to the Broca area."

"The what?"

"It's the region of the brain that controls language. It's located in the left hemisphere, which is consistent with the injury. If the patient regains consciousness, it may be that her ability to communicate has been severely affected." Doctor Medland glanced at his watch. "Are we done here? It's seven o'clock and I haven't been to bed yet."

Jack nodded. "Thanks doctor."

He looked through the observation window. Whoever the tattooed woman was, it was difficult not to feel a twinge of sympathy for her. Her life hung by a thread. And even if she found her way back to consciousness, she had the prospect of brain damage and a missing baby to look forward to.

He scrolled through the photos and sent the best ones to his colleagues along with an update on the woman's condition. The chances of identifying her had improved considerably. There couldn't be many women in the Greater Manchester area – or for that matter the entire country – with a tattoo like hers. If she'd ever come into contact with the police, it wouldn't take long to find her on the PNC database.

Jack returned to his car. The rain had diminished to drizzle. A watery sun was fighting its way through the clouds. Traffic was gathering as the city awoke. Naomi would be awake soon too and going through the usual pre-school rituals. Rebecca had used to brush and plait Naomi's hair every morning. Naomi could do her own hair, but she preferred someone to do it for her. If Laura wasn't around, that someone was Jack. He was fine with the brushing bit. Not so much with the plaiting. But he was improving. It was a running joke between Laura and him that when Naomi hit her teens he would have to help with her makeup too. He'd come to enjoy doing her hair – it was a chance for them to chat about what the day held in store – but he drew the line at messing around with lipstick and mascara.

He wondered whether the DCI wanted him to return to canvassing the neighbourhoods adjacent to the crime scene, or whether he had time to nip home and take Naomi to school. Chorlton was in the opposite direction to Clifton. Battling his way south at rush hour, then back north would take at least an hour. He dialled Paul. The call went through to an answering service. He hung up, muttering, "Prick."

He headed south. It wasn't professional, but neither was not picking up the phone on one of your DIs in the middle of an investigation. Paul obviously wasn't desperately in need of his services. In recent months, Paul had done everything he could to marginalise Jack, keeping him on the fringes of investigations, dumping every crappy duty going on him. No doubt, Jack reflected, he wouldn't have been called out last night if several team members hadn't been away on a training exercise.

In some ways, the current status quo suited him. The further you were from the sharp end of investigations, the less stressful the job was. Besides which, he got to spend more time with Naomi. In other ways, it was incredibly frustrating to be denied the chance to do his job properly. Several times he'd found himself wondering if his talents would be better used elsewhere, but he always brusquely dismissed the thought. He wasn't about to give Paul the satisfaction of pushing him out of serious crimes. If one of them was heading out the door, it wasn't going to be him.

Guilt tugged at Jack as the hospital receded from view. Paul might not need him, but the tattooed woman and her baby did. He resisted the urge to turn the car around. In the past he would already have been on his way back to Clifton regardless of any issues he had with his commanding officers. But his priorities had changed since Rebecca's death. Naomi had to come first.

Chapter 5

Naomi ran to greet Jack as he entered the modest, three-bedroomed semi they called home. He was disappointed to see that her hair had already been plaited – the traffic had been a bitch – but he smiled broadly as she hugged him and exclaimed, "Yay, Daddy. Aunt Laura said I wouldn't see you until after school. Why didn't you wake me and tell me you had to go to work?"

He stooped to kiss her cheek. "I didn't want you worrying. I know you don't like it when I get called out in the middle of the night. Your hair looks nice."

"Aunt Laura did it."

"She makes a much better job of it than me."

Naomi glanced around as if to make sure Laura wasn't behind her. "I like the way you do it better," she whispered.

Jack smiled at the compliment even though he knew it wasn't true. Whenever Laura was around, Naomi pestered her to plait her thick black hair into all sorts of styles. "Where is your aunt?"

"She's getting changed for work."

That reminded Jack. He grabbed a clean t-shirt and jeans from the linen basket in the kitchen. After changing out of his damp clothes, he made toast for Naomi and himself. They were munching on it at the table when Laura appeared in her nursing uniform. Her light brown hair was neatly pinned up. Black-rimmed glasses that gave her a stern look were perched on her nose. "I didn't expect to see you," she said to Jack, pinching a slice of toast from his plate.

He spread his hands as if to say, *Well here I am.* "Did you manage to get some sleep?"

"A couple of hours. How was your night?"

"I'll tell you later," Jack mouthed with a meaningful glance at Naomi.

"Someone's been killed, haven't they?" said Naomi.

Lines gathered between Jack eyes. "What makes you say that, sweetie?"

"You've got that look on your face. The one you always get when something really bad happens."

Jack smiled faintly. It was pointless trying to get anything past Naomi. She had his gift for reading people. Although there were times when he thought of it more as a curse. Everyone had their hidden side. The dark corner of their mind where they stowed the things they didn't want the world to see – secrets, fears, desires. It gave you a cynical view of life when the slightest tic, blink, frown or grimace laid those things bare. "Someone got hurt, but they didn't die."

"Did you help them?"

"I'm trying to." Jack felt that tug of guilt again. It was followed by a sense of urgency. "Right, come on, let's get you to school."

As Naomi grabbed her coat and rucksack, Jack said to Laura, "I'll call you later."

"Watch your back out there."

Jack rolled his eyes at her. "You're as bad as Naomi. It's just a run-of-the mill case."

"I'm not talking about the case."

Laura didn't need to say more. They both knew she was referring to Paul. She'd never had much love for Jack's boss and oldest colleague. As far as she was concerned, Paul was a snake in the grass, a backstabber.

With a nod, Jack headed for the front door.

As usual, the roads around Chorlton Primary School were snarled up with traffic. Stressed-looking parents were competing for parking spaces and hustling their kids through the school gates. "Oh the joys of the school run," Jack said sarcastically.

"Next year I'll be old enough to walk to school with my friends," said Naomi.

He glanced at her uncertainly. "We'll see about that." His instinct was to coddle her, shield her from all possible harm. But he was aware that in doing so he himself might inadvertently harm her. At some point you had to allow them a measure of independence or they became resentful and rebellious. Or even worse, they became over-dependent. He couldn't see that happening with Naomi. She was already straining at the leash. The question was how much slack to give her. He'd seen time and again what too much freedom too soon could lead to – delinquency, alcohol, drugs, underage sex. Being a parent was a fine line and walking it alone was no easy thing.

Naomi pecked Jack on the cheek and jumped out of the car. "Bye, Dad."

"Have a good day. Love you," he called after her.

He watched her and a friend run smiling into the school. He never got tired of seeing her smile. It made everything else – getting up before the sun, the school run, the job, even dealing with Paul – worthwhile.

As Jack accelerated away, his phone rang. It was Steve. "Where the hell are you?" Steve demanded to know.

"I've just dropped Naomi off at school. Where are you?"

"Where do you think? I'm still in sodding Clifton. You need to get your arse back over here ASAP."

"Why? Have there been any developments?"

"Yeah, I'm getting a cold from walking around with wet hair."

"You haven't got enough hair for that."

"Fuck you."

Jack chuckled. "See you soon."

Chapter 6

'Soon' turned out to be longer than expected. A jack-knifed lorry transformed the M60 into a car park for an hour or so. By the time Jack arrived at Clifton, Steve and the constables under his command had moved onto neighbouring Kearsley – a small town within the Metropolitan Borough of Bolton. Jack found Steve on Manchester Road chatting to a heavily made-up blonde in a beauty salon. Steve didn't appear to be in any rush to get through his questions. He seemed more interested in how much it would cost for a session of massage therapy. Jack moved things along by showing the beautician a photo of the red wing tattoo. She shook her head, saying, "I've lived in this area all my life and I've never seen anyone with a tattoo like that around here."

"What about anyone in camouflage clothing?" asked Steve.

"You mean a soldier?"

"Maybe. Or maybe just someone who dresses like a soldier. Someone big. At least six foot."

The beautician shook her head again. Steve gave her his card. "Call me if you think of anything. Anytime, day or night," he added smarmily.

Steve shot Jack a scowl as they headed outside. "Thanks a fucking bunch, mate. I was almost in there until you waltzed in and–"

"What was that about camouflage clothing?" interrupted Jack.

"The DCI sent out an updated description of the 'big figure' the lads saw." Steve showed Jack the message – 'Between 6′1″ to 6′4″, wearing camouflage trousers, a hooded camouflage jacket and possibly green netting'. "Didn't you get it?"

"No I didn't," Jack muttered darkly. He'd grown accustomed to being left out of the loop by Paul, but this was getting beyond ridiculous. His thoughts turned from Paul to the Little Owl showering on its branch. "What did you used to wear when you went birdwatching?"

"Depends. If you're in a hide, you can wear what you want. If you're outside, you need to blend in with your surroundings. Why, what's on your mind? Are you thinking of taking up a hobby?"

"I don't have much time for hobbies these days. I used to do a bit of birding myself down in Sussex."

"I didn't know that."

"Yeah well." Those two words spoke volumes about Jack's discomfort at talking about his life in Sussex. "I never took it all that seriously, but some birders wore all sorts of camouflage." He frowned in thought, then said, "Grab a couple of constables. I want to check something out."

Steve accosted the nearest two officers – a burly, bearded sergeant and a female constable who looked fresh out of Police College. As Jack drove the four of them back to Clifton, he explained what was on his mind. "What if the camouflaged figure is some bloke who goes to those woods to watch birds? He takes the victim to see the owl–"

"Then shoots her in the head," Steve put in dryly.

"He could be a married man having an affair with the victim. She gets pregnant and threatens to tell his wife, so he decides to kill her. Maybe he owns a small calibre rifle. The sort of thing used to shoot rabbits, which could explain why the bullet got lodged in her skull."

"Birders don't tend to go around shooting wild animals."

"Generally speaking, I'm sure you're right. But I know an odd little coincidence when I see one. You remember that nice old lady who invited me in for a cuppa? Well she had a stack of birdwatching books on her table. She might know the perp."

"Sounds pretty tenuous to me, Jack. But then again, we've got nothing better to go on right now."

Chapter 7

The car juddered along the potholed lane, splashing through puddles. To the west were the woods where one life recently came into the world and another almost departed it. An old man was digging on the allotments. A mechanic was working on a car in a breezeblock garage. They paused to eye the strangers. The row of pebbledash and redbrick houses overlooked a meadow that ended after a hundred or so metres at the M60, where streams of traffic generated a wall of white noise.

"Hang back for now," Jack told the uniformed officers. "We don't want to scare her."

Jack rapped on the front door. As before, it took Doreen a couple of minutes to get to the door. "Who is it?" she asked through the letterbox.

"It's Detective Inspector Anderson," replied Jack.

Doreen opened the door. She was wearing brown trousers and a knitted jumper. Her skin looked sallow in the insipid morning light. Her gaze moved slowly from Jack and Steve to the constables and back. "What can I do for you, love?" she asked. Jack noted that this time she didn't invite him in. Her demeanour wasn't quite so open and friendly. She looked as if something was bothering her.

"Sorry to disturb you again, Mrs Salter, but I forgot to ask whether you live alone."

"My son, Neil, lives with me."

"And how old is Neil?"

"He's fifty one."

"Is he a big bloke?" put in Steve.

"He's six-foot odd and built like a shire horse," Doreen said proudly. "Like his dad was."

"And is he interested in birdwatching like his dad was too," asked Jack.

"Oh yes. Bill used to take him all the time."

"Does Neil own a rifle or any other kind of firearm?"

Doreen's thin grey eyebrows bunched together. "Of course he doesn't," she said, as if the answer should have been obvious to them. "Neil wouldn't hurt a fly."

"Is Neil in the house?"

"He's in his room."

"Can we speak to him?"

For the first time, Doreen hesitated to reply. "Do you really need to?"

"I'm afraid so."

"He won't be of any help." Doreen lowered her voice as if admitting to something shameful. "You see, I had a bad time giving birth to him. They call it a..." She searched for the right words, "nu... nuchal cord. The umbilical cord was caught around his neck. He couldn't get any oxygen. It damaged his brain."

"I'm sorry to hear that," said Jack. A baby almost killed by the very thing that nourished it. The irony was too cruel. "Can Neil talk?"

"When he wants to, but he won't talk with this lot here." Doreen gestured to Steve and the constables. "He doesn't like being around people. He prefers his birds and badgers."

"What if I come in and talk to him alone?"

"I'm not sure that's a good idea," said Steve.

"My Neil wouldn't hurt a fly," repeated Doreen, giving him a sharp look with her gentle brown eyes.

"We'll leave the front door open," said Jack. "If that's OK with you, Mrs Salter?"

She sighed. "It's alright with me, love. But I'm telling you, you'll be lucky to get a word out of Neil."

"No harm in trying. Where's his room?"

Doreen pointed to a scuffed white door at the top of the steep stairs. Jack motioned for her to lead the way. Using two bannisters to precariously haul herself upwards, the old lady ascended the stairs. She tapped on the door and said a touch breathlessly, "Neil, love. There's a man here wants to talk to you."

Silence.

"There's nothing to worry about, Neil," said Jack. "I just want to ask you some questions."

More silence.

Doreen tried the door. The deep lines on her face became even deeper. "It's locked."

"Does he normally lock his door?"

"No. Only when something's upset him. Last month some children called him names. He locked himself in his room for two days."

"Has anything happened in the past couple of days that could have upset him?"

"Not that I know of." Doreen knocked again. "Come on now, Neil, love. Let me in and tell me what the matter is. Have those horrible children been calling you names again?"

There was a soft whimper from beyond the door.

"Something's really bothered him," said Doreen.

Jack wondered if it was Neil crying. It didn't sound like a grown man. It sounded more like a child. Possibly even a baby. "Do you have a key for this door?"

"Neil has the only key."

"Could you stand aside please?"

Doreen gave Jack an alarmed look. "You're not going to break down the door, are you?"

"Not unless it's absolutely necessary." Jack examined the lock. It was an old-fashioned mortice lock. Not the kind he could pick. The key was in the other side. He looked at the bottom of the door. There was a gap of two or three centimetres. "Do you have a newspaper and a wire clothes hanger?"

Doreen nodded and shuffled off through one of the other two doors on the little landing. She returned with the requested items.

Jack untwisted the hanger. He slid a sheet of newspaper under the door directly below the lock. At the same time, he prodded the wire into the lock. The key came loose and clattered to the floor. He pulled the sheet of paper back, bringing the key with it.

"Eee, you're a clever one," Doreen said admiringly.

Jack inserted the key into the lock, turned it and started to open the door.

"No!" boomed a deep voice from inside the bedroom. The door slammed shut hard enough to rattle the walls. Steve was at Jack's side in a few heartbeats. The detectives pushed with all their strength. The door didn't budge.

"Christ, this bugger's strong," gasped Steve.

"Neil, stop playing silly buggers and open the door," reprimanded Doreen.

"No!" the voice boomed again.

Jack stopped pushing, gesturing for Steve to do likewise. "Neil, my name is Detective Inspector Jack Anderson. You're not in any trouble. A woman's been hurt. Her baby is missing. All I want to do is find her baby. Do you like babies, Neil?"

"He loves them," said Doreen. "When Sally from two along had her twins, Neil couldn't stay away from them. He fed them their bottles, changed their nappies, the lot."

"Then you understand why I need to find this baby so urgently, don't you, Neil? It needs milk and clothes. It might need medicine. You wouldn't want any harm to come to the baby, would you, Neil? Of course you wouldn't. You love babies. So help me find this one."

There was a creak of floorboards on the other side of the door.

Jack turned the handle again and pushed. This time there was no resistance. Motioning for Steve to stay back, he stepped into a bedroom that was a shrine to wildlife. The walls were plastered with photos of birds, foxes, badgers, hedgehogs, deer, mice and the like. Shelves were bowed beneath the weight of birding books. A camouflage jacket, trousers and green netting lay in a heap on the floorboards. A tripod with a camera on it was propped against a wall. A huge slab of a man was standing by a single bed that looked barely big enough for him.

Neil was wearing an old grey tracksuit, its underarms stained with dark sweat patches. His hair was thinning and almost as grey as his mum's. Facially he looked like any other man in his early fifties, except for the eyes. There was something missing from his close-set eyes. Some spark of awareness. His stubbly cheeks glistened with tears. His rounded, bearish shoulders trembled like those of a child afraid of being scolded. There was no baby in the room.

"Now then, what's got you so riled up?" asked Doreen, approaching Neil, her expression both concerned and annoyed.

Neil whimpered – that same incongruous mewl that Jack had heard moments ago. Eyes lowered to the floor, Neil pointed at the camera. "Is there something on the camera that you want me to see?" asked Jack.

Neil nodded. Jack picked up the camera and searched for the On/Off button.

"Give it here," said Steve, stepping forwards.

Neil gave another, louder whimper. He quietened down as Doreen shushed him. Steve eyed Neil's ham-sized hands as if he didn't relish the thought of what they could do, before returning his attention to the camera. "This is a nice piece of kit," he commented. "Weatherproof, night vision, zoom lens. You don't get one of these for less than three or four thousand quid."

"Save the sales pitch for later," interrupted Jack. "Just show me what's on it."

Steve switched on the camera. A green-tinted image of a Little Owl perched on a branch appeared on its rear screen. "That looks like the same bird we saw." He scrolled through several night-vision images of the owl. In the final one, the bird was taking flight as if something had startled it. "There's a video here. It was taken at 11:43 last night."

Steve pressed play. The video started with the screech of an owl. The lens panned down to a view of the clearing taken from the top of the adjoining slope. There was a woman in the clearing – *the* woman. Her hair was tied back, fully exposing her facial tattoo. She was clutching her heavily pregnant belly. She dropped to her knees, one hand groping at the ground. From somewhere nearby came the sound of something running through the undergrowth. The woman's head jerked over her shoulder. She tried to stand, but her legs gave way again. She dropped onto her backside and began to bum-crawl towards the edge of the clearing.

She didn't get far. Five figures burst into the clearing from the direction of the motorway. They had torches that shone like phosphorous in the night-vision lens, eerily illuminating the woman's face. Two of them were identically dressed in dark trousers, jackets and balaclavas. They appeared to be of average height and stocky build. The other three figures were an altogether more bizarre sight. They were wearing similar baggy clothing to the tattooed woman. All three had long hair. At least one of them was a woman – large breasts hung low against her top as if she wasn't wearing a bra. Another might have been a short, slightly built woman or man. The third was tall and rake thin with clothes-hanger shoulders. Considering the reason for the cameraman's presence, they were wearing strangely appropriate masks. The woman's face was hidden behind what looked to be a fox mask. Her short companion was unmistakably badger. The tall figure appeared to be an eagle-like bird of prey with a hooked beak, slanted eyes and a long-feathered crest.

The tattooed woman struggled futilely as the figures in balaclavas grabbed her and dragged her to the centre of the clearing. She screamed, arching her back. Fox knelt to feel between the woman's legs. She held up her hand for her companions to see.

"Did her waters just break?" wondered Steve.

The woman screamed again. Grimacing, Neil clapped his hands over his ears. "Can you watch that somewhere else?" asked Doreen, worriedly rubbing her son's broad back.

Steve pressed pause. The detectives went downstairs. Steve beckoned the uniformed officers over. "Go upstairs and keep an eye on the big guy," he said. "And for Christ's sake don't do anything to upset him."

The detectives seated themselves at the living-room table and resumed watching the video. The balaclava-wearing figures restrained the woman's arms. The others pulled off her trousers. Fox and Badger held her legs wide apart. Eagle stooped to examine her vagina. He – assuming it was a man – pushed the fingers of one hand inside her. He kept them there for a long moment as if feeling for something. Then he withdrew them, placed both hands on the woman's swollen stomach and pushed down. Another scream tore from her. One of the figures restraining her arms put a hand over her mouth. She wrenched her head from side to side, but the hand remained firmly in situ.

"Piece of shit bastards," muttered Steve.

The pushing continued for several minutes. A tiny head emerged from between the woman's thighs, face to the ground. Shoulders followed... Arms... The woman suddenly became very still. Eagle straightened, holding a scrunch-faced baby still attached to its mother by the umbilical cord. The baby gave out a warbling cry.

"Wow, that was quick," said Steve. "My ex-wife was in labour half the night with our first. Is it a boy or a girl?"

Jack tilted his head at the screen. "I can't tell. The angle's wrong."

Eagle took out some sort of peg and clamped it onto the cord. He withdrew a penknife from a sheath at his belt and sawed at the cord. Jack remembered the feel of the umbilical cord from when he'd cut Naomi's – tough, sinewy, still palpitating with blood. It had taken him a good minute or two to cut through it with surgical scissors. It took Eagle considerably less time.

"They came prepared," observed Jack.

One of the balaclava-wearing figures took off their jacket, revealing a tight white t-shirt that clung to a male torso. The man had muscular, hairy arms. He handed his jacket to Eagle who swaddled the baby and passed it off to Fox. She cradled it in her arms with the sureness of someone accustomed to holding babies.

The figures released the tattooed woman and stepped away from her. She lifted her head, stretching her hands towards her baby. But Fox and Badger were already leaving the clearing. Eagle squatted by the woman. She feebly batted her fists at him as, lifting his mask slightly, he bent to kiss her forehead.

"He's got a beard," said Steve. "Looks blonde."

"Could be white or grey," said Jack. The night-vision made it difficult to tell. "Neil might be able to tell us which it is."

"If we can get him to talk."

From a cloth bag, Eagle took out something that looked like a klaxon. He lifted up the woman's baggy blouse, exposing bare, milk-swollen breasts. He placed the circular horn over a nipple and began pumping a handle.

"What the hell is he doing?" wondered Steve.

"It's a breast-pump," said Jack. "He's expressing the colostrum."

Eagle transferred the pump to the other breast and repeated the process. When he was done, he unscrewed the pump from the bottle and attached a teat. Again, he kissed the woman's forehead. Then he rose to his feet.

The muscular man removed a short-barrelled handgun from his waistband.

"Looks like a converted starter pistol," said Steve. "An Olympic .38 or something like that."

Olympic .38 BBM blank-firing pistols were a favourite amongst violent criminals, particularly gang members. They were cheap, easy to get hold of and even more easily modified to fire live ammo. Their mid-range accuracy was almost none existent, but they were effective up close, if somewhat unreliable.

Holding up his hands as if to say, *Not yet,* Eagle turned to hurry from the clearing. The muscular man aimed the gun at the woman's head.

"Don't you fucking dare," Steve hissed, even though he knew what the outcome had to be.

The woman stared into the barrel of the gun. It was impossible to tell if her expression was terrified, defiant or simply exhausted beyond caring. The gunman's identically dressed – apart now from the jacket the baby was wrapped in – accomplice moved out of frame briefly, returned with a spade and set to work digging up and stacking turves.

"See how they dug the grave before shooting her," said Steve. "These pricks know what they're doing."

The gravedigger piled soil on the opposite side of the hole to the turves. All neat and tidy. Nothing like the mess Jack had seen in the clearing. Steve fast-forwarded. He pressed play when the gravedigger started to pull up their balaclava to wipe away sweat. The gunman made a swift reprimanding gesture.

"Who's a cautious boy then," said Steve. "He's not taking any chances while the woman's still breathing."

Very cautious indeed, thought Jack. The woman wasn't showing any signs of trying to escape. She was clutching her stomach again and panting audibly. The afterbirth was on its way. The gravedigger climbed out of the hole, downed the spade and grabbed one of the woman's arms. She cried out in pain, fear or both as she was dragged to the lip of the hole. The placenta flopped out of her as she tumbled into her grave. The gravedigger kicked it in after her. The gunman took aim again. Jack noted that he was standing to the right of the grave, holding the gun in his left hand. A position consistent with the angle of the entry wound. The muzzle flashed. There was a pop like a firecracker going off.

Steve slammed his fist into the table. "Jesus Christ, just let me get my hands on these fuckers."

The shooter's accomplice rapidly filled in the grave, replaced the turves and covered them with leaves. After checking to make sure nothing had been left behind, both figures calmly departed the clearing.

Several seconds passed before the lens view rocked towards the woodland canopy. The scene shook with movement. Then the camera hit the ground in the clearing. The hulking, camouflaged figure of Neil dropped into view, partially obscured by grass and leaves. He tore up the turves and began scooping aside huge handfuls of soil. It didn't take him long to dig down to the woman. He ever so gently lifted her out of the grave and laid her on the ground. Her eyes were closed. One arm dangled limply over the edge of the grave. He stared at her as if unsure what to do. She twitched as if an electric current had passed through her.

Neil grabbed his camera and rose to his feet. Accidentally or otherwise, he must have pressed the stop button because the video abruptly ended.

Jack puffed his cheeks. "Well that was..." He trailed off as if uncertain exactly what it was that he'd just seen.

"That was enough to make you wonder if that poor little blighter would have been better off not being born. That's what that was," said Steve.

"I know what it wasn't," replied Jack. "It wasn't a random attack. Eagle knew–"

"You mean the bloke with the bird mask?"

"Yeah. He knew the victim. And that wasn't the first time he'd delivered a baby."

"You reckon he's done this type of thing before?"

"I'd say that's a distinct possibility."

Steve scowled. "What I wouldn't give for five minutes alone with that freak."

"So what do we know for certain?" Jack said as much to himself as to Steve.

Steve gave the obvious answer. "There are five scumbags out there who need putting behind bars asa-fucking-p."

"Fox is a woman. Not sure about Badger. And we know Eagle is a man."

"So is the one who took off his jacket. I'd put money on his mate in the balaclava being a bloke too. You wouldn't put the Animal Magic crew together with the balaclava buddies, would you? Those three look like extras from The Wicker Man and the other two look like small-time gangsters."

"They may well have a gangland connection," said Jack, thinking about the handgun. "I'll tell you something else. They weren't panicked by what went down. But they didn't intend it to go down there either. Otherwise they'd have had a grave ready and waiting."

"The balaclava buddies are definitely pros," agreed Steve. "The question is, what's the relationship between them, the other three and the tattooed woman?"

Jack thought about the broken glass on the hard shoulder. "All six came from the direction of the motorway. It takes about five minutes to reach the clearing. That means they were travelling in a vehicle or vehicles that passed the Junction Two camera at around half-past eleven." He glanced at his watch. It was almost twelve hours since the missing baby had been so cruelly pushed and pulled from its mother's womb. Time was slipping away and there was no more precious commodity in a case like this. "Let's go put Mrs Salter's mind at rest."

Chapter 8

"Like I said, he's as harmless as a lamb," Doreen was telling the uniformed officers as Jack and Steve entered Neil's bedroom. Mother and son were sitting on the bed. Doreen's liver-spotted hand was resting on her son's broad back. Neil was staring at the floor, hands clasped on his lap.

"My Neil's not in any trouble is he?" Doreen asked worriedly.

"Quite the opposite, Mrs Salter," replied Steve. "Your son saved a woman's life last night. He's a hero."

Doreen's mouth dropped open in an almost comical expression of astonishment that made Jack wonder whether anyone had ever said anything good about Neil before. She looked at her son, her eyes glistening with pride. "Did you hear that, Neil? He says you're a hero."

"Hero," Neil repeated quietly, wrinkling his face as if he didn't understand.

"That's right, Neil," said Jack, dropping to his haunches so that he could look into the big man's eyes. "That woman is only alive because of you. Now we need you to help us find her baby. Can you do that?"

Neil was stock-still for a moment, then he gave a little nod. Jack restarted the video and paused it on the tattooed woman. "Do you recognise her? What I mean is, Neil, had you seen her before last night?"

"No."

"What about the other figures? Have you ever seen anyone wearing masks like that before?"

"No."

Jack scrolled through the video to where Eagle raised his mask a few centimetres. "What colour is his beard?"

"Yellow."

"You mean blonde?"

Neil nodded.

"Is there anything else you can tell us about what you saw?" asked Jack. "No matter how silly or unimportant it may seem."

Neil held his hand out for the camera.

"You understand we need to take your camera for further examination?" said Jack. "You'll get it back once we're finished with it."

Neil nodded, but kept his hand out. Jack placed the camera in a spade-sized palm still dirty from digging up the woman. Neil rewound the video to the muscular man taking his jacket off. He zoomed in on the man's left forearm. Jack squinted at the screen. Through the dark hairs he made out what appeared to be a tattoo.

"I'll say it again, that's a bloody good camera you've got there, Neil," put in Steve, peering over Jack's shoulder.

At this praise, a shy smile touched Neil's lips. "Thirty-megapixels, 4K Ultra-HD."

"I can see you know your cameras. Can you zoom in and enhance the image?"

Like a puppy eager to please, Neil did so and displayed the results. There were two words running lengthwise along the man's arm, tattooed in crude block colour. "L... O..." said Jack, struggling to make out the letters.

"Love Alice," said Neil.

"He's right," said Steve. "It says Love Alice. You've got sharp eyes, Neil."

Jack pointed at several dark spots next to the words. "What are they? Moles?"

Steve bent closer to the screen. "No. They're too uniform. I'd say they're tattooed dots." He wrote on his notepad and showed it to Jack – 'LOVE::. ALICE:'

"What does it mean?" wondered Jack.

"That he's in love with someone called Alice."

"Obviously it could mean that, but what about the dots?"

"Could be some sort of code."

"I'm afraid you're going to have to come with us to the station and give a statement," Jack told Neil.

The big man's smile vanished. He shook his head hard.

"There's no need to worry, Neil, your mum can come too. And Police HQ is actually quite nice."

"Yeah, it's got a great café," said Steve. "Do you like cake?" Neil nodded and Steve continued, "Well they do a lovely bit of chocolate cake. You can eat as much as you want. I'm buying."

"Better take him up on that offer quick smart," smiled Jack. "He doesn't get his wallet out very often."

Neil chuckled, his face crumpling like a baby's. Jack glanced at Doreen, tapping his watch. With a nod of understanding, she rose to her feet and urged Neil to do likewise. "Come on, son, let's get your coat on."

Neil placidly did as he was told, reaching for his camo jacket. "Is that the jacket you were wearing in the woods, Neil?" asked Jack. "Forensic officers will need to check over the clothes you had on last night. Just in case there's any evidence on them that might help us."

"I'll make sure you get the clothes, but you'll have to wait downstairs," said Doreen. "Neil doesn't like getting changed in front of people."

"One of us has to stay in the room."

"I'll stay," said Steve. "That's OK with you, isn't it, Neil, mate?"

Neil gave another nod. Jack went downstairs with the uniformed officers. A few minutes later, Neil, Doreen and Steve descended the stairs. Neil had changed into different tracksuit bottoms and a jumper several sizes too small for him. Steve was on the phone. "Yes, sir," he was saying. "Thank you, sir, but it's Jack you should be congratulating. It was his hunch that led us here... OK, sir. Got it. I'll tell him."

Jack and Steve moved outside, leaving Doreen fussing around with coats, scarves and woolly hats. "That was the DCI," said Steve.

"I gathered that. So what have you got to tell me?"

"I'm to take Neil and his mum to HQ. You're to wait here for Forensics, then get back to knocking on doors."

Jack smiled wryly. He hadn't expected any acknowledgement of his work. Neither was he surprised to be palmed off onto jobs that almost certainly weren't going to turn up anything else of interest.

"I know, mate," said Steve, reading his expression. "It's bollocks, but what can you do? The bloke can't stand the sight of you."

"I don't much like his face either." Jack frowned at the ground. He gave a shake of his head. "You know what, screw him. He's going to be seeing me whether he likes it or not. You're right, Steve. It's time to sort this out."

Nodding approvingly, Steve rubbed his hands in anticipation. "How much is it for a front-row seat?"

Ignoring the facetious remark, Jack approached the sergeant and instructed him to stay put and coordinate proceedings. "Oh and if you happen to speak to the DCI, don't tell him I'm on my way to HQ." As an aside to Steve, he added, "I want it to be a surprise."

Chapter 9

The interview room wasn't the most welcoming of places: blank windowless walls, a red panic-button, four plastic-backed chairs – two on either side of a table with recording equipment on it. The air had a fusty, closed-in smell.

Neil didn't seem to mind. He was too interested in tucking into the six slices of cake on the table. Doreen was sipping a cup of tea beside him. She didn't seem to mind either. "I love a good police show," she was telling Jack and Steve. "Prime Suspect, Cracker, Taggart. I watch them all. Do you?"

Both detectives shook their heads. The last thing they wanted when they got home was to be reminded of work. Not that you could ever really stop thinking about it. The wail of grief that tore from a mother when she found out her son had been stabbed to death. The despair in the eyes of a rape victim. The remorseless face of a hardened criminal. Those weren't things you compartmentalised easily.

Jack turned at the sound of purposeful approaching footsteps. His gaze met with Paul's. Recent history had not been kind to DCI Paul Gunn. There was a lot more grey in his swept-back dark hair than there had been a few months ago. His face, once handsome in a world-weary way, now simply looked weary. Shuttling between his job in Manchester and his soon-to-be ex-wife and two kids in Sussex was clearly taking its toll.

Paul pulled up abruptly, frowning. "DI Anderson, didn't you get my orders?"

"I did."

"Then what are you doing here?"

Jack stepped out of the interview room, closing the door behind him. "We need to talk."

"What about?"

"You know what about."

Paul eyed Jack with a mixture of annoyance and uncertainty. "I hardly think this is the time for getting into personal issues. There's a baby missing."

"That's precisely why this game-playing has got to stop." Jack's sharp tone drew a curious glance from a passing constable. "We can do this here or in your office. It's up to you."

The detectives stared at each other for a moment. Paul turned to stride back the way he'd come. Jack followed him to a small, cluttered office. A desk was swamped by a tsunami of paperwork. Documents relating to various crimes overlapped each other on the walls. Paul had never been one for keeping his office tidy, but there had always been some discernible order to the chaos. Now all Jack saw was confusion – the outward expression of a disordered mind.

Paul shut the door and fixed his frazzled grey eyes on Jack. "Well?" he said impatiently.

"You sent me to North Manchester General to do a job anyone with a camera could have done. You didn't update me on what was our then prime suspect's description. Those things cost us two, maybe three hours."

"That description was sent out to everyone. If you didn't get it, the problem's on your end not mine."

Jack's lips thinned into a humourless smile. "I've had enough of your bullshit to last me a lifetime, Paul." Although his voice was tightly controlled, a tremor crept into it as he continued, "Natasha's divorcing you because you screwed my wife, not because of anything I said to her. All that shit that went on, it shouldn't have anything to do with what happens here."

Paul blinked, but kept his gaze fixed on Jack. "You're right, it shouldn't. But it does. It's why I always put you and that idiot Platts together and it's why I keep you as far away from the rest of the team as possible. You used to be a good copper, Jack, but not anymore. Oh you've still got the nose for it. I don't doubt that for a second. But you changed after Rebecca died."

Jack winced visibly. *Died.* Rebecca hadn't simply died. She'd thrown herself off a cliff. Maybe Paul wasn't the reason for that – Rebecca had struggled with mental health issues long before their affair – but at the very least he'd unwittingly helped facilitate her self-destruction. "Committed suicide," corrected Jack. "Why can't you just say it like it is?"

Paul shook his head. "You'll never get it right in here, will you?" He jabbed a finger at his temple. "Whether Rebecca jumped or fell, it makes no difference. She's dead. And we're still here, dealing with the fallout. You know what I think? If Rebecca could see us right now she'd be laughing at how pathetic we are."

"You're the pathetic one, Paul. Playing your petty little games."

Paul glanced pointedly at Jack's t-shirt and jeans. "I'm not the only one playing games."

"But I'm not putting lives at risk."

"Aren't you? When you talk to me like you did in the corridor, people lose respect for me. Do you realise how damaging that is?" Paul chopped his hand into his palm as if breaking something in two. "Before I know it other team members will be disregarding my orders, thinking they know better. I can't allow that to happen, no matter how bad I feel about what I did."

Jack's eyes dropped away from Paul's, furrows forming between them. As much as he hated to admit it, Paul was right. They were both as guilty as each other on that score. With a prickling of shame, his thoughts returned to the newborn letting out its first cries. "OK," he said, moving towards the door.

"Where are you going?"

"Back to Clifton."

Disappointment flashed over Paul's face – as if he'd hoped Jack would reply, *Home and I'm not coming back* – but it was quickly replaced by something else. It wasn't a look of apology or remorse, not even close, but neither was it a look of recrimination. "Did I say you were dismissed, DI Anderson?"

Jack stopped and waited for Paul to continue.

"The victim wasn't carrying ID or wearing a wedding ring. Her fingerprints aren't on the database. The doctors say there's a high probability she won't regain consciousness. Right now the only chance we have of identifying her quickly is releasing her image to the media. But of course that also lets her attackers know she's still alive, which could put both her and her baby in danger. What do you think we should do?"

The two men met each other's gaze again, their eyes cold but no longer openly hostile. "That's not our only chance," said Jack. "There are the motorway cameras. If they turn up nothing, releasing her image is a risk worth taking. If her attackers return to finish the job, we'll be ready for them. As for her baby," he thought about the way Eagle had carefully wrapped up the newborn before expressing the colostrum that was so vital to its immune system, "I don't think they'll hurt it unless they have to. Watch the video and I'm sure you'll agree with me. Was there anything else?"

"Yes, I don't need you in Clifton. I need you and DI Platts to concentrate on identifying the tattoos. Am I making myself clear? I don't want any more misunderstandings about who's giving the orders and who's taking them."

Another brief space of silence passed between them, then Jack said, "Yes, sir." *Sir.* It was only a small word, but there was a world of meaning in it.

Some of the tension faded from Paul's face as if an unspoken truce had been declared. He gave a jerk of his chin as if to say, *Then get to it.*

Jack wordlessly left the office.

Chapter 10

After fruitlessly searching the PNC databases for anyone with a tattoo matching the victim's or perp's, Jack and Steve headed out to do the rounds of local tattoo parlours. As soon as they were away from the prying ears of HQ, Steve said, "So come on then, let's hear it. Did you two kiss-and-make-up?"

"It's sorted," said Jack, although he knew things would never truly be sorted out between Paul and him. His oldest friend had had an affair with his wife – an affair that had quite possibly driven her to suicide. How did you ever get *that* right in your head? His tone made it clear there was nothing else to be said on the subject.

There were over a hundred tattoo parlours in the Greater Manchester area. It was going to take the rest of the day and probably the next day or two as well to get round them all. They'd decided to start in the city centre and work their way outwards. "What's the bet we don't find out anything until the last place on the list?" said Steve.

"If we find out anything at all," muttered Jack.

"God, you're a morose bugger sometimes. Would you rather be going door-to-door in Clifton?"

"No."

"Then try cracking a smile, why don't you?"

Jack formed his lips into an obviously fake smile.

Steve chuckled. "I think I prefer your miserable face."

The first tattoo parlour was in a trendy location with floor to ceiling windows, a neon sign and photos of the tattooist's handiwork in the window. The interior was all chrome, distressed wood and leather. Hip-hop was blasting out of hidden speakers. A guy with a hipster beard and two full sleeves of tattoos was working on a girl with a buzzing needle.

"Things have certainly changed since I was a kid," commented Steve. "Back then these places were hidden down backstreets and the only people you'd find in them were crims and slags."

"Every other teenager's got a tattoo these days."

"Yeah well if my daughter showed up with a tramp-stamp I'd hit the fucking roof."

"Do as I say, not as I do, eh." Jack glanced meaningfully at Steve's left bicep where under his sleeve there lurked a skull wearing the maroon beret of The Paras.

"That's different. I earned that tattoo. The only thing these kids have earned is a clip round the ear for being so stupid."

They showed the tattooist photos of the butterfly wing and 'LOVE::. ALICE:' tattoos. "That wing is a nice piece of work," he commented, "but I don't do facial tattoos. Kids come in here on a whim wanting something on their face. Five years later they're on antidepressants because no one will give them a job. The other tattoo's a piece of shit. This is the best tattoo parlour in Manchester."

"Do you know anyone who does facial tattoos?" asked Jack.

The tattooist wrote down the names of half a dozen parlours. "Some of these places have a very particular clientele, if you know what I mean. Confidentiality is a big deal to them. They probably wouldn't tell you even if they had done that tattoo."

They thanked the tattooist and left. "Change of plan?" said Steve.

Jack nodded. They checked out the nearest of the six parlours. It was on a congested city centre road above a shop with blacked-out windows that sold 'XXX DVDs and Magazines, Fetish Wear, Rubber and Latex Products, Special Interest Products'. The tattoo parlour's sign hadn't seen a fresh coat of paint in a long time.

"This is more like it," said Steve.

They climbed some gloomy stairs to a room painted all in black, its walls papered with images of tattoos. A slim, pale woman with a faceful of piercings, a necklace of tattoos and a head of raven black hair shaved down the sides exposing more tattoos said, "What can I do for you?"

"Well we're not here to get tattoos," said Steve.

The woman treated his suit, shirt and tie to a scathing up-and-down glance. "Really? I'd never have guessed."

Smiling at the sardonic response, Steve took out his ID. "Can I ask your name?"

"Viv."

Jack showed her the two tattoos. "Do you recognise either of these, Viv?"

She put on a pair of glasses and looked at the photos. She spent a full minute on the butterfly wing, tracing her finger over its ragged outline and delicately patterned surface. "Beautiful," she said. "Look at the detailing, the depth of the image. Someone with real talent did this." She handed the photos back. "Sorry, I don't know the artist."

"Are you sure?"

"A hundred percent."

"You wouldn't be lying to us, would you Viv?" said Steve. "This is a very serious matter. You could land yourself in a lot of trouble."

She fixed him with a steady stare. "Do I look like I'm lying? You've heard of Van Gogh, right?"

"Did he do those tattoos?"

Viv mouthed a sarcastic laugh. "My point is you'd recognise one of his paintings anywhere. It's the same with tattoos. When it comes to someone as good as whoever did that wing, I'd know their work at a glance."

"What about the other tattoo?" asked Jack.

Viv shrugged. "Anyone could have done it."

"Do any of your customers have a wife, partner or daughter named Alice?"

"Not that I can think of off the top of my head. I've been doing this twelve years. I've had thousands of clients. You hear a lot of names. A lot of stories. After a while, it all starts to blur together. It must be the same for you guys."

"Oh yeah, Viv, you definitely hear a lot of stories," agreed Steve. "A lot of bullshit."

She frowned. "Are you saying I'm lying? Because I don't have to take that kind of crap in my place."

"No one's suggesting anything like that," Jack assured her. "But as Steve said, this is an extremely serious matter. So if you can think of anything that might be of help we'd be hugely appreciative."

"Sorry if I offended you," said Steve.

Viv cocked an eyebrow as if she doubted his sincerity. Her gaze returned to the words 'LOVE::. ALICE:'. "I think maybe you're barking up the wrong tree. I don't think whoever has that tattoo is in love with someone called Alice."

"Then what does it mean?"

Viv took out a pen and wrote something below the words. Jack and Steve exchanged an uneasy glance. Below LOVE she'd written 'kilL tO liVE'. Below ALICE was 'kill AL polICE'.

"It's an acronym," explained Viv. "The dots represent–"

"I can guess what they represent," Jack broke in grimly. Each dot represented a kill. Seven civilians. Two police. This was bad. Civilians were one thing, but police... Only the worst of the worst knowingly killed police. "How do you know about this?"

Viv gave another shrug. "You hear about this kind of thing." She thumbed to a reclining leather chair. "I've had plenty of ex-cons in that." She added quickly, "I've never seen anyone with a tattoo like that though. And I wouldn't do any work on them if I did. I can't be doing with psychos like that. If you ask me they're all just limp-dicks with mummy issues."

"Can you give us the names of any of these ex-cons?"

Viv's frown returned. "Didn't you hear what I said before? I'm shit with names. And anyway, I don't even know if I'm right about that tattoo. It just kind of came to me as I was looking at it. Y'know, like when the answer to a question suddenly comes to you, but you don't know where from. Doesn't that ever happen to you?"

"All the time," said Steve. "It's called getting old."

"Cheeky sod," Viv shot back. "I'm not old."

"No, but I am."

Viv smiled, this time without any hint of sarcasm. "You don't look all that old to me. Lose that slug above your lip and the beer belly and you wouldn't be half bad."

Before Steve could counter with another comeback, Jack said, "Thanks for your time." He gave Viv his card. "If anything else comes to mind, give us a call."

"That's the second time you've done that today," Steve grumbled as they returned to the car.

"Done what?"

"Pussy-blocked me."

Jack gave him a sidelong glance. "Sometimes I think you've got mummy issues. That girl wouldn't piss on you if you were on fire."

"Nah. That whole bad bitch thing is just an act. Believe me, mate, I know a real bitch when I see one. My ex-wife's the biggest bitch in Manchester."

"Do you buy that, *It just kind of came to me,* line?"

"I don't see why not. But I hope she is lying. I'd love an excuse to talk to her again." Steve's expression suddenly turned serious. "A cop killer." He shook his head. "B-a-a-d news."

"On the plus side, we didn't have to speak to every tattooist in Manchester before coming up with something. I say we check out the other places that do facial tattoos, then head back to HQ. If Viv's right, our guy's walking around free after killing nine people. That's a lot of unsolved murders. Maybe we can find one that connects to him."

Chapter 11

It was late afternoon by the time they returned to HQ. They stopped off on the way to fill up on fast-food. Steve burped and patted his belly. "Viv's right. I should go on a diet. Start running again. Get back into shape."

"Forget it, you're too far gone," said Jack.

Steve stroked his salt 'n pepper moustache. "I've had this thing twenty-odd years. My first wife loved it. Said it tickled her–"

"I don't need to know what it tickled."

The daylight was dropping when they pulled into HQ's high-security carpark. Lights glowed behind dozens of alternating clear and blue-tinted windows. The glass walls and sharp modern angles were, doubtless, supposed to portray an open and friendly police force. But to Jack's eyes they only emphasised the cold, institutional nature of the building. The detectives made their way up to the incident-room. DC Olivia Clarke met them at the door with an armful of printouts. She treated them to one of her bright-and-breezy smiles. She had stylish hair, a slim-cut suit and an easy-going manner that combined to make Jack feel about a hundred-years-old.

"What have you two reprobates been up to?" she asked.

"We've been talking to tattooists," said Steve. "I'm thinking about getting 'past its sell by date' tattooed on my forehead."

"At least then no one could accuse you of false advertising," Olivia said dryly.

"You're supposed to say, *Aww, Steve, you're not past your sell by date.*"

"Aww, Steve, you're not past your sell by date," obliged Olivia.

Jack was looking at the uppermost printout – a high-angled, grainy colour image of a motorway carriageway. It was time-stamped 23:22

15/11/17. There was one car in the image. It was too dark to make it out clearly. "Find anything?"

"Yeah, take a look at this." Olivia leafed through the printouts to one time-stamped 23:28. There were three vehicles in the image. The foremost was a small car in the slow lane. Next came a bigger car, possibly a Range Rover or some other SUV. It was tailgating the small car, almost bumper to bumper. In the outer lane, slightly behind the other vehicles was what looked to be a minibus. Light from a lamppost was splashed across a front bonnet that had been amateurishly painted in a rainbow of colours. "That's the M61 southbound slip road adjacent to the crime-scene. Now look at this." She flipped to a CCTV-still of the multicoloured vehicle and small car time-stamped 00:23. "Those are two of the same vehicles on the M60 eastbound, just past junction fifteen. In almost an hour, they'd travelled less than a mile."

"That's got to be them," said Steve.

"We believe this is the other car." Olivia showed them an image of a black Range Rover with tinted windows. "It was picked up by the same camera half-an-hour later." She turned to the next image – a close-up of the SUV's front bumper. The registration was just about legible. The left-hand headlight was smashed.

"So assuming the victim was driving the foremost car, I think it's also safe to assume the perps in animal masks were in the minibus and the perps in balaclavas were in the SUV," said Jack. "They wait until there are no other vehicles around, ram her off the road, chase her down and do their thing. One of the perps from the minibus takes the victim's car. The shooter and his accomplice follow after filling in the grave."

"Sounds about right," agreed Steve.

"Have you got the other regs, Olivia?"

She nodded. "The Range Rover's reg comes up as an Audi hatchback that was stolen in Liverpool in 2016. The other car and minibus are both insurance write-offs. Someone probably bought them from a scrapyard. Pretty much untraceable."

"Shit," muttered Steve.

"Have we got any faces on camera?" asked Jack.

"Nothing clear."

"At least we know for sure that they used the motorway and came from somewhere north of Manchester," pointed out Steve. "Maybe Preston or Blackburn."

"Or Liverpool," said Jack.

"Liverpool's south of Manchester. You've lived here long enough by now to know that."

"I was thinking about the stolen Audi."

"I'm just on my way to show these to the DCI," said Olivia.

"One second." Jack jotted down the Range Rover's reg, thanked Olivia and headed for his desk. The Incident Room had a subdued, end-of-a-long-day atmosphere. Some officers were tapping away at laptops. Others were chatting quietly. DS Gary Crawley was slumped in his chair, heavy-eyed.

"I've spent the entire day traipsing around Walkden," he told them through a yawn. "Total waste of time."

"Why don't you go home?" suggested Steve.

Gary glanced at his watch. "I don't clock-off for another twenty minutes."

"Bollocks to that, you've been up since midnight."

"So what's new? I can sit around here or go home and have my ears abused by a stressed wife and two screaming babies."

"Well if you're hanging around, you can make yourself useful," said Jack. "We need to put together a list of every unsolved murder in the past... let's say ten years in Greater Manchester and Merseyside."

"That'll be a big list. Are you looking for anything in particular?"

"Yeah, anything with gangland connections."

"Especially suspected hits where the victim was killed by a single gunshot to the head," added Steve.

They left Gary to wearily get on with his task. "You didn't mention the possibility of two dead police," Steve said quietly to Jack.

"Say the words cop and killer in the same breath and you've got a roomful of angry people. That's not going to help anyone. If we come up with anything we'll take it to the DCI and find out what he wants to do."

Jack spent the next hour or so trawling through the PNC databases. He took a closer look at the stolen Audi first. The red hatchback had been stolen on February 2nd 2015 from the driveway of a house in Allerton, a relatively affluent suburb on the south side of Liverpool. The registration MY63 ARL indicated that the car was registered in Merseyside between September 2013 and February 2014. The thieves had forced a patio door while the owner was asleep, taken the car keys, the car and nothing else. Merseyside police believed the Audi had been stolen to order by a gang of professional car thieves from outside the city. The owner, a Mrs Felicity Booth, had spent the previous day shopping at the Trafford Centre. The thieves were thought to have seen her there and followed her home. No suspects were identified in connection with the theft.

Manchester was a hotbed of car crime. In recent years, organised gangs had targeted Audis, VWs and BMWS in the region. The cars were often exported to the Middle East and Eastern Europe where there was a booming market for high-end German cars. They could also be stripped and sold for parts or used as getaway vehicles. The scumbags stealing the cars were low-end crims, but the people they passed them on to were gangsters running multi-million pound operations. It would definitely be worth bringing a few of the higher-ups in for questioning. They wouldn't give up any names, but they might disapprove sufficiently of attempting to murder a woman and stealing her baby as to make life difficult for the perpetrators. They might even convince the guilty parties that returning the baby was in everyone's best interest.

Of course, that would give the perps a heads-up. But that was inevitable anyway considering the dead-end the motorway cameras had led to. Right now Paul was probably organising a press-conference to release the victim's image.

Next Jack looked into British police officers killed in the line of duty dating back twenty years. The list was fairly short, but still far too long. He scanned through thirty six names, mostly PCs but also a sprinkling of DCs, sergeants, an inspector and even a commander. The causes of death ranged from collapsing and dying whilst in hot pursuit of suspects to being deliberately rammed, run over, stabbed and shot. Similarly the killers encompassed the whole gamut of criminal humanity – violent drunks, petty thieves, drug dealers, armed robbers, gangsters, terrorists, sexual predators, psychopaths. In the vast majority of cases, the perpetrators had swiftly been caught. There were a handful, though, that had never been solved. One immediately caught Jack's eye.

On 28th April 2016, PC Andrew Finch had been on patrol in Leeds city centre. At approximately 2:15 pm, he approached an illegally parked car. In an apparently unprovoked attack, PC Finch was shot point-blank in the face by the driver. He died instantly. The car drove away at speed. A shop worker who heard the shot and went outside to investigate, photographed the car with their mobile phone.

Jack looked at a slightly out-of-focus image of the car. Registration: MA13 SOR. Colour: black. Make: Audi A3. The registration and colour were different, but the make and model were the same as the stolen Audi. The registration belonged to a BMW that had been stolen in Manchester a couple of months before the Audi. A cane with a hook on the end – or some such thing – had been pushed through the owner's letterbox and hooked the keys. Quick, easy, low risk and high return. As with the Audi, no suspects had been identified or arrests made. The photograph was of the rear of the Audi. Glare on the windows made it impossible to see the driver or any other occupants.

Another dead end.

After the shooting, a huge investigation had been launched. PC Finch was a family man with an unblemished record, well-liked by everyone who knew him. There was no reason someone might want to kill him. Hundreds of members of the North's criminal fraternity, particularly anyone who might bear a grudge against the police, had been questioned. But no solid leads were generated. The killer was either a lone-wolf or inspired such fear that no one dared speak out. The latter was entirely possible. A psycho who hated the police so ferociously that they were willing to kill a random constable in broad daylight was not someone you grassed on. The black Audi was never seen again. Was it the same car that had been stolen from Allerton? Were the killer of PC Finch and the man who attempted to kill the tattooed woman one and the same?

The possibility sent a cold thrill through Jack. There was nothing more dangerous than a killer with a gun and a grudge against coppers. His thoughts turned to Naomi. She worried about him just as much, perhaps even more, than he did about her. Recently she'd been pressuring him to go into a different line of work – preferably a primary school teacher or some other equally low risk profession. Cases like this made Jack wonder whether he should do just that.

He printed out the salient details and headed over to where Steve and Gary were working on the list of unsolved civilian murders. "Are you ready for this?" said Steve. "We're looking at sixty one unsolved murders in Greater Manchester and seventy two in Merseyside in the last decade. That's a shit lot of paperwork to go through."

"Well there's going to be even more," said Jack. "We need to expand our focus to West Yorkshire."

"Not me," said Gary, standing. "The wife just messaged me. She says she's divorcing me if I'm not home in the next half-hour."

As Gary trudged to the exit, Steve asked, "Find anything?"

Jack showed him the printout. Steve pulled his moustache uneasily. "I remember this case. Finch was about Gary's age. He had a couple of young kids. They held a funeral for him in Leeds city centre. Thousands of people lined the streets. You must have heard about it."

"It rings a bell, but I was going through a bad time back then. My wife Rebecca was seriously ill." Jack felt a sting of self-contempt at the vagueness of his words. Rebecca had been depressed, relentlessly slipping towards suicide. He'd berated Paul for not saying it like it was, yet here he was doing the same thing. *Depression. Suicide.* Were there any words in the English language harder to say?

"I'll end up seriously ill myself if I don't get some sleep soon," said Steve, displaying his usual insensitivity. Or perhaps, conversely, sensing Jack's discomfort and clumsily attempting to put him at ease. "Let's show the DCI what we've got, then we can bugger off home."

As they left the Incident Room, they spotted Paul emerging from the toilets at the far end of the corridor. His hair looked recently brushed. He'd put on a fresh shirt and tie. "Press conference," Steve murmured out of the side of his mouth.

The scent of aftershave preceded Paul as they approached him. "DI Anderson, DI Platts, I was just about to come looking for you two." He motioned for them to follow him into his office. "So how's your day been? Productive?"

"We might have something," said Jack.

"Just give me the gist of it." Paul glanced at a clock on the wall. "I've got about ten minutes before I speak to the press."

Steve told him about the tattooist's theory. Jack took over when it came to the Audi and PC Andrew Finch's murder. Paul listened with a gathering frown. "This is a..." he sought the right words, "disturbing development."

"I think we should begin bringing in all the usual suspects," suggested Jack. "Start at the top and work our way down."

"I agree, but I need to speak to the Super first. You know how emotive this kind of thing is. Leave it with me for now. Steve, you keep working on those unsolved murders. Jack, I want you to head back to the hospital. The victim's regained consciousness."

Jack's eyebrows lifted. He'd fully expected to hear that the woman had died. "Has she said anything?"

"Yes. She said she wants to talk to you."

Jack's surprise turned to puzzlement. "Me? How's that possible?"

"Apparently she heard you asking about her tattoo."

"But she was in a coma."

"They say comatose people can hear things," said Steve. "I watched this program about–"

"I'm sure it was very interesting, DI Platts," Paul cut in pointedly.

"And is that all she's said?" asked Jack.

Paul nodded. "Apparently she's having problems with her memory."

"So she can't remember what happened to her?"

"It seems that way."

"Then why does she want to talk to me?"

Sighing, Paul took another look at the clock. "DI Platts, you can return to your desk now."

"Yes sir."

Steve left the room. Paul waited until Steve's footsteps had faded away, then said, "I'm sensing some reluctance."

"My shift's over in five minutes. I have to pick Naomi up from her after-school club."

"Couldn't you get Laura to do it?"

"I could, but... well I had to wake her in the middle of the night to babysit Naomi. She's been at work all day. She'll be exhausted."

"If you can't go to the hospital, I'll just have to get someone else to do it. There are plenty of other things for you to be getting on with. I need someone to go over to Walkden tomorrow and do some follow-ups."

The implication of Paul's words was obvious – you wanted back on the team, this is the price. Jack couldn't help but wonder whether Paul was doing this out of spite because he rarely got to see his own children these days. He bit down on the impulse to say so. If he was going to stay in this job, he had to be all the way in. "I'll call Laura."

"Thank you, DI Anderson." Paul made it clear the conversation was over by shuffling some papers on his desk.

Chapter 12

Jack forgot his annoyance as he drove to North Manchester General. He was intrigued to find out what the tattooed woman had to say. He didn't intend to stay at the hospital long. As always, Laura had gladly agreed to look after Naomi. But Jack could tell from her voice that she was worn out. He made a mental note to buy a bottle of her favourite wine on the way home.

He parked up and made his way to ICU. Doctor Medland met him at the reception desk. "The patient regained consciousness about an hour ago," he explained. "Frankly, we were all amazed. But as I think I said to you before, it's incredibly difficult to predict how things will play out with brain injuries."

"I'm told her memory has been affected."

"Yes. The temporal lobe is essential for memory function. Even minor damage can cause anything from partial to total amnesia, along with all kinds of other complications – auditory and visual disturbances; changes in personality and behaviour. The good news is she's talking, which may indicate that the Broca area wasn't damaged after all."

"So what does she remember?"

"At this point the only thing she remembers is hearing your voice. It may even be that your voice started her along the pathway back to consciousness."

"Why would she respond to my voice in particular?"

"It could be something as simple as your southern accent. Perhaps you sound similar to someone she's close to."

"Does she have an accent?"

"It's difficult to say. Her voice is very weak."

Jack noted down, 'Victim might originally be from the south east'. Of course, that didn't do much to improve the chances of identifying her. As they made their way to the woman's room, Doctor Medland cautioned, "I must ask you to avoid mentioning anything that might cause stress."

"What about the baby? Does she know she recently gave birth?"

"No. And I think it should stay that way for now."

"Could mentioning the baby kick-start her memory?"

"It could, but it could also have a negative impact on her recovery."

Jack looked the doctor in the eyes. "If it was your child that had been abducted, wouldn't you take that risk to get them back?"

Doctor Medland considered this, then said, "OK, but if she becomes seriously distressed you must stop questioning her at once."

An armed officer was stationed outside the room. After the press-conference, the woman's face would be splashed across every TV screen in the country. Paul wasn't taking any chances.

Doctor Medland glanced disapprovingly at the officer's holstered sidearm. "Is it really necessary to have guns on the ward?"

Jack thought about PC Finch being shot dead for no apparent reason. "Yes," he stated.

The doctor motioned for Jack to keep his voice down as they entered the dimly lit room. The woman's eyes were closed. She was deathly pale, but if you looked closely you could see the shallow rise and fall of her chest. Doctor Medland touched her hand. Her eyes opened slowly like the petals of a flower in the sun. Her brown eyes were bleary, shot through with veins, so dilated as to appear almost black. They slid across from the doctor to Jack. There was nothing in them, just an anesthetised emptiness.

"I'm Detective Inspector Jack Anderson," Jack said softly.

A tiny spark flickered in her pupils. Her lips moved but no audible words came out. With one finger, she made a slight beckoning motion. Jack bent closer and she breathed woozily into his ear, "Who… am… I?"

She didn't have a southern accent. If anything, Jack thought he detected a faint Mancunian twang. "That's what I'm here to try and find out."

She closed her eyes as if she'd been afraid he would say that. She looked so painfully helpless that he put his hand on hers to try to comfort her. Her eyelids parted again. She looked at him numbly.

"Do you remember anything?" he asked.

Her lips trembled. Jack could see her mentally searching, groping for a light-switch in the darkness. She gave a barely-there shake of her head.

"Try not to move your head," cautioned Doctor Medland. "Do you know where you are?" He stooped to hear her whispered reply, then said to Jack, "That's a good sign. She remembers what I told her earlier. Her short-term memory appears to be functioning."

"Did you think you recognised my voice?" Jack asked her.

"I..." she faltered, then murmured, "don't know. What happened to me?"

Doctor Medland gave Jack a look that instructed him to tread with extreme care. "Someone attacked you," said Jack.

"Why?"

"We're not sure why." Jack hesitated. Something about this woman suddenly made him think of Rebecca. It wasn't her looks. Her face was broader and more angular than Rebecca's had been. Maybe it was her vulnerability. Or maybe it was the way she looked at him like a lost child. Whatever it was, it made him reluctant to say anything that could upset her. "We'll find out though. I assure you of that."

He made to remove his hand, but the woman curled her fingers lightly around his. Her skin was rough and calloused. Her nails were ingrained with dirt. "I had a dream... I... think it was a dream..." Her eyelids drifted down. Like someone talking in their sleep, she mumbled, "A man... with the face of a bird. He's... on top of me. I can feel him... inside... me..."

The woman's voice faded into a silence punctuated by the whoosh and beep of the surrounding machines. A jolt of concern passed through Jack as her fingers went limp. "Has she fallen back into a coma?"

Doctor Medland checked her vitals and EEG brainwave read-out. "She's asleep."

They left the room quietly. Jack was thinking about Eagle. Had the woman been in a relationship with the man behind the bird mask? The way Eagle had kissed her seemed to suggest so. Perhaps they'd been a couple. If so, Eagle could be the baby's father.

"You said it's a good sign that her short-term memory is working," said Jack. "Does that mean her long-term memory will return?"

"I'm afraid not. It merely means she's able to form new memories. Which is far more than we could have expected. I must tell you, though, her prognosis is still not good. That bullet is a ticking time-bomb. If we can't remove it, then..." Doctor Medland trailed off ominously.

Jack thanked him. As he headed for the exit, he heard a nurse asking the doctor, "How's our butterfly doing?"

"Butterfly," Jack repeated to himself. That was certainly an apt name for the woman. And not simply because of her tattoo. Back in Sussex, every summer the cottage's garden had been a riot of Painted Ladies that had migrated thousands of miles, evading predators and enduring disease and extreme weather along the way. Butterflies were a lot tougher than their delicate wings suggested.

He phoned Paul who greeted the update with a disappointed *hmm* and said, "So she might be from this area. She might be close to someone with a southern accent. And Eagle might be the baby's father. That doesn't give us much to go on. Anything else?"

Jack thought about the feel of Butterfly's skin. "She might do some sort of manual work. Her hands are rough."

"Perhaps she's a keen gardener."

There was an awkward pause. Rebecca had been a keen gardener. Before depression sucked the life out of her, she'd spent much of her spare time tending her flower beds – narcissi and tulips in spring, dahlias and cosmos in summer and autumn. Jack filled the silence with, "How did the press-conference go?"

"Fine. The hook's in the water. Now we just have to wait and see if we get a bite."

Jack held in a sigh of irritation at Paul's impersonal tone. Butterfly was the bait on Paul's hook. This very moment her attackers might be looking at her face on TV and debating what to do. Would they make another attempt on her life? Would they kill her baby? Perhaps they would do both. "Do you need anything else from me?"

"No. You can knock off. Thanks, Jack."

Thanks, Jack. Paul hadn't spoken to him in such a friendly – if that was the right word – way in a long time. Jack wasn't sure whether he liked the development. He could just about get to grips with them acting in a professional manner towards each other, but as for being friendly...

"Thank you, *sir,*" he replied and hung up.

Chapter 13

The instant Jack stepped into the house, Naomi flung her arms around him as if she hadn't seen him in months. Laughing, he cuddled her back. A hug from Naomi was the best pick-me-up there was. "You were supposed to finish work ages ago and you look really tired," she admonished.

Jack glanced at himself in the hallway mirror. Naomi was right. He did look tired. There were dark smudges beneath his eyes. "Sorry, sweetheart. I tried to get away earlier."

"But your *boss* wouldn't let you, would he?"

Boss. The way Naomi's lips curled on the word made Jack frown. She was as sharp as a pin when it came to picking up on people's emotions. Even if she didn't fully comprehend the reason behind it, she was well aware of his feelings towards Paul. The last thing he wanted was to infect her with his hate. That was the best reason of all to let go of what had happened. A therapist had once told him that the past was like a stick of dynamite that could explode at any moment, destroying you and the things you loved. Why would anyone choose to carry such a thing around?

I didn't choose this, Jack had retorted.

No, but you can choose to drop it, the therapist had said. *All you have to do is open your hand.*

All you have to do is open your hand. What could be simpler? He'd visualised himself doing it dozens of times. Yet the next time he looked down, the dynamite was always back, enclosed in white knuckles.

He stroked Naomi's hair. "Well I'm home now. Where's your aunt?"

Laura poked her head out of the kitchen. "I'm cooking tea. It'll be ready in about five minutes."

Smiling gratefully, Jack handed his sister a bottle of white wine. "Ooh my favourite," she said, smiling back. "What are you buttering me up for?"

"I just want you to know how much I appreciate everything you do for us."

"Aww, thanks little brother."

Jack went into the living-room and stretched out on the sofa. Naomi snuggled up against him like a cat. The worries of the day faded away as they watched TV and chatted about this and that.

After eating, Jack got Naomi ready for bed. She rested her delicate fingers on his as he read her a bedtime story. His thoughts returned to Butterfly. For her there was no past to let go of. Perhaps that was a blessing in disguise. Perhaps...

He kissed Naomi and went downstairs. Laura was putting her coat on. "Thanks again for everything, sis," he said.

"No problem. The bill's on the kitchen table."

Smiling at the dry remark, Jack kissed Laura goodbye. He returned to the living-room and put on the 24-hour news. It didn't take long for Butterfly's bruised and swollen face to appear on-screen. He paused the image. His gaze fell to his hand. When she'd touched him he'd felt something more than skin. He still seemed to feel it. A slight shivery sensation. Like static electricity. He thought about the lost look in her eyes. Maybe it wasn't his accent that had imprinted so deeply on her. Maybe on some unconscious level she'd recognised a damaged kindred spirit.

A yawn turned Jack's thoughts to bed. He dragged himself upstairs and got undressed. Butterfly's voice pulled him under into sleep, asking one question over and over – *Who am I?*

Chapter 14

Jack was woken by his phone. It was still dark. The alarm clock read 6:32. The phone's screen identified the caller as 'Steve'. Jack's heart gave a little kick. There must have been some new development for Steve to be ringing so early. He put the phone to his ear. "What's up?"

"Morning, sleeping beauty. You sound pissed off. Did I wake you from a dirty dream?"

Jack was in no the mood for Steve's bullshit. "Just tell me."

Steve chuckled as if Jack's brusqueness had answered his question. "OK grumpy arse. Maybe this'll improve your mood. We're off to The Lakes for the day. A call came in from a shopkeeper in Gosforth, a Mrs Barbara Boyles. She reckons our tattooed lady came into her shop early last year."

The news did improve Jack's mood, but not for the reason Steve alluded to. He was simply relieved that Steve hadn't rung to tell him Butterfly was dead.

"I'm on my way to pick you up," continued Steve. "See you in about twenty."

A quick shower and shave later, Jack phoned Laura to let her know what was going on. "Will you be back today?" she asked.

"I should be, but who knows what time."

"In that case, I'll take Naomi back to mine after school."

Jack got off the phone and looked in on Naomi. She was curled up beneath her duvet. He gently shook her awake. "Time to get up, sweetie." She followed him downstairs, blinking dazedly. Elsa – Naomi's black-and-white cat – greeted them with a meow as they entered the kitchen.

They were munching on cereal when there was a knock at the door. "That'll be Steve," said Jack, pushing his chair back. The burly ex-Para blocked out the thin November light as he stepped into the hallway. "Are you ready for a three hour drive to the arse end of nowhere?" he grinned.

"Hi Steve," said Naomi, poking her head through the kitchen doorway.

He ruffled her hair. "Look at you. You get more gorgeous every time I see you. It won't be long before boys are falling all over you."

She scrunched up her face. "Urgh! I can't stand boys. They're idiots."

Steve laughed. "You're right about that."

Jack ushered Naomi back to the table. The thought of boys falling over themselves to get at her was enough to make him want a cigarette. He reached into his pocket before recalling that he'd kicked the habit. He'd attempted to do so numerous times in the past, but always found some reason to light up again – stress at work, Rebecca's depression. Things were different now. It was all on his shoulders. He couldn't afford to take risks with his health.

Jack poured Steve a coffee as Naomi finished her breakfast. Neither man made any mention of what their day held in store. Steve had kids of his own. He knew how important it was to protect them from the cruelty and cynicism of life.

On the way to Laura's, Naomi chatted happily about school and her friends. But when they pulled over outside Laura's little terraced house, her expression grew worried. "You're going to be late home again, aren't you Dad?"

"Probably," admitted Jack.

"Don't you worry, I'll look after him for you," said Steve.

Laura appeared at the front door in her nurse's uniform. She waved. Jack and Steve waved back. "Have a good day, sweetheart," Jack called after Naomi as she got out of the car.

He heaved a sigh as they accelerated away.

"The guilt's a killer, isn't it?" said Steve. "It used to kick my arse every time I didn't get home in time to put the kids to bed. But then the wife ran off with some twat she met online, so now I don't have to worry about all that." His tone was blasé, but the way he reached for his cigarettes suggested he felt differently inside.

They drove in silence for a while, then Steve said, "I'll tell you what, your sister's not half bad. I wouldn't mind–"

"Don't even think about it," cut in Jack, darting him a sharp look.

Steve smirked and held his tongue. A smile found its way onto Jack's face too as they headed north out of Manchester. Laura and Steve. What a couple they would make. The smile disappeared as they passed the junction where Butterfly had endured her ordeal. The southbound slip road had reopened. The only sign that anything untoward had occurred was a fluttering strip of police-tape cordoning off the hard shoulder. A week from now there wouldn't even be that. It would be as if nothing had happened.

The M61 merged into the M6, taking them past Preston. A few miles beyond Lancaster, they left the motorway and headed west through rolling hills blanketed with woodland. "Have you been to The Lakes before?" asked Steve.

"No."

"Then you're in for a treat. Sharon and I used to bring the kids up here every summer. They loved it. Sharon couldn't stand it. She used to say all there is up here is rain and sheep shit. She'd rather have spent a fortnight cooking herself on a Spanish beach." Steve shook his head. "She was a pain in the arse. Only reason I married her was because she's got tits big enough to suffocate an elephant. But that's not enough to keep a marriage going."

"Then what is?" wondered Jack, thinking about Rebecca. They'd been drawn to each other physically, but they'd also enjoyed the same pastimes – hiking, gardening, movies. They'd shared a particular love of the coast.

Neither of them could have imagined not living near the sea. And now she was dead and he was living miles from the coast...

"Fucked if I know."

The road skirted past the south end of Lake Windermere. Sailing boats were moored along grassy banks. Signs advertised 'Lake Cruises'. The lake fed the broad River Leven, which ran parallel to the road. The sky was a palette of dark clouds and pale sunshine. Several miles further on, the river emptied into the vast tidal sandflats of Morecambe Bay. Jack felt the tension that had built up over the past couple of days ebbing away. "When this case is over, I might bring Naomi up here for a few days," he said.

Steve gave him the lowdown on the best places to visit as they headed into a rugged landscape of humpbacked brown fells laced with fast-flowing streams and rivers. Isolated buildings of weathered stone and pebbledash were scattered along the roadside. To the west they caught glimpses of the brooding Irish Sea. The landscape softened and the fells receded into the east as they neared their destination.

A terrace of white cottages and a few modern semis set amidst fields of grazing cows marked the outskirts of Gosforth. The village's centre was a picture-postcard assortment of cottages, inns and local shops with colourful painted brickwork bordering their doors and windows.

They pulled over outside the general store. "What do you say we talk to Mrs Boyles then have lunch in one of those pubs?" suggested Steve.

"Sounds good."

"The Gosforth Hall Inn's supposed to do some beautiful cask ales," Steve said, licking his lips in anticipation.

Jack smiled. "Been reading up, have you?"

"Let's put it this way. You're the designated driver for the return journey."

They entered the little shop, which managed to cram in a butcher's counter, bakery and delicatessen along with the usual groceries, beer, wine, spirits and other household items. A plump late-middle-aged woman with bobbed blonde hair and apple-red cheeks smiled at them from behind the till.

"Mrs Barbara Boyles?" asked Steve.

"Yes. Are you here about my phone call?" asked Barbara.

Steve nodded and introduced himself and Jack. He brought up a photo of Butterfly on his phone. "We understand you think you recognise this woman."

"I don't think it, I know it. You don't forget a tattoo like that. Especially when it's on the face of a pretty young woman." Barbara tutted as if to say, *What a shame.* "She came in here about a year-and-a-half ago."

"So last June," said Jack.

"Something like that. It might have been May, but no earlier. She was alone and she seemed a bit… well a bit lost."

Jack thought about the lost look in Butterfly's eyes. Had she been that way even before the amnesia?

"You get people like that around here sometimes," continued Barbara. "People running away from something, or trying to find something. Do you know what I mean?"

Jack nodded. He knew exactly what she meant. After Rebecca's death, he'd thought about taking himself and Naomi off to some far-flung corner of the world and never returning. "Can you describe her?"

"I'd say she was in her late twenties. Slim, but not skinny. Maybe five-four or five-five. Boyishly short blonde hair."

"Could her hair have been dyed?"

"Oh definitely. It was platinum blonde."

"What colour were her eyes?"

Barbara thought for a moment, then said, "I don't remember. Sorry."

"What was she wearing?"

"Nothing special as far as I recall. I do remember that she was barefooted."

"Did she buy anything?"

"No. She just asked for directions to Leagate Brow."

"Where's that?" asked Steve.

"You take the Wasdale Road to Wellington and follow the sign for Nether Wasdale. That takes you up Leagate Brow. There's nothing much there. You can go for a walk along the River Bleng or Low Lonning."

"Low Lonning?" said Jack.

"It's a bridleway. There's a lovely view of Wast Water from up there. But like I said, she wasn't dressed for walking."

"So why would she go there?"

Barbara's voice dropped a notch. "I thought maybe she was one of *them.*"

"Who's them?"

"Them that live out at Hawkshead Manor. It's a mile or so past Leagate Brow on the left-hand side of the road. You can't miss it. It's a beautiful place." Barbara tutted again. "At least it used to be before they moved in and turned it into some kind of commune or whatever you want to call it. You should see it now. What a mess. Weeds and rubbish everywhere. Livestock that look as if they haven't been fed properly in months. It's disgusting. I called the RSPCA but nothing's been done. Those people should be in prison for the way they treat those poor animals."

Jack and Steve exchanged a sidelong glance. Had Mrs Boyles dragged them all the way up here because she had a bone to pick and hoped they'd do it for her?

Jack's deep brown eyes grew interested as Barbara said, "And the way they treat their children isn't much better. Hair that's never seen a brush. Scruffy clothes. Half-starved. They don't go to school. God knows how many of them there are living there now. I've lost count. It seems like every time their mothers come down to the village one of them is pregnant or carrying around a new baby."

"How often do they come in here?"

"About once a month. Go back a few years and the only time I saw them was on the roadside selling fruit and veg and bits of tat they'd made."

"Was the woman you called us about ever with them?"

"No."

"Do you know any of their names?"

Barbara shook her head. "They never say a word. Not to me or anyone else in the village. They just buy what they came for and leave."

"How long have they lived at Hawkshead Manor?" asked Steve.

"Ooh, a good ten or twelve years. The previous owners, Mr and Mrs Lyons, both died a few months apart back in 2005 or 2006. Their son, Philip, lives down in London. He rents the place out through Swift Estate Agents in Egremont."

"And how many people live at the hall?"

"Like I said, I've lost count. I'd say six or seven women. Maybe ten or eleven children. And one man. Everyone around here calls them the quiet ones." Barbara shuddered. "It gives me the heebie-jeebies. It's not normal."

"Can you describe the man?"

Barbara wrinkled her nose. "In a word, ugly – weasel-faced, scruffy beard, long brownish-blonde hair, balding on top. He's about your height. Skinny. I'd say he's somewhere in his late forties or early fifties. He used to come in here sometimes, but I haven't seen him in..." she puffed her cheeks, "it's got to be two or three years. One other thing I can tell you, he's not from round these parts. He has a strong Scouse accent."

Jack exchanged another likeminded glance with Steve, thinking about the stolen Audi that might have been involved in the shooting of PC Andrew Finch. Another curious little coincidence. "Does he own a vehicle? Or have you seen any vehicles coming and going from the manor house? BMWs, Audis, anything like that?"

Barbara answered with a caustic laugh. "I've seen him driving the women and children round in an old banger of a minibus. No BMWs or Audis."

"Does the minibus have a rainbow painted on the bonnet?"

"I don't know. I can tell you this, it's not fit to be on the road." Barbara's voice fell almost to a whisper. "They say all the children are his."

"Really?" said Steve, sounding more impressed than appalled.

"It's not normal," repeated Barbara.

"No, absolutely I agree. It's definitely not normal."

The shopkeeper frowned as if she suspected Steve wasn't taking her seriously. Jack moved the conversation on. "Did anyone else from the village speak to or see the tattooed lady?"

"No. I've asked around. I'm the only one."

"And did she have a car or any other means of transport?"

"Not that I saw. There's a bus comes through here twice a day. She might have come on that. But then again, she didn't look the type to use buses."

"Is there anything else you can tell us about her?"

"Not that I can think of."

"And apart from the residents of Hawkshead Manor, is there anyone else we should talk to?"

"Philip Lyons. If you talk to him about what's going on up there, perhaps he'll do what he should have done years ago and kick *that* lot out of his house."

They thanked Barbara for contacting them. "Whoever that poor lady is, I hope she pulls through," she said. As they left the store, she added, "Will you be calling to let me know how it goes at the manor house?"

Steve answered with a wave, muttering under his breath, "Will we bollocks." He sparked up a cigarette and asked Jack, "So what do you make of what Hetty Wainthropp in there had to say?"

"The woman she described is roughly the right height and build. Obviously her hair was different, but she could have grown it out between then and now. There are some interesting coincidences. The pregnant women. The bearded bloke with the scouse accent. The minibus."

"And the name of the manor house. I mean because of the mask the bloke in the woods was wearing."

Jack hadn't thought of that. The coincidences were stacking up too high to be ignored. "Let's have a drive out Leagate Brow."

"What about lunch?"

Jack shook his head in reply. It was just after one o'clock. The baby had been missing for almost forty hours. Lunch could wait. He ducked into the car. Casting a mournful glance towards the village's pubs, Steve followed suit.

Chapter 15

Wasdale Road led them north east past rows of farm cottages and fields of grazing sheep. Towards the road's upper end, the River Bleng appeared on their right-hand side, bubbling through a stony channel lined by trees and bushes. They crossed the river on a low stone bridge and the road climbed steeply up Leagate Brow, narrowing to a single lane as it left behind the hamlet of Wellington. At the top of the slope, they pulled over by a bench. Like Barbara had said, there was nothing much to see. To the west, green fields rolled towards the sea. The bleak brown fells of Wasdale dominated the eastern horizon. Closer at hand, there was a patch of woodland, hedges, dry-stone walls, a pair of metal farm-gates, telephone poles marching down to the houses.

Jack looked askance at Steve. With a shrug, Steve got back into the car.

They continued along the lane, passing the woods on their left, descending steadily towards Wasdale. The precipitous scree-strewn slopes enclosing Wast Water came into view. At the head of the lake loomed the craggy summit of Scafell. They braked at a 'Public Bridleway' sign. "This must be Low Lonning," said Jack. The bridleway ran straight as an arrow towards a farmhouse with a stone barn attached to it. "Barbara said Hawkshead Manor is about half-a-mile further on."

The lane dipped into a wood of pale beeches and spindly firs whose branches drooped over a brick wall swathed in ivy and weeds. At the centre of the wall were wrought-iron gates set between crumbling stone posts. Only a few curls of black and gold paint still clung to the gates. A sign so faded as to be almost illegible read 'Hawkshead Manor'. Beyond the gates was a driveway well on its way to being reclaimed by nature.

Jack and Steve took a closer look at the gates. They were chained and padlocked, but hung at an odd angle. A shove from Steve created a gap wide enough to squeeze through. Jack pointed at the sign. Underneath the worn lettering someone had scratched 'Here Ends Civilisation'.

Steve grinned. "I can't wait to meet the lord of the manor."

Jack made a sweeping motion towards the gates. "Age before beauty."

Steve edged through the gap. "Not a bloody word," he warned as he sucked in his beer-belly.

A hint of caution came into their movements as they progressed along the driveway. If the lord of the manor and the man behind the eagle or, as it might be, hawk mask were one and the same, they were dealing with a dangerous individual. In amongst the trees were several tourer caravans streaked with moss and lichen. At some point in the distant past, one of the caravans had been painted red, green and gold. Others were graffitied with single staring eyes, anarchist symbols and slogans – 'FUCK THE GOVERNMENT. FUCK THE CHURCH. FUCK THE WORLD'; 'THE END IS NIGH LETS PARTY'. The ground around the caravans was strewn with rusting Calor Gas bottles, old tarpaulins and items of furniture that looked as if they had been ripped out of the caravans. The trees were decorated with coloured ribbons that fluttered in the breeze.

"We're not alone," observed Jack.

On either side, small figures slunk through the trees. Like the trees, the children were dressed in colourful, tatty clothes. Some had crewcuts. Others had long hair that was tangling into dreadlocks. Although thin, they didn't look to be quite the starving waifs the shopkeeper had described. They were grubby, but rosy-cheeked and bright-eyed. They moved as silently and swiftly as woodland creatures. Jack counted eight of them. The smallest looked to be only four or five-years-old. The largest was maybe ten or eleven. It was difficult to tell which were girls and which were boys. They all shared similar brownish blonde hair and narrow facial features.

"What do you want to do?" asked Steve.

"Let's keep walking."

The driveway degenerated into mud. "Bloody hell, these are brand new," grumbled Steve as the ground sucked at his shoes.

They emerged from the woods into an expansive area that might once have been landscaped gardens, but now was more akin to a broken-down farmyard. Several scrawny cows, goats and ponies were sniffing around for grass in a muddy enclosure. Hens were pecking at a patch of wheat that looked as if it had been left to rot. Rows of raised beds had been haphazardly planted with vegetables, but mostly left to go to weeds. Flies buzzed around a dead pig in a collapsed sty. Jack thought about Butterfly's dirt-ingrained fingernails and calloused palms.

"Looks like the good life gone bad," commented Steve, wrinkling his nose at the stench of decomposition.

"Explains why they've been using the village shop."

They continued past a cluster of vehicles in various states of disrepair – a double-decker bus mottled with rust, frayed curtains hanging in its windows; an old-fashioned ambulance on its axles; vans languishing in oil-stained grass. The garishly painted vehicle from the motorway CCTV wasn't amongst them. The children peered from behind a mound of tyres. Catching the eye of one who looked to be about Naomi's age, Jack smiled. Like a startled rabbit, the child darted out of sight.

Beyond the vehicles, the driveway flared out in front of a grand dilapidated three-storey redbrick house. Several of the house's ten tall arched windows were boarded up. The boards had been painted with the same staring eye as the caravans. The left-hand side of the double-fronted façade was almost completely enveloped in ivy, as were three of the six tall chimneys. White smoke rose from the foremost chimney. There were dark holes where slate tiles were missing from the roof.

"I'll bet this place costs a pretty penny to rent, even with the holes in the roof," said Steve. "I wonder how they pay for it."

"That's just what I was wondering."

The detectives climbed worn stone steps to a bolt-studded wooden door that looked strong enough to withstand a battering ram. Steve rapped on the door with a rusty knocker. His other hand lingered near his jacket pocket, which Jack knew contained a Taser. The door creaked open, revealing a thirty-something, five foot nothing, rake thin woman. Multicoloured beads were braided into her long blond hair. A shapeless brown dress hung down almost to her bare feet. Her blue eyes stared at them somewhat blankly from a face devoid of makeup. She said nothing.

Could this be Badger? wondered Jack. Her expression didn't alter as he introduced himself and Steve. He added, "If it's convenient, we'd like to talk to you and anyone else living here about a woman you may have seen hereabouts."

The woman continued to eye the detectives silently. Then she turned and walked away, disappearing around a corner. Steve motioned to his lips with his thumb and forefinger to signify that he reckoned she'd been smoking weed. Jack pursed his lips uncertainly. The woman's pupils hadn't been dilated. Rather, her eyes had seemed to be half there and half off in some other distant place. He got the sense that she was high on something less tangible but just as potent as cannabis.

"Should we follow her?" wondered Steve.

Jack lifted a hand to caution patience. His gaze moved around an entrance hall almost as big as the downstairs of his entire house. A brass candle-chandelier dangled from the ceiling. Stalagmites of wax had accumulated on the scuffed oak floorboards below. The walls were scrawled with childish drawings of flowers, trees, hearts, animals, suns, moons and smiling people. In stark contrast, hanging alongside the drawings in rough wooden frames were finely detailed paintings of a world in chaos. Buildings reduced to rubble. Forests on fire. Blood raining from the skies. Terrified multitudes fleeing some unseen enemy. The air was thick with musky incense. Lilting ambient music drifted from somewhere deeper within the house.

The woman reappeared, motioning them inside. She led them along a hallway decorated with more apocalyptic paintings. Jack detected the sweet tang of cannabis underlying the incense. Steve gave him an *I told you so* nudge. The smell intensified as they entered a large, high-ceilinged room. Flames crackled in a tall stone fireplace. Chopped logs were stacked carelessly against the fireplace's ornate wooden surround. Clusters of joss-sticks sent spirals of smoke into the air. The parquet floor was strewn with rag-rugs. Tie-dye throws and blankets were draped over a trio of shabby sofas. Sunlight seeped hazily through more tie-dyed sheets pinned over the windows. The music came from an old stereo system with tapes and records scattered around it. 'PEACE? LOVE?' had been daubed in six-foot-high letters on one wall and 'The land will be REBORN from its own ashes' on another.

A man with a scraggly blonde beard and matching hair tied into a top-knot – perhaps to conceal the bald-spot Barbara had alluded to – was reclining on a sofa. A frayed dressing gown, loosely tied at the waist threatened to expose more than Jack wanted to see. The man's scrawny legs were hooked over the back of the sofa. One of his paint-stained hands trailed towards an overflowing ashtray on the floor. He lethargically raised his other hand to wave hello, his lips curving into a smile that was neither friendly nor unfriendly. "Welcome to our waiting place," he said. He wasn't handsome – beaky nose, sunken cheeks, pock-marked skin – but neither was he as ugly as Barbara had made him out to be. His eyes were a warm brown and his Liverpudlian voice was soothingly mellow, more Paul McCartney than Cilla Black.

"What are you waiting for?" Jack couldn't resist but ask.

"The end of the world. What else?" the man replied as if it was the most obvious thing imaginable, lazily lifting a rollup to his lips.

Steve sniffed. "Is that a joint?"

"No."

"Mind if I have a drag?"

"Go ahead." The man held out his roll-up.

Steve stooped to take a drag. "Tobacco," he said to Jack.

"See, my friends, we have nothing to hide here." The man wafted a hand towards the other sofas. "Sit. Relax. Would you like something to drink? Dandelion wine? Tastes like piss, but it'll blow your socks off."

"No thanks," said Jack, remaining standing.

The man shrugged. "Suit yourselves." He gestured languidly to the woman and she left the room.

"Can I ask your name please?"

"Phoenix."

"What's your *real* name?" put in Steve.

"That's thc only name I've got."

"Do you have any ID?"

"ID?" Phoenix laughed as if the question was absurd. "ID is a badge of slavery. We've thrown off those shackles here."

"How many are there living here?" asked Jack.

Phoenix puffed thoughtfully on his roll-up. "Twenty one... I think."

"You think?"

"Hey man, I don't keep count. People come, people go. You know how it is."

Jack eyed the reclining man intently. "Not really."

Phoenix laughed again. "You guys are all the same. So uptight. No wonder you all get cancer and heart disease."

"You've had dealings with the police before?" said Steve.

"Sure. People like us make the authorities nervous. People who see the truth they work so hard to hide."

"And what is the truth?" asked Jack.

"That it's all ready to come crashing down. Not just this country. The entire world." Phoenix broke off as the woman returned with a glass of misty yellow liquid. She handed it to him and sat down cross-legged on the floor. He sipped his drink and stroked her braided hair. "Tell them how it is, Willow."

"We're building a better life away from the polluting influences of the corporate world," she said, her voice soft and sure, as if she was reeling out a well-rehearsed speech. "Soon that world will eat itself. When the end comes, we'll be ready."

"You don't look very ready," said Steve, glancing out of a window at the failed crops.

"You're not listening," said Phoenix, sitting up, his voice suddenly taking on a deep, resonant timbre. "Open your ears. This is about purity. When the physical body dies, the soul must be pure so that the astral body can progress upwards to the next level. Do you feel what I'm telling you?"

"Oh yeah, sure, I feel it," replied Steve, sliding Jack a sardonic glance.

Phoenix's intensity faded back to a serene smile. "OK, my man, but don't say you weren't warned." He lay down and resumed stroking Willow's hair. The smile didn't falter as Jack showed him Butterfly's photo. "I've no idea who she is, but I dig her tattoo. What happened to her?"

"Someone shot her and stole her baby."

Phoenix shook his head. "It's a sick, sick world. What's any of this got to do with us?"

"The woman claims she was here. She mentioned someone fitting your description," bluffed Jack, watching every movement of Phoenix's face.

Phoenix's eyes widened. "Really? That's crazy, man. What did she say about me?"

"Not much."

"Well we'll send her some meta."

"Meta?" said Steve.

In reply, Phoenix closed his eyes and took several slow deep breaths. He stretched a hand towards Butterfly's photo, saying softly, "May she be safe from further harm. May her injuries heal swiftly. May she be filled with peace and happiness." He inhaled deeply again, then opened his eyes and explained, "It's the energy of change. We all have a limitless supply of it within us. You've just got to break through the blockages of anger and fear and set it free."

"Set it free," Willow parroted like someone listening to an evangelical preacher.

Jack showed her the photo. She shook her head.

"Who knows, maybe she passed through here once," said Phoenix. "Like I said, people are free to come and go as they please. All are welcome so long as they leave the world at the gates."

"We need to speak to everyone who lives here."

Phoenix sighed, betraying the faintest trace of annoyance. "Gather them together," he said to Willow.

She rose to leave the room again. As they waited, Phoenix drank his dandelion wine and rolled another cigarette. Steve seated himself on an unoccupied sofa. Jack wandered around, listening to the silence. You could learn a lot from silence. Phoenix looked relaxed, but there was a restless intensity about the way he rolled his cigarette. As if he needed to keep himself busy. Jack noticed too that the glass of wine was nearly empty. Was Phoenix trying to lubricate away anxiety?

Steve lit a cigarette of his own. "You don't mind do you?"

Phoenix made a *go ahead* gesture. He seemed to have lost his taste for sermonising. Perhaps his nerves were getting the better of him.

Jack chanced his hand at another bluff. "Several people in the area say they've seen the woman hereabouts."

"You keep calling her *the woman,*" said Phoenix. "Doesn't she have a name?"

This one's not only a cool customer, he's got the nous to back it up, thought Jack. "Her injuries have affected her memory. But it's returning, little by little."

Phoenix flopped back against the cushions, puffing on his roll-up. "Did you know The Lake District is the most visited national park in Britain? Over twenty million people a year come on holiday here."

Steve smiled humourlessly. Jack could see his colleague was itching to make some retort along the lines of, *Clever bastard, aren't you*? "Quite the pad you've got here, Phoenix." Steve said the name with a faintly mocking emphasis. "Is it yours?"

Phoenix stared at Steve as if he was well aware the detective wasn't playing straight with him. "We're just travellers passing through."

"So in plain old English, you're renting this place. I'm curious, how does someone like you afford a gaff like this?"

"It's mind-blowing what can be achieved if people come together in pursuit of a single purpose."

"Tell me about it." Steve held Phoenix's gaze. "Right now there are about thirty detectives and god knows how many constables and forensic officers putting their heads together to try to crack this case. I say *try,* but really there's no doubt about it. We *will* crack this case. And the scumbags responsible are going to prison for a long time. And they'll count themselves lucky." Steve leant forwards, his eyes flat and hard. "Because if I had my way I'd put a bullet in each and every one of them and bury them in an unmarked grave. Just like they did to that woman."

Staring straight back at Steve, Phoenix shook his head slowly. "It fills my heart with sadness to hear you talking like that, Steve." There was something so soulfully earnest about his words that Jack momentarily found himself wondering whether he truly meant them.

The illusion was dispelled as Phoenix asked somewhat disingenuously, "Is it OK if I call you Steve?"

"I don't care what you call me," replied Steve. "As long as you tell me the truth."

"The truth. That's what we're all about here, Steve. Do you wish me to tell you the truth about yourself?"

Steve made a *be my guest* motion.

"You've got children, haven't you?"

Steve's silence was as good as a yes.

"You're a good man, but you're full of hate," continued Phoenix. "Hate for yourself for letting your children down. Hate for your ex-wife for leaving you. But most of all, hate for what society has done to you. You've given your life to your job and what has it given you in return? A broken family. Loneliness. The sins of the father shall be visited upon the children. That's what your God says. Is that what you want for your children? Do you want them to feel that same hate?"

Steve raised his hands, knuckles outwards. "You're right, there did used to be a ring on my finger. And you're right about some other stuff too. But you're wrong about my job. There's nothing I find more satisfying than getting these hands on lowlifes. Especially the kind of lowlifes that would steal a baby from its mother's arms."

Steve's voice was controlled, but Jack could tell Phoenix had got to him. He sensed that one or two more well-aimed observations might provoke Steve into doing something rash. His mind raced for something to say to diffuse the situation. All he could think of was, "What happened to your pig?"

Phoenix either didn't hear or simply ignored him. "You've been sold a lie, Steve. There's no such thing as God or justice. Once you open your eyes to that truth, you'll see there's no need for judgement. And where there is no judgement, there is no hate. There is only love."

Steve's lips twisted. "And you certainly like to spread your love around, don't you? How many women have you got living here? One for every day of the week, is it?"

Phoenix gave another sympathetic shake of his head. "There you go again, Steve. Judging."

Steve's voice jumped up a few notches. "You're damn right I'm judging. Shack up with as many women as you want. I couldn't give a toss. But when you start–"

Jack opened his mouth to interject. Throwing around accusations they couldn't back up with hard evidence was ammunition for a defence lawyer to claim the police were personally biased against the suspect. Before he could speak, the house's other inhabitants trooped into the room. First came Willow, followed by thirteen silent children. At the back of the line were six more women wearing homemade-looking clothes, their hair braided and dreadlocked, their faces free from makeup. They were an assortment of sizes – short, tall, slim, chubby – but all of them wore the same deadpan expression. Two were heavily pregnant.

They lined up behind Phoenix in two orderly ranks of ten. Laying his hands on their heads like a priest giving absolution, he reeled off their names, "This is Peace, Sky, Dharma, Krishna, Rebel, Rowan, Freedom, Star, Sun, Moon..." When he'd introduced them all, he added, "Children, these two men are detectives from Manchester. That's a big city far away from here. They're here to ask us some questions. There's no need to be afraid. Just tell them the truth."

Jack watched for any little signals Phoenix might give the children. There was nothing that he could see besides the laying on of hands. The detectives worked their way along the lines, showing Butterfly's photo. In response, they received twenty shakes of heads. Jack looked intently into each woman and child's eyes, but saw nothing to suggest they were nervous or hiding something.

"Have there been any additions to the household this week?" he asked them all.

A collective shake of heads.

Jack smiled at a girl who didn't shy away from his gaze. "A new little brother or sister?"

She stared at him silently, her eyes as unblinking as a rabbit's.

"Not that I'm aware of," Phoenix answered for her. He cupped a hand against one of the pregnant women's bellies. "But there will be soon."

"And is that a good thing?" asked Steve. "I mean if the world's such a terrible place, why would you want to bring so many children into it?"

Phoenix swept a hand towards his brood. "These children will populate the new world. They will show the way to those who are lost."

Lost. There was that word again. Had Butterfly been lost? wondered Jack. If so, and assuming she'd come here, she seemingly hadn't found what she was looking for.

Openly rolling his eyes, Steve took out his phone and made to photograph the group.

His smile faltering, Phoenix put up his palms. "No photos".

"Why not?"

"Because my children are not and never will be tracked by your databases. And because this is my house and what I say here goes."

Steve lowered his phone. Smile returning, Phoenix made a gentle *shoo* motion. The motley platoon filed from the room.

"Those are well-behaved kids," said Steve. "You've got them under your spell. That's for sure."

"There's no magic to it, Steve," said Phoenix. "Society teaches that if you give children too much freedom they will never learn to respect one another. But in truth it's the other way around. It isn't possible to have too much freedom. Just like it isn't possible to be half-free. You're either a slave or not. Which would you rather be?"

There was no irony in Phoenix's voice. He seemed to either not care or be unaware of the glaring contradiction between his homespun philosophising and his words of a moment earlier.

"I'll tell you what I know is true, Phoenix. If someone tells you something is free, you can bet your right bollock they're scamming you. Everything costs something."

The two men stared at each other. Neither was smiling now. "Do you need anything else from us?" Phoenix asked, keeping up his friendly tone.

"Not for now. Thanks for your time."

"No problem, my friends. I've enjoyed speaking to you. I hope you find whoever or whatever you're looking for."

Phoenix showed them to the front door. He filled his lungs with the chill November air. "What a beautiful day for the world to end." He looked from Steve to Jack, saying, "Peace and love. Peace and love."

As the detectives returned to the car, Steve showed Jack the sly photo he'd taken of Phoenix and his brood. Not bothering to conceal what he was doing, he photographed the house and gardens too, ranting, "Peace and love my arse. Fucking charlatan hypocrite. God, I would love to slap the bullshit out of him. And what about those women? Why do they fall for that shit? Are they all morons, or what?"

"They're just people like you and me," said Jack, Butterfly's face rising into his mind. "They're looking for the same things as all of us – friendship, security, a purpose in life."

"Then join the fucking army, not some batshit end of the world cult." Steve glanced from side to side. The children were back amongst the trees, darting from trunk to trunk. "The way those kids behaved... Brainwashed, the lot of 'em."

"They were expecting us. That whole scene in there felt rehearsed."

"Too bloody right it was rehearsed. I'll tell you what we should do. We should get a search warrant and turn this place upside down."

Jack nodded agreement. "But first let's see if we can find out who Phoenix really is."

Chapter 16

While Steve brought Paul up to speed, Jack got on the phone to Swift Estate Agents. "The manor house's tenant is a Mr Dennis Smith," the estate agent informed him. "Has Philip Lyons been in contact with you?"

"The owner of the house. No. Why would he have been?"

"Because the rent is seven months in arrears. Mr Lyons is starting eviction proceedings."

Steve laughed when Jack told him Phoenix's real name. "Dennis-fucking-Smith. Doesn't have quite the same ring as Phoenix, does it? Sounds like Dennis's little fantasy world is about to come crashing down on his head."

"Maybe that's what this is all about," mused Jack. "They're desperate for money so they sold a baby."

"But our tattooed lady doesn't play ball so they..." Steve made a gun sign at his head. "Sounds plausible." He laughed again, grimly amused. "It's not as if Guru Dickhead hasn't got sprogs to spare. But how would a bloke like that go about selling a baby? He'd need some heavy contacts."

"Phoenix mentioned he'd had previous dealings with the police. Perhaps he's got a record."

As Steve booted up the Toughbook laptop and accessed the PNC database, Jack contacted the nearest police station, which was in Whitehaven, a small port town fifteen or so miles away on the coast. A man with a strong Cumbrian accent came on the line. "This is Police Sergeant Eric Ramsden."

Jack told the sergeant who he was and what he needed.

"Yes, I've had several run-ins with Mr Smith," confirmed Sergeant Ramsden. "There have been complaints about animal welfare and selling food produce from unlicensed roadside stalls. But we've never had reason to charge him with anything. To be honest, I think the complaints have more to do with certain people not liking the way Mr Smith and his err... family live than any real concern about criminal offences. You say this woman you're up here about asked for directions to Leagate Brow."

"That's right."

"Hawkshead Manor is on Lane Side. Leagate Brow leads to Lane Side. So that makes sense, but still it's a fair distance further on..."

The sergeant's uncertain tone piqued Jack's interest. "What's on your mind, Eric?"

"I can't see how it could be connected to your case, but Leagate Brow is... Well it's notorious in these parts. Something terrible happened there. A family of four from Manchester – Marcus and Andrea Ridley and their two young daughters, Tracy and Charlie – were staying at The Rose and Crown Inn in Gosforth." Eric paused as if sifting through memories he hadn't thought about in years. "It was erm... July 30th 1998. The Ridleys went for a walk at midday on Low Lonning."

"Barbara Boyles mentioned Low Lonning."

"It's popular with hikers. I've walked it myself many times. Anyway, the Ridleys had walked northeast for about 150 metres when a masked figure emerged from the trees to the left-hand side of the path."

"What type of mask?"

"A balaclava."

Jack thought about the balaclava-wearing figures who'd shot Butterfly. This was getting more interesting by the moment.

"He – we believe the figure was a 'he' – was carrying a shotgun," continued the sergeant. "He tied up the Ridleys and put bags over their heads. At this point we believe a second man became involved in the incident. He started to remove the older daughter Charlie's clothes. Marcus was making a lot of noise so the attackers dragged him into the woods. The younger daughter, Tracy, managed to get free. She tried to free her mum and sister, but fled when she heard the attackers returning. She ran to a farmhouse and raised the alarm. I was the first on the scene. Andrea and Charlie had been shot and mutilated. Marcus's throat had been cut." Eric's voice snagged on something that might have been shame. "We never caught the men who did it."

"Did you have any suspects?"

"We interviewed a local guy – Phil Beech. He's a gamekeeper who looked – still looks after – the woods where the murders took place. He'd been drinking in The Rose and Crown earlier that same day. We also spoke to a pal of his who was being investigated at the time for statutory rape – Dale Sutton. He lives in Seascale."

"Two men," Jack murmured thoughtfully. "What do they look like?"

"Beech is tall – at least 6'4" – and thin." A note of distaste found its way into the sergeant's voice. "A real lanky streak of piss, if you'll excuse the language. Sutton's of average height and fat. And when I say fat, I mean obese. I've got family in Seascale. I see him around occasionally. Grey beard, mean eyes, stomach hanging down to his knees."

Jack conjured up a mental image of Butterfly's attackers – medium height; trim, muscular build. Beech and Sutton weren't the ones he was after. "Do you think they murdered the Ridleys?"

"I don't know. I'll admit, I can't stand either of them. I would have liked to see them put away if only to get them off my streets. Tracy Ridley described the man she saw as average height and stocky build, which fitted Sutton's description back then. But we didn't have enough to charge them."

"Do you have photos of the Ridleys?"

"Yes. I'll email them to you along with the case file."

Jack thanked Sergeant Ramsden and got off the phone.

"That sounded like an interesting conversation," said Steve. His eyebrows lifted as Jack recounted the grim tale of the triple murder. "This shit just got deeper. And it gets deeper still Listen to this. Our Dennis isn't quite what he makes himself out to be. He's done time. A two year stretch in Strangeways from 2003 to 2005 for dealing Class As. He was picked up in a nightclub sting in Manchester city centre with a bagful of cocaine and MDMA. Even more interestingly, he did fourteen months in HMP Liverpool from 2000 to 2001 for burglary and aggravated car taking. The dickhead broke into a house in Wavertree – that's on the south side of Liverpool – and made off with the usual crap and a VW Golf. Only thing was, he crashed the car and put two people in hospital. It made me think about that Audi that was stolen in Allerton in 2015. I know there's a fifteen-year gap between the crimes, but still..."

Steve let his words hang meaningfully. Jack thought about PC Andrew Finch being shot point blank in the face. Could Dennis Smith have pulled the trigger? To all appearances, PC Finch's shooting had been unprovoked. His killer had merely been illegally parked. PC Finch hadn't run a check on the Audi's number plates. He hadn't known they were stolen. All he'd intended to do was tell the driver to move their car. Of course, the driver couldn't have known that. But instead of waiting to find out why PC Finch had approached them, they shot him before he could get a word out. Imagine what it took to aim a gun at a stranger – policeman or otherwise – and end their life for no good reason. The pathology of it was terrifying.

Dennis's crimes were serious, but not violent. Nothing in his past suggested he'd been building up to such a catastrophic outburst of aggression. But then again, there was also nothing to suggest that shortly after his release in 2005 Dennis would relocate to Cumbria and start up his own little cult. Dennis was a character of extremes with a loathing for society. Maybe he'd killed PC Finch in some sort of insane attempt to provoke the apocalypse he was preparing for.

Jack's phone pinged as an email came through from Sergeant Ramsden. Jack looked at a photo of Tracy Ridley. She'd been eleven when it was taken.

Wavy reddish-brown hair tumbled down over her narrow shoulders. There was a spray of freckles on her soft-round cheeks and button nose. Her cupid's bow lips and brown eyes were smiling into the camera. Had this girl grown into Butterfly? Her hair and eye colour roughly matched Butterfly's. As for the rest of her face... Jack swiped back and forth between photos of Tracy and Butterfly. It was difficult to tell. Butterfly's face was currently a mass of swelling, bruising, scratches and bandages. The tattoo didn't help either.

"What do you reckon?" Jack asked.

"I suppose they could be the same person," Steve replied uncertainly. "I'd better get back on to the DCI."

Jack got out of the car and stared through the manor house gates. He couldn't see the children, but he could feel their eyes on him. He thought about Tracy – the fear that must have gripped her, the agony of leaving her family behind to die, the grief and loneliness afterwards. Was that why Butterfly had formed a connection with him? Was she instinctively drawn to the loss in his voice?

Steve spoke to him from the driver side window. "The DCI wants us to stay put."

Jack's thoughts turned to Naomi. He'd hoped to be back in Manchester in time to put her to bed. "For how long?"

Steve shrugged. "I'm starving. How about we head back to Gosforth?" He jerked his thumb towards the manor house. "These whackos aren't going anywhere."

"You go. I'll stay."

"Suit yourself. Do you want me to bring you something back? How about a Cumbrian sausage? I know how much you like a nice bit of sausage."

Jack smiled crookedly at the typically inappropriate remark. The smile faded as Steve drove away. He wondered if he was right about Butterfly's baby. Perhaps it had been sold to a couple who would love it like their own.

He hoped to god that was the case because the other possibilities didn't bear thinking about.

Chapter 17

As the afternoon wore away, dark clouds gathered above the desolate peaks of Wasdale. The sun made a brief appearance, casting cold shadows. Jack watched the entrance to Hawkshead Manor while Steve snoozed off a pub lunch on the backseat. Apart from the occasional glimpse of a bird or squirrel, there had been no movement beyond the gates. A deep stillness had settled over the manor house's grounds.

A skim through the Ridley murders case file revealed some interesting details about Tracy. She'd grown up in Prestwich on the north side of Manchester, only four or five miles from where Butterfly had been shot. Was that where Butterfly had been heading when she was rammed off the motorway? Did she still have relatives or friends in the area? If so, not only would they be able to identify her, maybe the sight of them would bring her memory back.

The question was – if his suspicions were correct, why hadn't any of them responded to the police's appeal for help?

Steve's phone rang. He woozily groped for it and put the receiver to his ear. "Yes, sir... No, nothing. All quiet... Right... OK, sir." He proffered the phone to Jack. "The DCI wants to talk to you."

His voice carefully business-like, Jack said, "Hello, sir."

"I need you at North Manchester General ASAP," Paul said with an exasperated breath. "It seems you've made quite the impression on the victim. I sent DI Crawley over there to try and find out if she's Tracy Ridley, but she's refusing to speak to anyone other than you."

A little flutter rose from Jack's stomach. It made him feel all at once strangely privileged and uneasy to know Butterfly had attached so strongly to him. "I'll set off right away. Do we know anything else about Tracy?"

"Not much. No one on the databases fits her particulars."

"Could be because she's been living off-grid at Hawkshead Manor and other places like it."

"We have managed to track down Tracy's only living relative. After the murders, Tracy was brought up by her grandparents, William and Shirley Ridley. William died in 2002. Shirley's now living at the Golden Years care home in Rochdale. DC Clarke's on her way there. But I don't hold out much hope of Shirley identifying the victim even if she is her granddaughter. Shirley has Alzheimer's."

Jack's forehead creased. Tracy was seemingly all alone in the world. If Butterfly and she were one and the same, it didn't take a great leap to see how she could have been seduced by Phoenix's radical worldview. She must have yearned for a sense of belonging. "What about Dennis Smith?"

"As far as we can tell, he was involved in low level gang activity until his second prison stretch. We're putting together a list of criminal associates, people he's served time with and suchlike. He's got plenty of family in Greater Manchester and Merseyside. We've contacted several of them. They claim they haven't seen hide nor hair of him in years."

There was an awkward little silence.

"Anything else?" asked Paul.

"No, sir."

Jack was relieved to get off the phone. Every conversation with Paul was a tightrope act. One false step could send him plummeting into the same old pit of anger and resentment. "We're heading back to Manchester," he informed Steve.

"Not me," said Steve. "I'm staying put. Sergeant Ramsden's on his way over from Whitehaven to keep me company."

"Maybe you'll get a chance to properly sample the local beer after all," pointed out Jack.

Steve got out of the car, grinning sleazily. "Tell your sister I'm thinking about her."

Jack flicked him the Vs and accelerated away.

Chapter 18

Jack was almost at the hospital when Paul phoned to confirm that Shirley Ridley was indeed in no fit state to identify anyone. She hadn't recognised either Butterfly or the eleven-year-old Tracy. Nor was she in possession of any recent photos of Tracy. Tracy had never visited Shirley. The nurses at the home hadn't even been aware that Shirley had a granddaughter. According to them, it was only in rare moments of lucidity that Shirley remembered her own name. Paul was arranging for DNA testing to determine whether Tracy and Shirley were related. But Shirley's inability to give consent meant a court order was required.

Jack was struck by the strange synchronicity between Butterfly and Shirley's memory loss. Perhaps it was a mercy for both of them.

Another flutter rose from his stomach as he headed up to ICU. What was it? Nerves? He couldn't tell, but he realised that he wanted to feel Butterfly's hand on his again and find out if that shivery electric sensation had been a one off or something else – something he hadn't felt since Rebecca. He reprimanded himself for the unprofessional thought. As with Paul, he needed to keep his mind solely on the job.

"How's she doing?" Jack asked the nurse who escorted him to Butterfly.

"A lot better than any of us expected," replied the nurse. "She keeps asking for you. Every time she wakes up it's, *Where's Jack? Can I see Jack?*"

Jack's anticipation spread like wings as, with a nod at the armed officer on the door, he entered Butterfly's room. Her eyes were closed. Her pallor hadn't improved. The nurse stooped over her and said, "Butterfly." As an aside to Jack, she told him what he already knew, "That's what we call her."

Butterfly's eyelids parted. She looked blankly at the nurse. A flicker of something – relief or perhaps simply recognition – came into her eyes as she saw Jack. She mouthed his name, her voice just barely there.

He smiled at her. "Hello again."

"I..." Butterfly drew in a breath and found some strength for her voice. "I didn't know if you were real."

"I'm real." Jack seated himself at her bedside.

Butterfly reached for his hand as if to check he was telling the truth.

"Please don't touch the patient," cautioned the nurse. "It's important to minimise the risk of infections."

Somewhat reluctantly, Jack drew his hand away from Butterfly's. He thought he glimpsed a glint of disappointment in her eyes, but maybe he was just seeing what he wanted to see.

"Where have you been?" she asked.

"I've been trying to find out who you are."

"And have you?" There was no hopefulness in Butterfly's voice, just a sort of numb curiosity.

"Possibly. Have you heard of a place called Gosforth?"

"No."

"What about Hawkshead Manor?"

"No."

"Have you ever been to The Lake District?"

"I don't know."

Jack brought up the photo of Dennis Smith and his family that Steve had taken. "Tell me if you recognise anyone in this photo."

Butterfly looked at it and gave a slight shake of her head.

Jack zoomed in on Dennis. "Are you sure?"

"I'm sure."

He swiped through the photos of Hawkshead Manor. Each one met with the same negative response. Finally he came to the photo of Tracy. Butterfly stared at it for a long moment. Her lips quivered as if she wanted to say something. Instead, she shook her head and closed her eyes as if exhausted by the effort of trying to remember.

Jack felt a tug of disappointment. He'd thought for a second that the photo had sparked Butterfly's memory.

"That's enough questions for now," said the nurse. "Butterfly needs to rest."

"No," said Butterfly, opening her eyes. "I need to know who those people are."

Jack told her about Dennis Smith and the peculiar world he'd created for himself at Hawkshead Manor. Butterfly listened with interest, but no recognition. Jack grew hesitant when it came to Tracy's tragic story. DNA testing would prove whether Butterfly was Tracy. He didn't want to needlessly upset her if she wasn't Tracy, so he limited the information he gave to, "The young girl is someone we're trying to track down. That photo was taken in 1998. So she'd be about your age now. It may well be that her case is unrelated to yours."

"What happened to her?"

"We can talk about that another time if needs be."

"Can I see the photos again?"

Jack held out his phone. Butterfly's bloodshot gaze lingered on Dennis. "Phoenix... Dennis... Phoenix... Dennis..." she mumbled to herself, as if repetition would repair the connections that the bullet had damaged. She trailed off into frustrated silence.

Jack rose to his feet. Butterfly looked at him with frightened eyes. "My mind is so empty."

Although she was talking about her memory, her hands moved towards her swollen stomach. Jack read a heart-wrenching plea in her eyes for him to stay. Even if the nurse had permitted him to do so, he knew it wouldn't be a good idea. It would only encourage Butterfly to become more attached to him, and maybe vice versa. And he couldn't see how that could lead to anything good.

"Go back to sleep, Butterfly," he said as softly as if he was soothing Naomi after a nightmare. "I'll see you again soon."

Chapter 19

Jack had nothing to say that was worth the risk of talking to Paul. On the way to his car, he texted him the news, or rather lack of it. 'Have spoken to the vic. She has no memory of Gosforth, Dennis Smith or Tracy Ridley.' Paul replied 'OK. Court order being fast-tracked through. Should have it by tomorrow.'

Jack thought about what the DNA test might reveal with mixed emotions. If Butterfly and Tracy were the same person, it would give her back her identity. But what was that identity? A woman haunted by her tragic past? A dropout waiting for the end of the world? Someone so lost and alone that they could be taken in by a charlatan like Dennis 'Phoenix' Smith? Perhaps it would be better if Butterfly remained unidentified. No past. No family. A clean slate.

Naomi was waiting for Jack at the front door of Laura's house with a big smile that washed away the mental grime of the day.

Laura peered past him towards the car. "No Steve?"

"He's still in The Lakes."

"Oh."

Jack looked at his sister intently. Was that disappointment he detected in her voice? And why was there a smudge of fresh lipstick on her teeth? Oh god, she couldn't possibly... He dismissed the idea before it was fully formed. Surely she had better taste than that...

"Why are you looking at me like that?" asked Laura, sucking her glossy lips somewhat self-consciously.

... Or maybe she didn't. "I'll tell Steve you asked after him."

Laura frowned. "Don't bother. I don't want that sexist dinosaur getting any funny ideas."

Jack held in a laugh at the overly defensive response. He'd spent his adult life honing his ability to spot when people said one thing and meant another. So Laura had a thing for Steve. So what? As she'd said, Steve was a sexist dinosaur. She could have added selfish, chauvinist bigot to the list of negative character traits. Basically, he was everything she wasn't. But who knew? Maybe that was a good thing. If nothing else, any relationship she and Steve had wouldn't be lacking a spark. And what was the alternative? Loneliness? No one to confide in? No one to comfort you when your fears came calling? No one to love? Jack's thoughts returned to Butterfly. The desire to laugh subsided.

"I may have to go back up to The Lakes myself tomorrow."

"Well just call if you need me."

"Thanks, sis."

As Jack drove home, Naomi gave him the tale of her day. He tried to put Butterfly to the back of his mind. This was Naomi's time. He'd made himself a promise not to let the job intrude on their relationship. But Butterfly's face kept returning. Her eyes had cried out for someone to comfort her, someone to be at her side while she slept. *No, not someone,* he corrected himself. *You.*

"Dad, you're not listening to me, are you?" Naomi exclaimed.

He blinked and glanced at her. "Sorry, sweetheart. It's been a long day."

"You work too much."

At the concern in Naomi's voice, Jack reached to squeeze her wrist. "Tell you what, I'll book some time off. We can go on holiday."

"Yay! Where?"

Jack smiled, delighted by her delight. "Wherever you like."

"I don't know where I want to go."

"Then have a think about it. There's no rush. I won't be able to get time off while we're in the middle of a difficult case."

Naomi's porcelain-smooth forehead pulled into furrows. "I saw that lady on the news. The one who was shot. It made me feel sad."

"It makes me feel sad too."

"Why would someone do that?"

Jack's forehead mirrored Naomi's as he replied, "That's not something you need worry about." Naomi had already been through so much in her short life. He couldn't erase what had happened, but he could do his best to shield her from further evidence of life's unforgiving nature. He was coming to realise that it was an impossible task though. Naomi seemed to have inherited the same sense of curiosity and adventure that had led him to the police force. He just hoped she hadn't also inherited the sensitivity that had made life too much for her mother to bear.

The sky was softening into twilight by the time they reached Chorlton. Jack went through Naomi's bedtime routine – supper, bath, story. He kissed her cheek. "Night, sweetheart. I love you."

"I love you too, Dad."

As Jack left her bedroom, Naomi asked, "What's life about, Dad?"

He felt like frowning – the question was eerily reminiscent of the things Rebecca used to say – but managed a smile instead. "What do you think it's about?"

Naomi shrugged. "I don't know."

"I can tell you what it should be about for you – having fun, enjoying yourself, not worrying about what you see on the news. Now close your eyes, sweetie. It's late and you've got school tomorrow."

Naomi did as she was told and Jack went downstairs. He took paracetamol for the ache behind his forehead. A glass of something strong would have achieved the same effect, but that wasn't an option. He knew from experience where drinking to blot out pain – be it physical or emotional – led. His thoughts drifted over the months he'd spent mired in the oblivion of alcohol after Rebecca's death. He'd been dry for nearly a year now, and he intended to keep it that way.

What's life about, Dad? The question nagged at him as he stretched out on the sofa. His gaze moved to a photo of Rebecca inconspicuously positioned on a shelf. It and the one on Naomi's beside table were the only photos of her on display in the house. He'd boxed up the rest and stowed them in the loft. He didn't want the house to be a shrine to her memory, but neither did he want to pretend she'd never existed. He wanted to be able to look at her, if only for a fleeting moment, without sadness, regret, guilt, anger and all the other painful emotions her face brought rushing back. For an instant, he could almost hear her yelling at him, *Life is nothing but shit. It's all just shit, shit, shit!* He felt a panicky tightening in his abdomen. What if Naomi turned out to be like her mother? *Then you'll deal with it,* he told himself sharply. *But she's not like Rebecca. She's like you. She's a survivor.*

His mobile phone's ringtone interrupted his train of thought. 'Steve' flashed up on the screen. He put it to his ear. "What's up?"

He expected to either get an earful about being bored of watching the manor house or a drunken account of the quality of the beer in Gosforth's pubs. Instead, Steve said, "There's something funny going on at the house."

"Funny as in ha-ha?"

"Funny as in bloody odd. I can smell smoke and there's an orange glow in the sky. I think they've lit a bonfire."

"They could be disposing of evidence."

"Or maybe they're having their own little festival. It sounds like they're banging drums in there. I'm tempted to go have a look-see."

Another disturbing possibility occurred to Jack as he thought about Dennis's paintings – buildings in rubble, forests on fire, blood raining from the skies. "I'm not sure that's a good idea. Is Sergeant Ramsden there?"

"Uh-huh."

"Put him on."

Eric Ramsden's deep Cumbrian voice came through the receiver. "Hello, Jack."

"Has anything like this happened before?"

"Not to my knowledge, but I don't often come over this way. There's not much call for it."

"I think you should get more officers out there. Firemen too. Tell Steve I'm about to set off back to you. I'll be there ASAP." Jack got off the phone to Eric and got on it to Laura. "I'm really sorry, sis, but I've–"

"I'm on my way," she interjected purposefully. She sounded almost glad that he'd disturbed her evening. *Friendship, security, a purpose in life.* Those words came back to him. He felt a twinge of sadness for Laura. He always thought of her as thick-skinned, but her tone was a reminder that she had the same need to feel needed as anyone else.

As he waited for Laura, Jack looked in on Naomi. She was fast asleep. *What's life about, Dad?* He pushed the question away. He knew that if he allowed himself to dwell on it he wouldn't be able to leave the house. All he'd be able to do was sit around fretting about things he had little or no control over. He padded downstairs and made himself a sandwich. It was going to be a long night.

Chapter 20

The hellish glow in the night sky was visible from miles away. A smoky smell tickled Jack's nostrils. Something big was on fire.

A police car was blocking the little stone bridge over the River Bleng. A few people were milling around, some in dressing-gowns and slippers. Displaying his ID to a grim-faced constable, Jack asked, "What's the situation?"

"The manor house is on fire and..." The constable faltered as the wail of a siren filled the air. Rapidly approaching blue and white flashing lights appeared at the top of Leagate Brow. The constable sprang into his car and reversed off the bridge, allowing an ambulance to race past.

"Who's in the ambulance?" Jack called to the constable.

The constable pointed towards Leagate Brow as if to say, *You'll find the answer up there.* An ominous feeling gathering in his stomach, Jack accelerated up the hill.

He pulled in sharply, his wing-mirror scraping along a hedge, as another ambulance screamed by. Whatever was going on, there appeared to be more than one casualty. Several hundred metres up ahead, flames licked at the darkness through a billowing pall of smoke. He found his path blocked by another police car. Beyond it the lane was clogged with ambulances, fire engines and police vehicles. He got out, surveying a scene like something from a war zone. Paramedics were hauling bodies on stretchers. Firemen were directing arcs of water at a strip of blazing woodland. Police officers were dashing around, trying to make themselves heard above the hiss and crackle of burning branches, the revving of engines and the whump-whump of a helicopter circling overhead. Flames and flashing lights threw wild shadows across the chaotic scene.

Jack's gaze was drawn to a team of paramedics working on a small, unconscious figure. The child's sooty limbs were flopped at awkward angles. The paramedics were inserting an airway adjunct. A short distance further on, paramedics were attending a woman who was spasming violently and frothing at the mouth. Nearby, two children lay heartbreakingly motionless in the back of an ambulance. Wrenching his eyes away from the bodies, Jack approached a cluster of police at the manor house gateposts. The gates had been cut off their hinges and moved aside. Steve was nowhere to be seen. The police were geared up with shields, helmets and batons, ready to go in hard. *What the hell are they waiting for*? wondered Jack.

"Sergeant Ramsden," he called out.

A solidly built forty-something man with neat brown hair and a matching beard turned to him. "Detective Inspector Anderson?"

Jack nodded. "What's going on? Why haven't you gone in?"

Before the sergeant could reply, a shout went up for paramedics. A young boy came staggering between the gateposts, clutching his stomach, his face scrunched in agony. The boy doubled over suddenly, vomiting a toxic soup of bile marbled with thick veins of blood. As paramedics rushed to the boy's aid, Eric Ramsden said, "We think they've taken some kind of poison."

"So why haven't you put an end to this madness?"

"Because they've got DI Platts."

Jack put his head back, mouthing, "Fuck." He should have guessed. The stupid sod had ignored him.

"Not long after speaking to you, DI Platts went into the manor house grounds. About twenty minutes after that, Dennis Smith contacted us through DI Platts's radio, said they had Steve and would kill him if we entered the grounds."

"Did he say anything else?"

"No."

"Did you ask to talk to Steve?"

Eric nodded. "Mr Smith refused to let me."

"So you don't know for sure if Steve's still alive."

"No we don't. We decided it was best to wait and see if Mr Smith made any demands. Then about..." Eric glanced at his wristwatch, "quarter-of-an-hour ago. Christ, has it only been fifteen minutes?" He shook his head as if doubting his eyes. "A child appeared at the gates in the same state as that one." He pointed to the boy. "When more sick women and children started appearing, we decided to go in. But then we got a call from the helicopter. Four masked figures have come out of the house. One of them is a white male, naked with tied wrists."

"It has to be Steve. Maybe they want to talk."

"What could they want to talk about? Seems like they're more interested in dying than talking."

As if on cue, Dennis's voice crackled through Sergeant Ramsden's radio. "I want to talk to the head pig."

Jack motioned for the sergeant to hand him the radio. There was a calmness to Dennis's demand that made Jack feel like spitting obscenities into the radio. Instead, he replied with equal calm, "This is the head pig." There was no irony in his voice. Dennis wanted to speak to a figure of authority, an enemy he could use to help him play out his fantasy. Jack wasn't about to give him that satisfaction.

There was a pause as if Dennis had been caught off guard by the response. Then he said, "Detective Anderson, is that you?"

"It is, Dennis."

A rise of annoyance came into Dennis's voice. "There's no one here by that name. I'm Phoenix. I've lived a thousand lives. Out of the ashes I–"

"You're Dennis Smith," broke in Jack. He didn't want Dennis to get into his stride. He wanted to keep him on the back heel. It was a risky strategy, but no riskier than allowing Dennis to work himself into a self-righteous froth. "You're a petty criminal and not a very successful one if your prison record's anything to go by."

"I will rise!" Dennis shouted over Jack. "Purer. Wiser. Stronger. And you shall bear witness to my transformation. Come see. Come alone."

With that, the radio fell silent. Jack gave it back to Eric and turned his gaze towards the driveway.

"You're not thinking of doing as that madman says, are you?" asked the sergeant.

"How many people have come out of there?"

"Six children and two women."

"That means there are seven children and five women still in there. I don't see that I have any other choice."

"We could all go in."

"They'll kill Steve."

"Then we use snipers. An armed unit is on its way. They'll know how to deal with this nutcase."

Jack shook his head. "That's what Dennis expects us to do. He wants to be martyred. We kill him and we might as well give up any hope of getting those others out alive. Besides, this guy doesn't want to hurt us. He just wants an audience to spout his message at."

"OK," Eric said in a tone of reluctant assent. "Well what *can* we do to help?"

Jack's reply was grimly deadpan. "A stab-vest and a Taser wouldn't go amiss."

Chapter 21

Water from the hoses fell like sheet-rain as Jack advanced along the driveway. Burning trees crackled, popped and sizzled. Despite the firemen's efforts, the fire was spreading. The caravans were on fire too, belching black smoke out of their broken windows. 'THE END IS NIGH LETS PARTY' and the other apocalyptic slogans daubed over them were rapidly being scorched into oblivion. It wouldn't be long before the Calor gas bottles started going off like mortars. There were no inquisitive, rosy-cheeked faces peering from behind the trees this time.

The scene that greeted Jack beyond the woods was almost enough to make him wonder whether Dennis's predictions were indeed coming true. The goats, cows, and ponies lay dead in their pens, their eyes bulging, their mouths ringed with bloody froth. Even the hens hadn't been spared. Their decapitated carcasses were piled alongside the driveway. The dead pig had also been decapitated. Its rotting head faced Jack from atop a tall stick thrust into the driveway.

A few metres beyond the pig, the double-decker bus had been positioned across the driveway. Someone had spray-painted it with 'THIS IS THE END OF THE FUCKING WORLD'. Flames leaping from the manor house's roof made it seem as if the sky itself was on fire.

Jack peered inside the bus. It appeared to be unoccupied. He squeezed between its front-bumper and the pig-pen, pausing to take in the full scale of the fire ripping through the manor house. The right-hand side of the house was engulfed in flames. Large sections of the roof and walls had collapsed. The opposite side was intact, but tongues of flame were darting out of the tall windows. Even from that distance, the heat made Jack's eyes water.

Anyone still alive inside the house wouldn't remain that way for much longer.

Something nearby caught Jack's eye. He broke into a run and dropped to his haunches at the side of a small, motionless figure. The girl couldn't have been more than seven or eight-years-old. He recognised her from earlier in the day. Her name was 'Star' or 'Moonbeam' or some such thing. Her eyes gaped sightlessly. Blood stained her lips and nose. She lay horribly contorted in a slick of vomit and diarrhoea. Jack checked for a pulse in vain.

Rage surged up his throat. Dennis fucking Smith and his wives, or whatever they were, deserved the same fate as the pig for this. He took a deep breath. He couldn't afford to let emotion get the better of him. Not while other lives hung in the balance.

His gaze swept the grounds and fixed on four figures in the shadows to the left of the house. He rose and strode towards them. The figures were naked except for animal masks. Jack had seen three of the masks before.

The woman in the badger mask was short, skinny and flat-chested. She might have been mistaken for a boy if not for the absence of male genitalia. Blonde hair braided with multicoloured beads had found its way out from beneath the mask, identifying her as Willow. The woman in the fox mask was a few inches taller, with heavy hips and pendulous breasts. Her stomach was riddled with stretch-marks as if from multiple pregnancies. Dennis was wearing his sharp-beaked, red and brown plumed phoenix mask. A single eye was painted in what looked like blood on his scrawny, hairless chest. He was holding a knife to the throat of the final figure.

Steve's face was hidden behind a grotesque Orwellian pig mask – Jack knew it was Steve because of the grinning, beret-wearing skull on his colleague's left bicep. The pig had wolfishly sharp teeth and a snakishly long tongue. A top hat was perched at a jaunty angle on its head. Steve's hands were tied behind his back. Streaks of blood glistened on his neck and chest.

"Steve, this is Jack," said Jack. "Are you alright?"

"Yeah, I'm alright. The fuckers jumped me from behind." Steve's tone suggested the only serious injury he'd suffered so far was to his pride.

Jack turned his attention to Dennis. "What do you want?" He managed to keep his voice steady. It wasn't easy. What *he* wanted was to tear off Dennis's mask and pummel his fists into the murdering bastard's face.

"I want everyone to know the truth," Dennis said in his infuriatingly Zen voice. "This world is a lie. Religion, government, the media – all of it a lie with one purpose, control. I tried to escape its corruption, but there's only one way to truly be free." He theatrically flung out a hand. "Fire! No lies can survive the purifying flames."

"Where are the other women and children?" asked Jack.

"The same place I'll soon be."

Jack's stomach coiled into a sick knot at the thought of all those lives snuffed out to gratify Dennis's fantasies

"Prison's the only place you're going, you piece of shit," shouted Steve. He flinched as Dennis pressed the knife into his throat, drawing fresh blood.

"Please don't," exclaimed Jack. "I'll make sure everyone knows the truth. But first you've got to do something for me, Phoenix. Let Steve go."

"I'm doing this for love," said Dennis. "No father could love his children more than I do."

"I know." Jack held up a pacifying palm. His other hand hovered near to the Taser in his pocket. He wondered if he could get off a shot before the blade plunged into Steve's throat. He doubted it.

Fox suddenly crumpled to her knees. She pulled up her mask and a torrent of blood spewed from her mouth. Her eyes goggled towards Dennis, seemingly ready to pop out of their sockets.

"What's going on?" demanded Steve as Jack instinctively made to go to Fox's aid.

"Stay where you are," warned Dennis, applying more pressure to the blade.

"She's dying!" retorted Jack.

"Her body is dying," corrected Dennis. He gave Fox one of his soulful looks. "Goodbye for now my beautiful Vixen. Don't be afraid. We'll be together again soon."

A final gout of vomit darkened the grass, then Vixen pitched face-first into it.

"What have you taken?" Jack's question was directed at Willow. "Tell me and we might be able to save you."

"I've already been saved," she retorted defiantly.

"OK then," Jack said to himself as much as anyone else. He mentally wrote off Willow. Now it was all about Steve and the missing baby. "Where's the baby?" he asked Dennis.

"What does it matter? This is the beginning of the end. The fire I've started will spread across the entire world."

Jack had expected some such response. For a narcissist like Dennis, the world began and ended with him. Appealing to his conscience was clearly a non-starter. Maybe appealing to his vanity would be more productive. "You're right, Phoenix. What you've started here is too big to be stopped. So what difference will it make if you let your child spend the little time there is left with its real mother?"

Dennis laughed, a sound that was all the more chilling because of its warm, rolling quality. "You wouldn't think the child was better off with her if you knew who she really is."

"So tell me." There was an edge of uncertainty in Jack's voice. As if he wasn't sure he wanted to know who Butterfly really was.

"Enough talk. The time has come!"

Prompted by Dennis's proclamation, Willow picked up a canister. Jack smelt petrol as she poured the canister's contents over Dennis. Steve squirmed as it splashed over him too. Jack glanced nervously at the glowing sparks drifting down around them.

"Don't do it," he pleaded.

Dennis no longer seemed to hear. He spread his arms like a bird taking flight. His voice rose feverishly. "The bird of paradise. Born in flame, ending in flame!"

As the blade left his throat, Steve threw himself forwards. Willow sparked a lighter and held it to Dennis. The petrol ignited with a whoosh. Jack sprang forwards too, grabbing Steve and dragging him clear. For one second, maybe two, Dennis stood motionless, his skin sizzling like roasting pork. Then a scream of unimaginable pain tore from his lungs. He whirled around and sprinted towards the house, flapping his arms wildly. All three onlookers watched as if mesmerised as Dennis disappeared through the flaming arch of the front door.

There was a moment of silence almost as loud as the scream, then Steve said, "Take this fucking mask off me."

As Jack did so, Willow sat down cross-legged on the grass. She closed her eyes, rocking gently and humming to herself. Steve's hair was matted with dry blood. Jack untied his colleague's wrists. Steve tentatively felt at the cut on his throat. It wasn't deep. Jack took off his jacket and offered it to him.

Steve shook his head. "I'll look more ridiculous with that on than without it." He glanced at the house. There was a glazed, haunted look in his eyes, as if he'd seen things that couldn't be unseen. "Mad bastards," he murmured.

Jack got on the radio and relayed the situation. "We're on our way to you," replied Eric.

Jack handed Steve the Taser and pointed at Willow. "Watch her." He started towards the house. Its left side was fully ablaze now. Fingers of flame were pushing through the roof and pulling it down. There didn't seem much chance of anyone being alive in there, but he had to make certain.

"They're all dead," said Steve, guessing Jack's intention.

"Are you sure?"

Steve nodded. Tears were streaking through the soot on his cheeks. He swiped at them as if they annoyed him, repeating, "Mad bastards."

"*Are* they all dead?" Jack asked Willow.

She either ignored or didn't hear him. Blood was trickling from her nostrils. Her fingers were convulsively flexing.

From the direction of the woods came the sound of approaching vehicles. Blue flashing lights competed with the flickering red flames. Steve lowered his head. "I could have saved them." He pounded a fist into the ground. "I could have fucking saved them."

Chapter 22

It was getting light by the time the firefighters got the multiple blazes under control. A state of numbed calm had descended over the scene. People were getting on with their jobs as quickly but quietly as possible, as if in reverence for the dead. Steve, Willow and Vixen had long since been whisked away to hospital. A sweep of the grounds had revealed the bodies of three more children. A pair of large barns had been found in woodland to the rear of the house.

Jack hitched a lift to the barns in Eric's Land Rover. They arrived as officers were cutting the padlocked doors of the windowless, breeze-block and corrugated steel structures. The barns looked as if they'd been built during Dennis and his tribe's tenure of Hawkshead Manor. Their roofs were covered with a thick layer of cut pine tree branches, camouflaging them from sight from the sky. A large extractor fan on the wall of one barn gave a clue as to what it might contain.

Between the barns was a minibus also camouflaged with branches. The bus's paintwork was a mess of psychedelic swirls. The number plates were missing, but this was surely the same bus that had been caught on CCTV on the M61 slip road.

Armed police entered the barns first. Jack and Eric followed when they were given the all clear. The pungent, sickly sweet scent that flowed out of the first barn confirmed Jack's suspicion. He stepped blinking into the brightly lit interior. Rows of high-wattage bulbs dangled on wires from the roof, bathing hundreds of neatly potted cannabis plants in warm white light. Silver venting ducts snaked their way between the wires. Hoses fed a sprinkler system. The floor and walls were insulated with white plastic. Bags of fertilizer and peat were stacked against the walls.

"Someone's been hard at work in here," commented Eric. "No wonder they didn't have time to look after their other crops."

"It would cost serious money to light and heat this lot too," said Jack. The plants hadn't yet come into bud. In order to do so, they required thousands of watts of light running twelve hours a day. Maybe Butterfly's baby had been sold to tide the operation over until the harvest came in.

They moved on to the second barn. Jack's eyebrows lifted when he saw what it contained – eight high-end cars. There were two BMWs, four Mercedes, a Porsche and an Audi. Number plates, spare parts and tools were laid out on workbenches. One car was shrouded in a respray tent. "This doesn't look like the sort of operation a burnout like Smith would run," said Eric.

Jack made a noise of agreement, moving in for a closer look at the Audi. It was a black hatchback. Registration MA13 SOR. His heart quickened. Same colour, same make and model, same registration. Surely this had to be the car that was driven by PC Andrew Finch's killer.

"Come and have a look at this," Eric called from the far end of the barn.

The sergeant was squatted next to a deep bed of soil dotted with conical white mushrooms that gave off a faint ammonia aroma. "These are death caps," he said. "Just half of one of these would be enough to kill you."

"You'd better call the hospital."

Eric was already pulling out his phone. Jack ushered everyone out of the barn. A Forensic team were on the way from Manchester. He didn't want anyone even breathing on the Audi before they got here. He phoned Paul and brought him up to speed. "Well, well," Paul said upon hearing about the Audi. There was no triumph in his voice. Even such a major breakthrough paled into insignificance next to the children's deaths.

"How's DI Platts?" asked Paul.

"He'll be OK." *Physically at least,* Jack added to himself. Mentally he wasn't so sure. He'd never seen Steve so broken up before. Jack had tried to tell him that none of this was his fault, but he hadn't wanted to hear it.

"What about the unaccounted for women and children?"

"We're still searching." There was little hope in Jack's voice. According to Steve, the manor house's lounge had been littered with the dead and dying. That part of the house was now nothing more than ash.

"Dennis Smith was some piece of work. Makes you wonder about our nameless victim, doesn't it? Seems convenient that she has no memory of being involved with him. What do you think, Jack? Is she pulling the wool over our eyes?"

Jack was thoughtfully silent. He hadn't seriously considered the possibility that Butterfly was lying. His instincts told him she was telling the truth. But instincts could be wrong, especially when emotions became involved. If Butterfly's memory was intact surely she would have an idea where her baby was. And if she'd fled Hawkshead Manor to protect her baby, then pretending otherwise would make no sense. But what if she hadn't fled to protect her baby? What if she'd fled to protect herself? Maybe she'd discovered Dennis's crop of death caps, guessed what he was planning and it panicked her into running. "I don't know," he admitted reluctantly.

"Listen, I know you're exhausted, but I need you to get back here and talk to her again. I think it's time she got the full story."

Jack got off the phone, heaving a sigh at the thought of telling Butterfly that she was mother to a missing baby. How would she react? How was she supposed to react? The sight of Eric approaching with a sickened expression pushed the questions to the back of his mind.

"I was too late," said Eric. "The last of the children just passed away."

"What about the women?"

"They're all dead too."

Jack put his head down, closing his eyes and pressing his fingers to his forehead. With a sudden movement, he dialled home. Laura picked up and said in a voice heavy with sleep, "Morning, Jack."

"I need to speak to Naomi."

"She's asleep."

"Then wake her."

He knew it was selfish – Naomi didn't have to be up for another hour – but he needed to hear her voice. A moment later her soft little voice came down the line. "Hi Dad. Are you OK?"

"I am now. I love you, sweetheart, more than anything."

"I love you too, Dad."

"Go back to bed."

Laura came back on the line. "What's going on, Jack?"

"I'm heading back to Manchester. I should be able to pick Naomi up from school. I don't think I'll be coming up here again. I'll call you later." As an afterthought, he added, "You know how much I love you, don't you, sis?"

"Now you're really starting to worry me, Jack."

He smiled at Laura's dryly concerned reply. The smile vanished as someone nearby said, "They're bringing out the bodies."

Chapter 23

Jack swallowed the dregs of his coffee as he entered Intensive Care. He told the duty nurse why he was there and she went off to check whether Butterfly was awake. The armed constable approached him and said, "I heard about what's going on in The Lakes. Is it as bad as they're saying?"

Jack nodded. He didn't have the energy for unnecessary conversation.

"Bloody hell," the constable murmured with a shake of his head. "Makes you wonder what the world's coming to, doesn't it?"

Yes, thought Jack. *It makes you wonder.*

The nurse returned. "She's awake, but try to keep your visit brief. She had a bad night."

Jack's forehead wrinkled. "Nothing too serious I hope."

"Dizziness. Vomiting. We've adjusted her medication, and that's done the trick. But she's worn out."

Jack's mind was suddenly full of an image of bloody bile surging from Vixen's mouth. Strange how life kept throwing up – for want of a more apt description – these little coincidences. He sighed. Butterfly's night had been bad, but her day would not be any better.

He entered her room. She looked at him with heavy-lidded eyes. "Hello again," she said, smiling tiredly as he sat down at the bedside.

"How are you feeling?"

"They've got me on so much medication that I can't feel much of anything at all. You look tired."

"I had a long night."

"That makes two of us."

Jack stared into Butterfly's eyes. He saw no artifice in them, only weariness and vulnerability.

"What is it, Jack?" she asked, seemingly sensing his reluctance to say what needed saying.

Dennis's words echoed back to him, *You wouldn't think the child was better off with her if you knew who she really is.* They spurred him to reply, "Dennis Smith is dead, along with everyone else at Hawkshead Manor. They committed suicide."

Jack studied Butterfly's reaction like a scientist looking through a microscope. Her lips hung apart. Her eyes drifted off as if searching for something that wasn't there. After a long silence, she asked, "Why?"

"I can't say for certain."

"It's because of me, isn't it?"

"No–" began Jack.

"Yes," Butterfly cut in, her eyes returning to his, glazed with self-loathing. "You found them because of me. They killed themselves because of me."

Jack shook his head. "Dennis had been planning this for a long time."

"How do you know?"

Jack told her about the death caps. "There were other things in the barns too. Stolen cars. A cannabis farm."

Butterfly was silent for another space, her eyes shot through with a pain that had nothing to do with her injury. "What sort of person would get involved with a man like that?" she wondered. "Was I stupid or desperate? Am I a bad person?"

Jack resisted an urge to put his hand on hers. Whatever feelings he might have, he couldn't let them colour his judgement.

"Did I know what Dennis planned to do?" she continued, speaking as much to herself as Jack. She echoed the questions on his mind. "Is that why I ran away? To save myself? Did I leave those children to die?"

"I don't know. Did you?"

The look of wounded realisation that overtook Butterfly's face at the question made Jack hate himself. "You don't believe me, do you? You think I'm lying about my amnesia."

"I'm just doing my job."

"Just doing your job," Butterfly said sadly. "I thought you were my friend. I thought..." She trailed off, lowering her eyes again. "I don't know what I thought."

"I am your friend," Jack couldn't stop himself from saying. "But this isn't about me. Right now, it's not even primarily about you."

"Then who is it about?"

This was the moment Jack had been dreading. "Something else happened to you in those woods. Your attackers took something from you."

"*Something,*" Butterfly echoed, her hands moving towards her belly. "What something?"

"You were pregnant."

"Oh god," Butterfly gasped. "They took my baby, didn't they? I knew it. Somehow I knew it. Oh god, my baby..." Her eyes bulged as she desperately tried to sit up.

"I don't think you should be moving around." Jack put up his palms to emphasise his words.

Ignoring him, Butterfly raised herself halfway up. Propping herself on trembling arms, she demanded to know, "What have they done with my–" She fell silent and collapsed onto the mattress, her eyes rolling back in their sockets. Suddenly the machines she was hooked up to were emitting a chorus of rapid beeps and alarm sounds.

"Butterfly," exclaimed Jack, patting her hand.

She didn't respond. Her jaw hung slack. He couldn't tell if she was breathing. "Nurse!" he shouted, reaching for the red emergency cord. Before he could pull it, the door swung open and several nurses and doctors hustled into the room.

"She passed out," Jack told them.

He darted anxious glances at Butterfly as a nurse ushered him out of the door. A curtain was swished around Butterfly's bed. The door clunked shut.

Jack paced the corridor, ears straining for clues as to what was happening. Minutes crawled by like hours. Finally, Doctor Medland emerged from the room and informed him, "She's regained consciousness."

"Oh thank god," breathed Jack. "Can I see her?"

"Absolutely not. Another event like that could prove fatal. Did you say anything to her that could have brought on such a reaction?"

"I told her about the baby. She said she somehow already knew. Could her memory be returning?"

Doctor Medland frowned thoughtfully. "Possibly. Or she could simply have picked up on the fact that she has a postpartum belly and there's a lot of swelling where we stitched a perineal tear."

"Do me a favour, doctor. Tell her I believe her and I'm going to do everything in my power to find out what they've done." Jack handed Doctor Medland his card. "Let me know when she's up to seeing me."

On the way out of the hospital, Jack phoned Paul and said, "She's not lying. Either that or she's the best actor I've ever met."

"OK, Jack. Go home and get some rest."

Jack hung up, his forehead pinching into sharp lines. He wasn't thinking about the bitter history he shared with Paul. He was thinking about the way he'd felt when Doctor Medland told him Butterfly was conscious. It had gone beyond simple relief into something else. Something that told him he was in trouble.

Chapter 24

Jack spent a long time in the shower scrubbing off the scum of the night. But he couldn't wash away the memory of the small, motionless bodies. Afterwards, he went downstairs to make himself a bacon sandwich. His throat tightened with nausea at the sizzle of frying flesh. He binned the bacon and settled for toast. He ate it in the car on the way to Naomi's school. His throat grew tight again at the sight of children running around happily in the playground. Tears threatened to fill his eyes. He took a moment to compose himself before leaving the car.

Naomi's smiling face was like a light shining in a dark place. He smiled back as she exclaimed, "Hi Dad." Her expression turning serious, she treated him to a disapproving look. "Were you up all night?"

Jack nodded. "But I'm OK," he said and he meant it – as long as Naomi was OK, he was OK.

They returned to the car hand in hand. On the way home they stopped off at a supermarket. After the surreal events of the night, the mundanity of shopping comforted Jack. The dead faces receded from his mind as he chatted to Naomi. They came rushing back, though, when he saw a pregnant woman. He halted abruptly, his gaze fixed on her belly. It wasn't until the woman moved out of sight that he realised Naomi was talking to him.

"Dad. Dad."

He dredged up an unconvincing smile. "Sorry, sweetheart, I was miles away."

The rest of the way around the shop, he was uncomfortably aware of Naomi casting concerned glances at him.

Back at the house, he made spaghetti Bolognese. As they ate, Naomi rattled on about this and that. In the small silences between conversation, Butterfly's face kept rising into Jack's mind. He wondered what it would be like to have her and the baby there with them. Could it work? Could they be a family? He shook his head at himself. It was crazy to entertain such thoughts. Even if Butterfly felt the same way as him, how could he risk letting her into Naomi's life?

The remainder of the evening consisted of chores and Jack helping Naomi with her homework. By the time Naomi was in bed, Jack was almost asleep on his feet. Before heading to bed, he phoned Steve and asked, "How you doing?"

"Never better, mate," Steve replied jauntily. There was a tell-tale slur in his voice and a babble of voices in the background.

"They let you out of hospital then."

"They wanted to keep me in overnight, but fuck that. I needed a pint or two or three..." Steve trailed off into a drunken chuckle.

"Are you still in The Lakes?"

"No." Steve's forced jauntiness deserted him. "And I'm never going back up there again. I thought Manchester was full of nutters, but it's got nothing on that place."

"Are you in the office tomorrow?"

"Yeah. Post Incident Procedures and all that crap."

"You'd better get some sleep then. You're going to need a clear head."

"OK, Dad. Don't worry. You know me. Skull like a rhino."

Jack made an unconvinced noise. Steve was an old school copper. He avoided talking about feelings like the plague. Better to bottle it all up. And if that didn't work, nine or ten pints would do the job. "Yeah I know you, Steve. So I know you won't take me up on this, but if you need to talk you know where I am."

"Shit happens. People die. What else is there to say? Who knows? Maybe that mad bastard was right. Maybe it would be better if we burnt the whole place down and started again."

"Say that when you're sober and I'll tell you to stop talking bollocks."

Steve rediscovered his chuckle. "Talking bollocks is what I'm best at." He added sincerely, "Thanks Jack."

There was a lot in those two words and the silence that followed. Steve wasn't simply grateful for the offer of an ear to bend. He was thanking Jack for putting his life on the line for him.

"Now bugger off and let me finish my pint," Steve said with characteristic gruffness.

"Remember what I said. I want you home by eleven at the latest."

Steve laughed at the half-jokey comment. "Yeah, yeah. Night, Dad."

Jack got off the phone and, somewhat reluctantly, headed to bed. As exhausted as he was, he knew that when he closed his eyes he would see the dying and dead children again. Had Butterfly known what Dennis planned to do? Had she abandoned them to their fate? *You wouldn't think the child was better off with her if you knew who she really is.* With those words seeming to reverberate in his ears, he fell into a troubled sleep.

Chapter 25

The first thing Jack thought about when he woke up was Butterfly. Was she OK? He had to know. He phoned the hospital. A nurse informed him that she'd a better night. There had been no repeats of yesterday's 'event'. "And how about her amnesia?" asked Jack.

"No change there as far as I'm aware."

Jack thanked the nurse and got off the phone with a sigh. He'd hoped to wake up with a clearer head, an acceptance that his and Butterfly's relationship could never be anything more than policeman and victim. But the yearning to see her had grown stronger. He could feel it like a physical ache in his chest.

After dropping off Naomi at school, Jack drove to headquarters with a heavy sense of what the day held in store. There was a mind-numbing expanse of post-incident reports and statements to wade through. He reflected that at least it would distract him from thinking about Butterfly.

As he parked outside the monument to progressive policing that was Greater Manchester Police HQ, Steve pulled up alongside him.

"Morning, Dad," said Steve. The bags under his eyes betrayed that he'd got to bed a lot later than eleven o'clock. A gauze pad was taped over the wound on his neck.

"How's your head?"

"Fine," replied Steve, although the way he winced as someone slammed a car door nearby suggested otherwise.

Jack opened his mouth to say something else, but snapped it shut and did a double-take. "Where's your moustache?"

"You remember that tattooist?"

"Viv?"

"Yeah. I met her for a drink last night." Steve stroked the bare skin above his upper lip. "She shaved the old slug off while I was asleep."

Jack smiled at Steve's not-so-subtle disclosure that drinks had led to bed. "Asleep or passed out?"

Steve shrugged. "Do you think it makes me look younger?"

"Oh yeah definitely, you'll be getting ID'd down the pub."

Steve grinned, as comfortable with sarcasm as he was uncomfortable with sincerity. "I'll tell you, that girl got me into positions I haven't been in since I was a teenager. My cock feels like it's been put through a–"

"OK, OK, I get the picture."

Chuckling, Steve jerked his chin at HQ. "Come on, let's get this over with."

As they caught the lift to SCD's floor, Jack glanced appraisingly at Steve. He didn't buy the *I'm alright Jack* act. He knew Steve was hurting. He read it in the lines between the veteran inspector's eyes and the tightness of his lips. He thought about the way Naomi looked at him when she was trying to work out what was going on in his head. He'd promised himself he would keep his job and family life separate, but maybe that wasn't the way. Dennis Smith had kept the world away from his family. And look at how that had turned out. Perhaps it was better to let it all in. Teach her to deal with it. Jack exhaled heavily at the idea.

"Don't worry, mate," said Steve. "It'll be over before you know it."

Paul poked his head out of his office as the detectives passed by. He beckoned them inside. Jack could tell from the gleam in Paul's eyes that he had something to tell them. Paul was mostly a closed book, but breaking a big case made him as excitable as a kid in a sweet shop. First, though, there was a dutiful show of concern to get out of the way.

"How are you both holding up?" asked Paul, seating himself behind his perpetually cluttered desk.

In reply, he received a simultaneous, "Fine, sir."

"Glad to hear it. Terrible, terrible thing that happened up there." Paul's eyes strayed to a photo of his children. "Unimaginable. If you need to speak to someone. Myself. A counsellor..." He let the offer hang, his gaze moving between the two men. Neither said anything. With a nod, he got down to what he really wanted to talk about. "We've recovered fingerprints from the Audi in the barn."

Paul handed Jack a mugshot of a man with slicked-back black hair and heavy stubble. Deep-set, unreadable eyes stared out of a broad face with a boxer's squashed nose. Not the sort of bloke you'd want to stumble into down a dark alley. He looked to be in his mid-to-late-thirties.

"The prints belong to this..." Paul paused for the right description, "rather unsavoury character. His name's Ryan Mahon."

"Mahon," echoed Steve, his brow creasing. "Why is that name familiar?"

"Ryan has a record as long as my arm. This is one serious guy. We're talking the cream of Manchester's scumbag crop. His first serious conviction came in 1998. He was convicted of Section 20 Assault and sentenced to two years in HMP Altcourse. Some guy was making eyes at Ryan's girlfriend in a pub, so Ryan punched him and stamped on his head. Put him in a coma for a month."

"Nice," Steve commented wryly.

"When exactly was Ryan arrested?" asked Jack.

Paul consulted Ryan's rap-sheet. "May 21st. Why?"

"I was thinking about the Ridley murders. They took place on the 30th of July that year, which rules Ryan out of the running for them."

"But not Ryan's younger brother Gavin," said Paul, producing a mugshot of Gavin Mahon – crewcut hair a few shades lighter than his brother's, narrower face, same deep-set deadpan eyes, but a faint devil-may-care smile on his lips.

"He looks about thirty-five."

"Close. He's thirty-four."

"So he would have been what? Fourteen or fifteen in '98. A bit young to be committing a triple murder."

"Maybe he was a child prodigy," Steve put in with a humourless little laugh.

"Neither of the brothers has a history of sexual assault," said Paul. "Besides the Ridleys were killed a good seven or eight years before Dennis Smith moved into Hawkshead Manor. The two cases would appear to be unconnected."

"Doesn't mean our vic's not Tracy Ridley," said Jack.

"We'll have an answer on that score one way or another soon enough." Paul returned his attention to the rap-sheet. "In 2000 Ryan graduated from GBH to extortion. He and Gavin set up Mahon Security Consultants. They provided bouncers to dozens of doors around here. If business owners turned down their services, their pub or club would be flooded with troublemakers. One landlord who refused to cave in recorded Ryan making thinly veiled threats and went to the police. While Ryan was on remand in Forest Bank, Gavin threatened the landlord with a gun, tried to intimidate him into retracting his statement. Unfortunately for Gavin, we'd bugged the premises. Gavin got four years. Ryan got eighteen months. Guess where Ryan did his time."

There was only one answer Jack could think of that would explain the thrill of triumph in Paul's voice. "HMP Liverpool."

"That's the one. And for six of the twelve months he spent there, his cellmate was–"

"Dennis Smith," said Steve, stabbing a finger at the air as if pressing an invisible buzzer.

Paul nodded. "I've spoken to Rob Jones. He was Director of HMP Liverpool at the time. By all accounts, Ryan was a big deal in there. He was the go-to-man for drugs, alcohol, mobile phones. He had six months added to his sentence after being caught with an ounce of cannabis. He got out in early 2003. Gavin still had two years left to do in Forest Bank, but that didn't stop Ryan from getting back into business. This time he stepped up to the big show – armed robbery. From May 2003 to December of that year two men carried out a series of robberies across the North West, targeting cash deliveries to banks. They'd take the guards down with stun guns and hammers and make off with the cash in a stolen getaway car."

Paul handed his detectives a case file and timeline of the robberies:

May 10th 2003 - Two men wearing balaclavas assault guard outside Barclay's Bank, Crofts Bank Road, Urmston. £42,750 stolen.

June 12th 2003 - TSB Bank, Stockport Road, Manchester. Two masked men jump out of a silver VW Golf and assault a guard. £12,436 stolen.

July 20th 2003 - TSB Bank, Barlow Moor Road, Manchester. A guard fled dropping a cash case after being approached by two masked men with hammers. £16,570 stolen.

The robberies continued like that at a rate of roughly one a month. They were meticulously planned and executed. Any resistance met with a brutal response. Getaway cars were torched. No forensic evidence was left behind. By December well over £200,000 had been stolen. But the robbers weren't about to take a break for Christmas.

On December 6th, they targeted a cash delivery to Allied Irish Bank on Hardman Street, Manchester city centre. This was a risky move – the previous robberies were in suburban areas – but also held out the possibility a greater reward. The robbers followed their usual strategy – pull up in getaway vehicle, subdue guards, make off with cash. In this instance £87,390. They only made it as far as Deansgate Interchange, half a mile from the bank, before police intercepted them.

The robbers crashed into the A57's central reservation and fled their vehicle. One of them was caught in the grounds of a block of flats adjacent to the south side of the ring road. At approximately the same time, a Toyota was stolen from a carpark on Great Jackson Street on the opposite side of the ring road. It was believed the car was stolen by the other robber. He escaped with the money.

"Dennis Smith," said Jack. It was surely no coincidence that stealing a VW Golf had landed Dennis in HMP Liverpool or that the same brand of car had been used in several of the robberies.

"If you mean the escapee, I can't think of a better candidate," agreed Paul. "Ryan was, of course, the other half of the duo. He refused to give up his accomplice. Not a penny of the £279,988 they stole was recovered."

Steve whistled. "Nice little nest-egg for Dennis to kick-start his new life at Hawkshead Manor."

"Well while Dennis was planning for the end of the world up in The Lakes, Ryan was doing a ten year stretch in Strangeways. He got out in eight."

"Eight years in a Cat A. Hard time," reflected Jack. By the time Ryan was released he would have been ready to take his place amongst the North West's criminal elite. "So where did Ryan go from there?"

"Moss Side. And as far as we know that's where he's been for the past seven years."

"He went straight?" Jack's tone was dubious. For career criminals like Ryan, more often than not the only way out of their life of crime was in a coffin.

"I don't know about that, but he disappeared off our radar. So did Gavin." Paul showed them a third mugshot. "This may explain their low profile and some other things too." The mugshot was of an older man whose face was a mashup of Ryan and Gavin's features – salt 'n pepper hair and stubble, craggy brown eyes, broken nose, lantern jaw. It was the sort of face you would struggle to put a dent in with a sledgehammer. "That's Glenn Mahon. Ryan and Gavin's dad."

Steve clicked his fingers. "I knew I'd heard the name Mahon before. He was killed a few years back during an armed robbery, wasn't he?"

"That's right. A tipoff came in that an armed gang was planning to hit a security van outside a branch of RBS in Eccles. A firearms unit was lying in wait when three masked men jumped out of a white van and put a handgun to a guard's head. Officers opened fire killing two of the men. The third fled the scene and managed to escape. The dead men were Glenn Mahon and a pal of his, Billy Hardy. This was in July 2010, not long before Ryan got out of prison."

"But Gavin wasn't inside at the time, was he?" said Jack.

"No. He was picked up for questioning, but he had a ready-made alibi. Apparently he was with his wife and kids at the birthday party of a friend's child."

Steve snorted. "Did they give him a party bag to prove he was there?"

"There was a big hoo-ha after the shooting when it turned out the gun was a replica. The Mahons made a lot of noise about GMP having a vendetta against Glenn. He had a long history of run-ins with us, including blinding an officer in one eye while resisting arrest for drunk and disorderly in 2007."

"What a gem. And his boys have done him proud," Steve remarked dryly.

"Kill all police," said Jack, thinking about the 'LOVE::. ALICE:' tattoo on the forearm of one of Butterfly's attackers. "So assuming the men who shot and buried our vic are Ryan and Gavin, and assuming the tattoo means what we think it does, these guys have killed at least two of ours."

The room was momentarily silent. Jack could see his colleagues were thinking the same as him. PC Andrew Finch had seemingly been shot dead because he was in the wrong place at the wrong time. Ryan and Gavin would have no issue doing the same to anyone attempting to arrest them. They might even relish the opportunity to exact further revenge for their dad's death.

"So what's our next move?" asked Jack.

"What do you think?" said Steve. "We take the murdering bastards down. Make them wish they'd never been born."

"I wouldn't put it quite like that, but yes," said Paul. "The brothers live next door to each other on Broadfield Road. We're raiding both houses today."

"They won't be there," said Jack. "Not after everything that's happened."

"They're probably in the Costas by now working on their tans," agreed Steve.

"I don't doubt you're right," said Paul. "But their wives and children are there." He consulted a file on his desk. "Ryan is married to Beth Mahon. They have three children. Gavin is married to Leah Mahon. They have two children. We've got eyes on them. The children are at school. Both women are at home. If we turn their houses over and bring them in for questioning, it might bring Ryan and Gavin out of the woodwork."

Jack's forehead wrinkled. "Are you sure you want to try and poke the snakes out of their hole?"

Paul replied with a frown of his own. "Are you saying we should be intimidated by these thugs?"

"Of course not, sir," Jack said respectfully. Paul's irritated tone reminded him that their relationship was still balanced on a knife edge. Irritation could quickly turn into outright anger and, before he knew it, he might be back to knocking on doors in Clifton. "I just think we should tread carefully. We know what the Mahons are capable of. Do we really want to risk angering them?"

"I hope we do make them angry, because angry people do stupid things."

You mean like when I punched you in the face after I found out you'd been fucking my wife. Jack caught the thought before he could give voice to it.

"Please let them try something," snarled Steve. "I'd love an excuse to put them in hospital."

"No one will be putting the Mahons into anything other than a prison cell, DI Platts," admonished Paul.

"No word on the street about the whereabouts of the brothers?" asked Jack.

"Not a whisper. All our informants are saying the same thing – no one who values their neck will give up the Mahons."

Jack wasn't surprised. Fear. That was the best weapon scumbags like the Mahons had at their disposal. The more fear they commanded, the safer they were from being grassed up, double-crossed and the myriad other ways in which their kind fucked each other over. The idea that the brothers would be protected by some sort of code of silence was as laughable as it was naïve. It was an almost certain bet, for example, that the only reason Ryan hadn't named his accomplice in 2003 in return for a reduced sentence was because it would have meant losing his share of the loot. "What about known associates? Have we got eyes on any?"

"The only people the Mahons regularly associate with are other Mahons. They're a tight bunch."

"Fucking inbreeds," Steve muttered.

Casting him a disapproving glance, Paul continued, "The exceptions to the rule seem to have been Billy Hardy, who was a childhood friend of Glenn, and Dennis Smith, who as we now know was useful to the Mahons in all sorts of ways."

"What about wiretapping their phones?" suggested Jack.

"That takes time and the baby's been missing for the best part of four days. Do you want to sit around twiddling your thumbs on the off-chance the Mahons would be stupid enough to contact each other using traceable phones?"

Jack shook his head. As reluctant as he was to admit it, poking the snakes seemed to be their best option. "When are the raids taking place?"

"As soon as the relevant warrants are issued." Paul glanced at his watch. "Which should be anytime now. Do you feel up to coming along?"

"Just try to stop me, sir," grinned Steve.

Jack merely nodded.

Chapter 26

A convoy of police vehicles headed by a Firearms Unit van sped along a claustrophobically narrow street of redbrick terraced houses. Some bystanders rubbernecked. Others barely afforded the vehicles a glance – they'd seen it all before. The van screeched to a halt outside two bay-windowed houses with postage-stamp front-yards. To an uneducated eye nothing marked the houses out as the homes of notorious criminals. But from his car at the rear of the convoy, Jack picked out a few tell-tale signs – CCTV cameras above the front doors, a matching pair of white Land Rover Discoveries with tinted windows parked outside.

A conga line of officers in full body armour exited the van, semi-automatic rifles slung around their shoulders. They split into two lines, moving in rapidly on both houses. "Armed police!" The shout echoed along the street. "Open the door!"

Only a few seconds passed between the demand and the deployment of officers with Enforcer battering rams.

"Go on lads," encouraged Steve as the officers swung the steel rams.

Echoing thuds boomed out as the doors were repeatedly struck. Neither gave way. "Must be reinforced," said Jack, getting out of the car for a better view.

Officers set to work on the downstairs windows with sledgehammers. The glass shivered but didn't break. An old lady poked her head out of a front door next to Jack. "They say the windows are bulletproof," she informed him.

"Please go back inside, madam," he said. The woman remained where she was, craning her neck to watch the action. Other people were hanging their heads out of doors and windows.

"Fuck off," shouted one man. "Haven't you already done enough to their family?"

"Back inside!" retorted a firearms officer. The man gave him the finger. A gang of tracksuited kids on BMXs were weaving in and out of the police vehicles, laughing and jeering as constables chased them away.

The sledgehammers were still pounding ineffectively at the windows. Sparks flared as an officer took an angle grinder to one door. Jack puffed his cheeks as Steve perched himself on the bonnet beside him. "Well we're certainly making an impression."

Steve lit a cigarette. "This lot should be grateful. You can't buy entertainment like this."

The angle grinder fell silent as it broke through the lock. The officer wielding it stepped aside and six or seven of his colleagues with rifles raised and ready filed through the doorway, bellowing, "Armed police! Stay where you are!"

From inside the house came a shrill voice accompanied by a chorus of deep barks. As the officer with the angle grinder attacked the neighbouring house's door, two officers reappeared hauling along a pair of thickly muscled white bulldogs. The dogs looked skittery and nervous, more scared than ready to fight.

A woman in a tight vest, skinny jeans and high-heels tottered after the dogs. She was five-foot-nothing and whippet-thin with breasts like over-inflated balloons, bleached blonde hair and a 'You've been Tangoed' face. She was holding her own in a wrestling match with an officer twice her size. "You've got no right to take my dogs. Let go of me! Fucking bastards. Cunts. Let go. Police brutality! Police brutality!"

The kids on bicycles took up her chant. "Police brutality!"

"She's a bit tasty," Steve said to Jack.

The woman's tirade continued as more officers ran to restrain and escort her into the back of a van. Paul lowered his car window. "Leah Mahon," he told Jack and Steve. "Gavin's wife."

The neighbouring door's lock gave up the ghost. Firearms officers entered the property. There were more shouts of, "Police!" and "Don't move!" This time they were greeted with silence.

A woman emerged from the house. She too was a buxom blonde done up like something out of The Only Way is Essex. But unlike Leah she carried herself with an air of aloof superiority, chin held high. She eyed the scene icily from her front gate. Several officers stood ready should she try anything. She gave them no excuse to lay a hand on her.

"That must be Beth Mahon," said Jack.

"She looks like a duchess," said Steve. "My type of woman."

"Are there any women that aren't your type?"

Steve chuckled. "Now you come to mention it..."

Paul got out of his car and motioned for Beth to be brought over. She approached them with the poise of a model on a catwalk.

"There she is," the old woman said just loud enough for Jack to hear. "Queen bloody bee."

Beth was preceded by the click-click of her designer high-heels, the jangle of her gold jewellery and the heavy scent of her perfume. Her catlike blue-green eyes were as inscrutable as her husband's. They slid across to the old woman who swiftly retreated into her hallway and closed the door. Jack had seen it many times before. Families like the Mahons lorded it over their streets like robber barons. They could doubtless have afforded to live in a more salubrious area, but preferred to remain where people knew them and their reputation. No one in Moss Side would pick up a phone to inform on them. That didn't mean the Mahons' neighbours were bad people. Most would probably have loved to see the back of the Mahons. But soaring levels of crime, poverty and unemployment had left them jaded, apathetic and, above all, sceptical of the police's ability to protect them.

"Beth Mahon?" said Paul.

"Who's asking?" Beth replied in a broad, flat-vowelled Mancunian accent.

Paul displayed his ID and Beth made a sound in her throat as if she was gathering phlegm to spit.

"We'd like you to accompany us to the station, Mrs Mahon," said Paul.

"Am I under arrest?"

"No."

"Then I'm not going anywhere."

"I could place you under arrest."

A knowing smile played at the corners of Beth's glossy lips. "If you coulda, you woulda."

Paul returned an exaggeratedly polite smile. Beth clearly would not be bluffed into cooperating. A constable approached. "Both houses are clear, sir. No sign of the suspects."

"Why didn't you open the door?" Paul asked Beth.

"Would you if murderers were trying to break into your house?" she replied loudly enough to be heard by the faces lining the doors and windows.

Paul's gaze swept uneasily over those same faces. "Would you prefer to talk somewhere private?"

"Makes no difference where we are. I've got nothing to say to you."

"Don't you want to know why we're here?"

"I couldn't give two fucks why you're here."

"You've got three children, haven't you?" put in Jack.

Beth looked at him for the first time. "What if I have?" There was an edge to her voice, like the warning growl of a mother wolf.

"What are their names?"

Beth said nothing, but Jack could feel the hate behind her slanted eyes.

"Callum, Jade and Anya," said Paul, perhaps sensing that Jack was mining a potentially productive seam.

"Anya," said Jack. "That's an unusual name. Why did you call your daughter Anya?"

Beth bit her upper lip and held her tongue.

"It's funny," went on Jack. "Before my daughter was born I never used to notice kids. But afterwards I couldn't stop noticing them. Especially babies. They seemed to be everywhere. Crying their lungs out. Scrunched up little faces. Tiny fingers. And I'd say to myself, what kind of monster could hurt a baby? I think all new dads feel the same way... Well, nearly all. There are some that don't care who they hurt just so long as they get what they want. You know the kind of people I'm talking about, Beth. The lowest of the low. Even in prison they have to be kept in isolation for their own safety."

The sandpaper-rough laughter of a heavy smoker drowned out Jack's voice. "Sorry," said Beth, theatrically gripping her sides. "Go on, finish what you were saying. I could do with a good laugh."

"Real piece of work, aren't you, love?" said Steve. Now it was his turn to make sure his voice was loud enough to be heard. "Your husband sells babies to god only knows who. There's a baby out there right now possibly being abused because of Ryan and Gavin. And you find that funny?"

Beth eyed him unflinchingly. "*You* put four bullets in my dad," she hissed as if Steve had pulled the trigger. "*You* said Dad had a gun. That was a lie. Billy Hardy had the gun. And even that wasn't a real gun."

"An investigation ruled that the shooting was lawful," pointed out Paul.

"Pigs investigating pigs," Beth spat contemptuously. "State hired murderers. That's all you are. Justice is whatever you decide it is. Well if we can't get justice by the law, we'll make our own." She pumped a fist into the air. "Justice for Glenn Mahon!"

"Justice for Glenn Mahon!" parroted the BMX gang and a scattering of other onlookers.

"I hope that's not a threat, Mrs Mahon. Because we won't tolerate threats."

Beth jutted her chin at Paul. "What are you gonna do? Take me down the station and beat me up?"

Paul sighed. "We don't tolerate police brutality either."

"I reckon she's watched too many episodes of The Sweeny," said Steve.

"Perhaps we should show her the footage from the woods," Jack suggested.

"That sounds like a good idea," agreed Paul.

Jack fetched a laptop from his car. "Shall we go inside?" said Paul. "I don't think you want your neighbours seeing this, Mrs Mahon."

Beth stared at him, her eyes narrow and calculating. With the same slow movements that let the onlookers know she would go at her own speed and no one else's, she returned to her house. Paul, Jack and Steve followed her into a hallway that was done out like a mini palace complete with plush red carpets, fluted bannister and angelic murals. Officers were none-too-gently rooting through mahogany kitchen cupboards and piling bone-china on marble work-surfaces.

"Oi! Careful," Beth yelled at them. "That stuff costs more than you pricks make in a year." She shifted her attention to officers carrying hard-drives, laptops and iPads downstairs. "Hey, those belong to the kids."

"We have the right to take anything that may aid us in our enquiry, Mrs Mahon," said Paul. "They'll be returned as soon as we're finished with them."

Scowling doubtfully, Beth stalked into a living-room that had been thoroughly turned over. Gold-framed family portraits had been taken down from the wood-panelled walls. A top-of-the-range flat-screen TV had received the same treatment. What looked like a whole antiques emporium's worth of china vases, plates, ashtrays, tea sets and the like lay in a jumble on the carpet. The cushions had been removed from a red leather three-piece-suite and tossed aside. An officer was rifling through an ornate drinks cabinet.

"Give us a moment," said Paul.

"Yes sir." The officer handed Paul two bundles of fifty-pound notes sealed in bank wrappers marked '£2,500'. "These were in the cabinet."

Paul looked at Beth. "Can you explain this?"

She stared back as if she would have liked to do the same to him as had been done to the room. "Pocket money."

Paul cocked an eyebrow. "I'm afraid this will have to be booked into evidence."

"And how am I supposed to feed my kids if you take my money?"

"You could try getting a job like everyone else," Steve suggested.

"Think you're fucking hilarious, don't you?" Beth retorted. "Thieving bastards," she muttered as Paul returned the money to the officer.

"Make sure Mrs Mahon gets a receipt for this," Paul said pointedly.

Jack fast-forwarded through the night-vision footage to where Butterfly stumbled into the woodland clearing. "Have a look at this please, Mrs Mahon."

Beth looked uninterestedly at the laptop. A hush descended over the room as on-screen Butterfly dropped to her knees, clutching her pregnant belly. Jack watched Beth watching the footage, partly to gauge her reaction, but also because he couldn't stomach watching it again himself. As the video unfolded, her expression remained inscrutable. But shade by shade the colour leached from her sharp cheekbones. Her jaw muscles pulsed when one of the balaclava-wearing figures handed over his jacket for the baby to be swaddled in.

Jack paused the video. "You recognise that man, don't you?"

"Which man?"

"You know who I mean. I would show you the rest of the footage, but I know it wouldn't bother you seeing your husband shoot a woman. Killing people is just a job. But stealing babies? That's something else entirely. Imagine how you'd feel if someone tore a baby out of your womb and sold it."

Beth wasn't laughing now. "Depends, doesn't it?"

"On what?"

"On whether I was fit to be a mother."

"Are you fit to be a mother?"

Beth's eyes flashed fiercely. "A good mother wants her children to be safe. If she can't keep them safe herself, they're better off with someone else."

Her words made Jack uneasy. Was she implying that Butterfly couldn't be trusted to care for her baby? Dennis's voice echoed in his ears again – *You wouldn't think the child was better off with her if you knew who she really is.* "Is that why Ryan took the baby, because he thinks it will have a better life with someone else?"

"I don't have the faintest fucking clue what you're talking about."

"Thing is, Beth," Jack persisted, "people aren't always what they seem. Sometimes someone might seem like they can't be trusted, but the exact opposite turns out to be true. Others might seem like they can be trusted with your most precious possession, but..." He let his words hang meaningfully for a second, before adding, "I once worked on a case involving a retired headmaster. This guy did charity work in his spare time. No one had a bad word to say about him. That is until one of his granddaughters told a friend that grandad kept touching her 'down there'. The friend told their parents and the parents told us and... Well, then it all came out. For forty years this guy, this pillar of the community had abused his own kids, his grandkids, the kids he'd taught–"

"Shut your filthy gob and get out of my house," scowled Beth.

"Where are Ryan and Gavin?" pressed Jack.

"Get out! Out!"

"I can tell you're a good mum, Beth. Forget Ryan and Gavin. Just tell us where the baby is. You have the power to make sure that baby comes to no harm."

"And if the baby's real mother isn't fit to take care of it, she won't get it back," put in Paul. "We'll make certain it ends up in good hands. Trust us."

Trust us. At those words a shutter seemed to slam down over Beth's face. "I've got nothing to tell you," she said in a voice like a full-stop.

"OK, Beth," said Jack. "If that's the way you want to play it. I just hope for the sake of your children that you don't come to regret your decision."

Very calmly, Beth turned to Jack and spat in his face.

"That's assault," said Steve, reaching for her.

Jack blocked his hand. "Forget it." He held Beth's gaze for a heartbeat before retrieving his laptop and leaving the room.

Paul followed him outside. "Sorry, Jack. I shouldn't have stuck my oar in."

Jack wiped saliva off his face. "She wouldn't have given up any information regardless."

"I'm not sure. I think you were getting somewhere. If you press charges we can take her in and sweat her."

Jack shook his head. "I doubt she's got the answers we need. Ryan would know better than to put her at risk of being charged. Besides, I deserved that. I was wrong to bring her kids into it."

"So what do you think our next move should be?"

"I don't know." *If we can't get justice by the law, we'll make our own.* Jack turned Beth's words over in his mind. "Maybe we should just wait and see what happens."

Paul made no reply. Both men knew waiting wasn't an option. As Jack headed for his car, Paul said, "You *didn't* deserve it, Jack."

Lines gathered between Jack's eyebrows. It was surreal to hear Paul talking to him like a friend. Only a few days ago he would never have believed it possible. Could he return the gesture? Rebecca's beautiful, brittle face flashed through his mind. No, he wasn't ready to do that. But neither did he feel like listening to the part of his mind that urged him to retort, *Who are you to tell me what I do or don't deserve?* Instead, he simply continued on his way.

Chapter 27

The air in the windowless box that served as an interview room was thick with the scent of perfume and cigarettes. Leah Mahon had been allowed several cigarette breaks during the course of the afternoon. The nicotine appeared to have done little to calm her nerves. Her long painted nails tapped out a ceaseless rhythm on the table-top. Her small eyes were constantly on the move too, flitting around like trapped bluebottles. She worked over a piece of gum, stretching it out of her mouth, balling it up and shoving it back in. Jack watched her silently. Neither of them had said a word in five or six minutes. He'd tried the same tack on her as on Beth and got the same result. She was a different beast to Beth – younger, less adept at controlling her emotions. During her viewing of Butterfly's ordeal, she'd trembled uncontrollably. But she knew how to do one thing extremely well – keep silent. In two hours, she hadn't spoken more than fifteen words and most of those had been 'no' or 'fuck off'.

Jack skimmed over Leah's personal details once again – 'POB: Moss Side, Manchester, DOB: 10-04-1982.' She'd gone to the same high-school as Gavin, although she was three years younger than him. They'd married in 2005. A year later she'd given birth to twin brothers – Tyler and Liam. She had no criminal record. She'd never had a job – at least not one that involved paying tax. There was one smudge on her record – she'd been flagged up to social services when the twins kept turning up to school covered in bruises. A 'child in need' case had been opened, but it was determined that neither parent posed a threat to the twins.

Jack sighed. He was reluctant to use her children as leverage, but it was all he had. "In 2015 social services interviewed you after concerns were raised about the welfare of your sons."

Leah's over-plucked eyebrows twitched as if she'd been waiting for Jack to play this card. "Yeah, so fucking what? Nothing came of it? The boys had been fighting. What's wrong with that? It's just normal boy stuff, isn't it?"

"Is it?" asked Jack, encouraged that Leah had said more in the past few seconds than during the entire interview. "I don't remember fighting with my brother like that." Laura was Jack's only sibling, but truth and lies were only tools to be used as required when there was a baby missing. "Did Gavin fight with Ryan when they were kids?"

Leah chewed her gum. This time her silence told Jack all he needed to know. "Ryan's what, three or four years older than Gavin?" he continued. "Bigger too. I'll bet he used to beat the shit out of Gavin, didn't he?"

Leah's fingers balled into fists. "No one beats the shit out of my Gav."

"I believe that. When it comes to everyone except Ryan that is. It's obvious which one of them is the boss. How old is Ryan's son Callum?" Jack answered his own question. "Fifteen. So there's about the same age difference between him and your boys as between Gavin and Ryan. Is that what happened to Tyler and Liam? Did Callum beat them up? He did, didn't he? He's doing the same thing to your boys as Ryan did to Gavin. And when your boys grow up, they'll be under Callum's thumb just like Gavin is under Ryan's. Is that what you want?"

Leah let out a sharp laugh. "You must think I'm stupid or something. I know what you're game is and it won't work." She pushed her chin out proudly. "I'm a Mahon. Do you understand what that means?" A sneer twisted her lips. "Nah, how could you? You don't have a fucking clue what loyalty is."

"Oh I know what loyalty means, Leah. And I know what it doesn't mean too. It doesn't mean letting your children get beaten up on a daily basis. And it certainly doesn't mean allowing them to be forced into a life of crime. Because you know where that life leads, don't you?" Jack motioned to the room. "Here." Then he pointed downwards. "Or there."

Leah resumed chewing her gum even more intensely than before.

Jack saw the opening and went for it. "It doesn't have to be that way. You can decide here and now that you want something different for your boys. All you have to do is help us."

Leah's thick foundation cracked like a dry riverbed as she wrinkled her forehead. "I don't know nothing."

"I believe you, but Gavin will contact you at some point. You just have to let us know when and what he says. Simple."

Thirty seconds passed. A minute. Jack let the silence continue. He knew when to twist the screws and when to back off. Two minutes. Leah was staring at her fingernails as if she hated them. Three... Four minutes. *Give her a gentle nudge,* Jack said to himself. "You don't want social services sticking their nose into your business again, do you? Because all it would take is for Tyler and Liam to show up at school with more bruises and another case could be opened against you."

Leah stopped chewing. The lines on her forehead disappeared. She lifted her eyes back to Jack's. When he saw the look in them, he knew he'd overplayed his hand. "They're not afraid of you." Her voice was barely a whisper.

"Who isn't?"

"You know who I'm talking about. You started this, but they're gonna finish it."

"Is that a threat?"

"It's a fact. They've been getting ready for this ever since you murdered Glenn."

The certainty in Leah's voice sent a cold tingle through Jack. "Glenn was an armed robber. I'd say getting shot is a hazard of the job, wouldn't you?"

"It doesn't matter what I think. And it doesn't matter what I know. You won't have to find Gavin and Ryan. They'll find you."

Jack glanced towards a CCTV camera in a corner of the ceiling through which Paul was watching proceedings. "What are they going to do?"

Leah bared her too-white teeth. "What do you think they're gonna do?"

"I think they're going to get themselves killed. And you're going to end up a widow. And your boys are going to grow up without a dad. You can stop that from happening, Leah."

She gave out a laugh that told Jack his chance of cracking her had passed. "Are you afraid?" she asked with a taunting edge. "You should be." She looked at the camera. "All of you."

Jack sighed again. "I hope you change your mind, Leah. Take it from someone who knows, it's no fun bringing up children on your own."

They faced each other for another silent moment. Jack's eyes were sympathetic, but Leah's expression remained set like concrete. "Is there anything else you'd like to say?" he asked without expectation.

Leah shook her head.

"OK, so I'm now handing you the notice that explains what happens to the interview recordings." Jack passed Leah a sheet of paper and glanced at his watch. "The time is three fifteen PM, the interview is concluded and Detective Inspector Anderson is switching off the recording equipment."

Jack stood to leave, but paused. "Gavin and his brother put a bullet in a new mother's head. How can you love someone like that?" There was no provocation in the question, just curiosity.

"I don't know nothing about that, but if they did it, it was just a job," Leah replied matter-of-factly. "They take pride in their work. They never let a customer down," she added as if she was talking about a firm of plumbers or builders.

Just a job. Jack gave a little shake of his head. People could rationalise almost anything if they wanted it badly enough. His thoughts returned to

Butterfly. What if she *had* known what Dennis Smith planned to do? How would he rationalise that? He knew the answer because it had already passed through his mind. Whoever Butterfly had been back then, she was a different person now. Wasn't she? Surely she couldn't be held accountable for things she had no memory of. Could she?

"Someone will be along shortly to escort you from the building," Jack informed Leah.

He made his way to a neighbouring room where Steve was lounging in front of a CCTV screen. "Where's the DCI?" asked Jack.

"He had to take a phone call." Glancing at the grainy camera image of Leah, Steve gave a snort. "Maybe we should get a logo made up – *Ryan and Gavin Mahon. Scumbags for hire. Guaranteed to get the job done or your money back!*"

Paul entered the room. "How'd it go?"

Jack gave him a quick rundown.

"Well we can be fairly sure of one thing," said Paul. "The brothers aren't hiding out on the Costas."

"The Force needs to be put on high alert. And I mean the *entire* Force, not just GMP. Armed response should be at the ready around the clock."

Steve snorted again. "Don't you think you're overreacting, Jack?"

"Why don't you ask Andrew Finch's widow? Find out what she thinks?"

"Jack's right," said Paul. "We have to take this threat seriously. I'd better let the Super know what the situation is. Jack, I need you to head over to the hospital."

"Butterfly won't recognise the Mahons."

"Butterfly?"

"That's what the nurses call her."

"Well they can start using her real name. I just had a call from the DNA lab. We got a match. The victim is Tracy Ridley."

Jack winced internally. Although his instincts had told him this was coming, he'd held onto a slender hope that Butterfly had a loving family waiting for her somewhere. But girls with loving families didn't tend to fall under the spell of charlatans like Dennis Smith. That fate was reserved for people whose lives were blighted by tragedy, people desperate for something to make sense of the world and their place in it. People like Tracy Ridley.

"I can get someone else to do it if you're too tired," said Paul, mistaking Jack's troubled silence for weariness.

Jack shook his head. He would have taken any reason to see Butterfly – he wasn't ready to think of her as Tracy – even if that reason was to tell her a pair of unidentified psychopaths had murdered her family.

"Watch your back," Paul cautioned as Jack turned to leave.

"You too," said Jack, wondering what Rebecca would think if she could see him showing concern towards the man she'd had an affair with. Would it make her happy? He hoped so. He would have thrown his arms around Paul and sworn undying friendship if it helped Rebecca find the peace that had eluded her in life.

His thoughts moved from the past to the present. How would Butterfly take the news he had for her? Would it bring on another 'event'? Maybe it would be enough to finish the job off for the Mahons. The possibility weighed on him as he headed for his car.

Chapter 28

Jack padded into Butterfly's room as if trying not to wake her, but she wasn't asleep. The sight of her eased the knot of tension in his stomach. Her cheeks were devoid of colour – except for the tattoo – but her eyes were the clearest he'd seen them. She granted him the briefest of glances before sliding her gaze away. The knot tightened again. "How are you feeling?" he asked.

She shrugged as if to say, *What do you care?*

"Did Doctor Medland tell you what I said?"

"You mean about believing me?"

"Yes." Jack approached the bed and tried to catch Butterfly's eyes. "I'm sorry for doubting you."

She looked at him, her expression shifting from annoyance to uncertainty. "Do you really mean that?"

"Yes," he replied with absolute conviction.

"I don't blame you for doubting me, Jack." Her eyes fell away from his again, this time wracked with guilt. "I can't stop thinking about those poor children. What if I could have saved them?"

"If you could have saved them, you would have."

"How can you know that?"

There was a pained appeal in the question. "Because of who you are," was the only answer Jack could think to give.

"What do you mean?"

"I've got something to tell you, but I need you to stay calm."

The tattoo fluttered as Butterfly's eyes flew wide. "Have you found my baby?" Her voice was anything but calm.

"No, it's not that," Jack said quickly. She released a breath that mingled disappointment with relief. He got the easy part out of the way first, bringing up a photo of the Mahon brothers on his phone. "Do they ring any bells?"

Butterfly's eyebrows pinched together. "They're the men who shot me, aren't they?"

"What makes you say that?"

"Because they look like killers. Who are they?"

Not wanting to make Butterfly any more agitated than she already was, Jack limited himself to saying, "They're small-time gangsters."

"Gangsters." Her voice was tight and low, as if constricted by the thought of such men laying their hands on her baby. "Have you spoken to them?"

"We don't know where they are."

The lines between Butterfly's eyes sharpened. "I don't understand. How does this prove I didn't abandon the children?"

Now came the hard part. "There's something else." Jack swiped to the photo of eleven-year-old Tracy – wavy brown hair, freckles, smiling eyes. "You remember I showed you this photo before? Her name's Tracy Ridley." He readied himself to pull the emergency cord if necessary. "*Your* name's Tracy Ridley."

Butterfly looked from the photo to Jack and back as if struggling to comprehend what he'd told her. She reached for the photo, but drew her hand back as if it might bite her. "Are you sure?"

Jack nodded. "We ran a DNA comparison."

Her gaze flicked up to his, hopeful now. "On who?"

"Shirley Ridley. Your grandma. She's in a care home in Rochdale. She has no memory of you." By way of explanation, Jack added gently, "Alzheimer's."

"No memory." Butterfly's lips curved into a sadly ironic smile. "We should get on well then. What about the rest of my family?" When Jack didn't reply, her eyes searched his face as if looking for an answer. "Surely there are others?"

Jack shook his head. "I'm sorry, Butterf–" He broke off and corrected himself, "Tracy."

"How's that possible? How can I not have a mum and dad?"

Drawing in a long breath, Jack swiped to a photo of Tracy standing alongside a slim woman with curly brown hair, a similarly built man with receding red hair and a young girl beaming cheekily into the camera. He pointed. "That's your mum Andrea, your dad Marcus, and your older sister Charlie."

Butterfly stared at the photo for a long moment, then said, "They're dead, aren't they?"

"They were murdered."

She closed her eyes as if shutting out something she couldn't bear to see. "By who? Those gangsters?"

"Their killers were never identified… Are you sure you're up to hearing this right now?"

"Just tell me, Jack."

He took another breath. Then he recounted how two men wearing balaclavas tied up the Ridleys and sexually assaulted Charlie. And how when the men dragged Marcus into the trees to cut his throat, Tracy got free and ran away. All the time he watched for any sign that Butterfly was about to suffer another seizure. But her face remained strangely serene, like a patch of smooth water on a windy day. When he was finished, she said in a fatalistic, matter-of-fact way, "So I ran away and left them to die. Just like I did with the children."

"No. You tried to free them and when you couldn't you ran to get help."

"How do you know I tried to free them? Maybe I lied to the police."

"What reason would you have had to lie? You were eleven-years-old. You'd have been terrified. In shock."

Butterfly's face twitched with uncertainty. "When I look at that photo all I see are strangers. People who mean nothing to me. Perhaps they never meant anything to me."

"You're wrong. How do you think you got involved with Dennis Smith? You were searching for the place where your parents and sister were killed. You must have bumped into Dennis. He saw how vulnerable you were and exploited it. That's how people like him operate. It wasn't your fault. None of this is your fault."

Guilt flowed like tears from Butterfly's eyes. "I wish I could believe you, Jack." Her fingers traced the outline of her eleven-year-old self. "Who are you?" she murmured.

"I'll tell you who she is." Jack took Butterfly's hand. It was cold and clammy although the room was warm. "She's someone who lost her way. That doesn't make you a bad person. It just means you're human."

Butterfly withdrew her hand from his, turning to the wall.

"Look at me, Tracy," said Jack.

"Don't call me that. I'm not Tracy."

"You're right about that. Maybe your amnesia is a blessing in disguise. You don't have to be Tracy anymore. You're free to be whoever you want to be." Jack touched her chin, gently angling it towards him. "Butterfly."

"Butterfly," she echoed, lacing her fingers into his.

They stayed like that for the space of several breaths, looking into each other's eyes. When they drew apart, Jack knew there was no point fighting it. He didn't care who Tracy had been. All he cared about was Butterfly.

A clock on the wall caught his eye. It was past five. Time to pick Naomi up from Laura's. *Naomi.* He noticed the knot in his stomach again. Could it work? The three – hopefully four of them – together. A family. *You can make it work,* he told himself with as much conviction as he could muster.

"I've got to go," he said. "I have to pick up my daughter Naomi."

Butterfly's eyebrows lifted. "You have a daughter."

Jack smiled. "Why is that so surprising?"

"I don't know. I don't suppose it is." A faintly fearful note came into Butterfly's voice. "Do you have a wife?"

Jack's smiled faltered. "I did. She died."

"Oh. I..." Butterfly seemed uncertain how to respond. "I'm sorry to hear that. How did it happen?"

"I'll tell you another time. It's a long story. I'll come at the same time tomorrow and you can ask me as many questions as you like."

"Same time tomorrow," Butterfly echoed as if making certain Jack's words were imprinted on her mind.

On his way out of the ward, Jack spoke to the firearms officer – a young man with eager-to-impress eyes. "Craig, isn't it?"

"Yes, sir."

"You don't leave this doorway, Craig. Not even for a second. If you see anything that strikes you as odd – and I mean *anything,* like if someone sneezes funny – you contact me at once. Understood?"

Craig nodded.

Jack returned to his car on feet that felt light. One word kept replaying in his head – *tomorrow.* Tomorrow couldn't come soon enough.

Chapter 29

As usual, Naomi was waiting for him with a hug at Laura's little house. "Hi Dad! Have you had a good day?"

Smiling into her blue eyes, he replied, "Yes." Relative to the previous two days, almost anything would have qualified as a 'good day'.

Naomi gave him one of her looks that always made him feel as if he was the child and she the parent. "What was good about it?"

Jack's mind raced for a reply that didn't involve Butterfly. He was a long way from ready to negotiate that minefield. To his relief, Laura approached saying, "Hello little brother. Are you two stopping for tea? It's spaghetti Bolognese."

"Yay, my favourite," exclaimed Naomi.

Jack laughed. Naomi never seemed to get bored of spaghetti Bolognese. "We'd love to," he gladly accepted the invitation. As Naomi skipped into the kitchen, he added, "Thanks, Laura."

"What for? It's only spag bol."

"I'm not talking about the spag bol."

Laura looked at him curiously. "Then what are you talking about?"

"I'll tell you later."

Jack wasn't sure how Laura would react to learning that he'd fallen for a woman with no memory and, to say the least, a chequered past. She was intensely protective of Naomi, but she'd also been encouraging him to dip his toe back in the dating pool. Most likely she would try to convince him Butterfly was bad news. And she'd be right. He knew that. But he also knew that he hadn't felt this way about anyone besides Rebecca. How many chances did life give you to meet someone you had that kind of connection with? Not many. This might be the last one he got.

He ate quietly, content to listen to Naomi and Laura chatting. His mind kept drifting to Butterfly. He knew she was safe, yet he had a strong urge, almost a compulsion to go to her. He became aware that Laura was talking to him.

"Hello, earth to Jack, are you receiving me?"

"Sorry, I was miles away."

"I can see that. What are you thinking?"

"That I need a good night's kip. It's been a long week." Jack's phone rang. He took it out. "It's Steve." He pushed back his chair, moved into the hallway and put the phone to his ear. "What's up?"

"Are you near a TV?"

Jack's stomach lurched. Steve's voice was shaking. He'd never heard Steve like that before. Had something happened to Butterfly? "Yeah why?"

"Turn on the news."

Jack quickly did so. The screen displayed a street of terraced houses and small shops cordoned off by police tape. Beyond the cordon, armed officers were standing guard while paramedics worked on a figure on the ground. A swatch of bloodstained skin and a limp hand were visible between high-vis jackets. A few metres away a police car with a shattered windscreen appeared to have reversed into a car parked outside a café. A table and chair were overturned on the pavement. A handbag lay next to them. Whatever had happened, it hadn't happened long ago.

Jack felt a rush of relief and guilt. It wasn't Butterfly lying there, but someone – from the looks of it, a fellow officer – was fighting for their life on that street.

"Have you seen the video those fuckers made?" asked Steve.

As if responding to the question, a reporter appeared on-screen and said, "I must warn you, the footage we're about to show contains extremely disturbing images. The police have asked us to keep showing it in the hope someone comes forward with information that leads to the capture of the perpetrators."

"No, but I think I'm about to," Jack said as the news cut to shaky footage that appeared to have been shot on a mobile phone from the front passenger seat of a fast-moving vehicle. Built-up streets swept by the windows as the lens panned across to the vehicle's driver – a well-built figure in black combat fatigues, a balaclava and a bulky bulletproof vest. A soundtrack was provided by a constant murmur of voices and beeps from a police scanner on the dashboard. The car suddenly braked. The driver reached to retrieve a sawn-off shotgun from the backseat before getting out. As the passenger got out too, Jack glimpsed what looked to be a Glock 9mm in their right hand.

The scene outside the car was instantly familiar. A police car was parked in front of a café. A woman was smoking a cigarette at a table on the pavement. The shotgun-wielding figure calmly crossed the road, putting up a hand to halt oncoming traffic. Catching sight of what was heading her way, the woman sprang up, overturning the table and chair in panic. She fled, leaving behind her handbag.

A man's face could be seen through the glint of the low winter sun on the police car's windscreen. He looked young, fresh-faced, like he hadn't been in the job long. As the figure levelled the shotgun at him, he ducked out of sight. There was an echoing boom and the windscreen exploded in a puff of shattered glass.

"Run!" Jack urged futilely as the masked figure moved in closer. Instead, the policeman started the engine. The car bunny-hopped backwards, crunched into another car and stalled.

The shooter took aim again – this time from directly beside the car – and blasted the second barrel through the passenger window. There was a muffled scream. As the shooter turned to run back across the road, the footage abruptly ended.

The reporter reappeared saying, "That shocking footage was sent to us anonymously a short time ago along with this chilling message, 'An eye for an eye, a tooth for a tooth, blood for blood'. The injured officer, Police Constable Tim Finch has since been taken to hospital. We're awaiting an update on his condition."

"I'll give you an update," Steve put in, his voice clogged with emotion. "He died on the way to hospital."

"The Mahon brothers just declared war on us," said Jack.

"Yeah well if they want a war, they'll fucking get one. And maybe sooner than they realise."

"Sounds like we've got a lead on their location."

"When those morons sent that footage they didn't conceal their phone number. We've traced the phone's location. The fucker's are hiding out in Carrington."

"Carrington," echoed Jack. Carrington was a village to the west of Manchester best known for its close proximity to Manchester United's Trafford Training Centre. Steve – a diehard Red Devil's supporter – had taken Jack by the training ground once when they were out that way. It had heavy security and a regular police presence.

"The firearms lads are on their way there – along with half the other officers in Manchester – and they're out for blood."

"Seems like an odd choice for a hideout. Small place, but with lots of journalists and TV crews always hanging around. Do the brothers have relatives or known acquaintances there?"

"No. We think they're holed up in a warehouse on Carrington Business Park. It's a big site. Way bigger than the village. Loads of empty buildings. I'd say that's a pretty good place for a hideout. Listen, I'm only a couple of miles away from you. Do you want me to pick you up?"

"No. I'll go in my own car."

"OK, see you there. Remember to bring your truncheon. If you're lucky, you'll have a chance to use it."

Jack couldn't tell whether Steve was serious. Steve was mostly bark and not much bite, but there was a different note in his voice, an edge of raw hate, an eagerness to do violence. Jack wondered whether Steve's anger was about more than wanting to avenge a fallen comrade. When people became police officers, they accepted that they could be killed in the line of duty. But those children up in The Lakes had accepted no such risk. They'd been led to their deaths by the very people they should have been able to trust most. And Steve had had a front-row seat to the slaughter. No one – no matter how thick-skinned – could walk away from something like that unscathed.

"And you remember that there's a missing baby out there," cautioned Jack.

"Oh I haven't forgotten that," Steve growled.

"Well let's just hope we get a chance to talk to the brothers, because I get the feeling they're looking to go down in a blaze of glory."

"In which case I'll have to be satisfied with pissing on their corpses."

Steve hung up, leaving Jack with a knot between his eyes. He was worried about Steve, but more than that the entire turn of events troubled him.

"What's wrong, Jack?"

He turned at the sound of Laura's voice. "An officer's been..." Glancing past his sister towards the kitchen, he lowered his voice, "shot dead. I'm sorry for dropping this on you, Laura, but-"

"Of course I'll look after Naomi," she pre-empted his request.

With a faint smile of thanks, Jack went to Naomi. Looking up at him with big eyes, she said, "Something bad's happened, hasn't it?"

Jack nodded. There was no point trying to say otherwise. The truth was written all over his face. "I have to go out for a while." He stooped to kiss her soft hair. "Be good for your aunt."

"She always is," said Laura.

"Be careful, Daddy," said Naomi as he headed for the front door.

He smiled back at her. "Don't worry, sweetie, I won't be in any danger."

Laura and Naomi followed him to the door. They waved as he got into his car and sped away.

Chapter 30

Jack headed west out of Chorlton. In the distance he caught snatches of sirens – a lot of sirens. A hurricane of anger was racing towards the Mahon brothers. His frown intensified as he thought about the footage they'd sent to the media. Ryan – Jack would have put money on it being the older brother – hadn't panicked when the first shot missed its target. He'd calmly adjusted his aim for the kill shot. The Mahons were stone-cold professionals, but not concealing their phone number was an amateur's mistake.

Something occurred to him. Perhaps Steve was right about Carrington being a good choice for a hideout, only not in the way he'd meant. Carrington was on almost the opposite side of Manchester to North Manchester General Hospital. And very soon so too would be a large percentage of the city's police.

They take pride in their work. They never let a customer down. Leah Mahon's words rang through Jack's mind like an alarm. He braked hard, forcing a car to swerve around him. What if the phone number hadn't been a mistake? What if Steve and all the rest of them were heading towards a warehouse with nothing but a phone in it? Perhaps the Mahons were creating a diversion so that they could get to–

"Butterfly," he breathed the name like a warning.

He did a U-turn and floored the accelerator, reaching for his phone to call for backup. He hesitated as something else occurred to him. This was no longer about Butterfly and her baby, it was about Glenn Mahon. Ryan and Gavin wanted revenge for the killing of their dad. They were challenging the police to a fight. That was why they hadn't concealed the number. They *wanted* the police to find them. He'd said it himself, they were looking to go down in a blaze of glory.

He eased up on the accelerator, but didn't alter course again. He wouldn't be missed in Carrington. Butterfly needed him. And, he realised, with a strange lightness in his head, he needed her too. He needed to look into her eyes, feel her touch, hear her voice. But above all he needed to know she was safe.

Jack skirted the city centre, leaving behind the sirens. The rush-hour traffic had slackened off. The last glimmers of twilight lingered on the steel and glass towers flanking the road. It was the type of crystal clear evening when he would have loved to ramble through the gentle East Sussex countryside with Rebecca and Naomi. Those days were gone forever, lost at the bottom of the English Channel along with Rebecca. But perhaps one day Naomi, Butterfly, her baby and he would stroll through Chorlton together. Not long ago the idea that he would ever again be part of a 'complete' family would have seemed like an impossible dream. All he had to do was get through this day and maybe, just maybe, it would become a reality.

Keeping an eye out for anything remotely suspicious, he parked near the hospital's main entrance and hurried through the automatic sliding doors. A series of seemingly endless corridors led to Intensive Care. He felt a loosening in his chest at the sight of the armed constable – Craig – outside Butterfly's door.

"No one is to be allowed onto the ward without my being consulted first," Jack told the nurse on the duty desk. "Not even your colleagues."

Eyeing him grimly, Craig said, "I thought you'd be heading to Carrington, sir."

"I'm of more use here."

"I wish I was there." The constable's voice was strained. "Tim was a mate of mine. I only spoke to him the other day." He shook his head as if struggling to get to grips with knowing he would never speak to his friend again.

"I know it's difficult, but I need you to stay focused." Jack's tone was sympathetic, but firm.

Craig frowned, glancing at Butterfly's door. "You don't think the Mahons might still come after her, do you, sir?"

"I doubt it, but I wouldn't put it past them. They're crazy enough."

Craig's hand moved to his holstered pistol. "Just let them try."

Jack caught a tremor of bravado in the young constable's voice. Ten years earlier he might have said something similar himself, but that was before Naomi's birth and Rebecca's death had beaten the bravado out of him. "If the Mahons do come here, you're not to engage them unless absolutely necessary. The ward is on lockdown, so whatever happens we'll be safe until backup arrives."

Craig nodded and Jack entered Butterfly's room. A smile flickered across her pale lips. It wasn't much, but it was enough to make Jack's heart pound. Seating himself at her bedside, he somewhat self-consciously reached for her hand. She curled her callused fingers into his, saying softly, "Hello."

Her voice made the hairs on his neck prickle. "Hello."

They looked silently at each other. There was no longer any pretension in Jack's eyes. His need was laid bare. Did he see the same in Butterfly's deep-set brown eyes? He felt afraid to ask. His talent for reading people had failed him when it came to Rebecca. It had been like reading instructions in a language he couldn't quite understand. He'd grasped the basics, but the subtleties always seemed to elude him. What if he was reading Butterfly wrong?

He told himself that this wasn't the time to ask her those kinds of questions. But he knew it was an empty excuse. This was *exactly* the time to ask. If the Mahons really were on their way, then there wasn't a second to spare. The same applied if they weren't on their way. That sense of having time was an illusion. The time was always now. Rebecca had taught him that.

"There's something I need to say," Jack began. "I like... No, like's the wrong word. What I mean to say is, I..." He had the right words – *I want to be with you. I want us to be together* – but before he could get them out, there was a bone-shaking crunch like a wrecking ball had hit the building. The room shuddered, the lights flickered, then all hell broke loose.

Chapter 31

"What was that?" gasped Butterfly, staring bug-eyed at the door.

"Stay there!" Jack said needlessly. He sprang to his feet and opened the door a crack, ready to slam it shut if need be. Thick white smoke with a zingy metallic flavour was billowing along the corridor. Someone was coughing. Someone else – maybe more than one someone else – was crying out in pain. An alarm was emitting a shrill, intermittent whine.

Craig was squinting into the smoke, gun drawn and at the ready.

"What's going on?" Jack shouted over the alarm.

"I don't know. Sounded like a bomb went off," Craig yelled back, breathless and shaky.

"Have you radioed for backup?"

"No, sir."

"Then do it now!"

As Craig reached for the radio handset in his chest rig holder, there was a flash of reddish-white light ten or fifteen metres away to the left. The concussive boom that accompanied the flash set off a high-pitched squealing in Jack's ears. Craig went down as if he'd been poleaxed, screaming and clutching his face. Through the smoke, Jack made out two bulky figures as black as silhouettes. He ducked to grab Craig's arms. There was another flash and boom! The doorframe above Jack's head disintegrated in a shower of broken plaster and splintered wood. He jerked backwards, hauling the injured constable with him. Blood was streaming between Craig's fingers. Jack got a stomach-churning glimpse of shredded flesh and shattered teeth.

"It's them!" cried Butterfly. "It's the men who took my baby, isn't it?"

Jack thrust the door shut. He dragged Butterfly's bed in front of it and kicked on the brakes. As gently and quickly as possible, he lifted her off the bed and carried her to the far corner of the room. Taking care not to dislodge the tubes attached to her, he laid her on the floor tiles. He ran to fetch the mattress. The door handle turned. The door opened a sliver and clunked against the bed. As Jack lugged the mattress to Butterfly, from behind him came the *thud, thud* of someone trying to batter their way into the room. He propped the stiff orthopaedic mattress against the wall in front of Butterfly, then darted back across the room to hook his hands under Craig's armpits. The constable was silent and limp. That wasn't good. The Mahons seemed to have given up on attempting to bludgeon their way in. Jack wasn't sure whether that was a good or bad thing. The answer came as he was manoeuvring the unconscious constable towards the mattress.

A second explosion shook the room. The shock-waves knocked Jack flat onto his back. There was a whoosh like air being expelled from a pressurised container, then came the clatter of debris raining down. Something flat and jagged – possibly a large fragment of the door – landed on Jack's chest, forcing out what little breath was in there. His mouth working like a fish out of water, he heaved the object away and struggled to sit up. The room was lost in suffocating smoke.

"Butterfly," he wheezed, scrambling to the mattress.

The mattress was dusty and torn, but had withstood the blast. Jack ducked into the triangular space between it and the wall. It was gloomy in there, but less smoky. "Butterfly," he said again, feeling for her hand.

"Jack," she replied tremulously.

Her voice sounded far away to his ringing ears. "Are you OK?"

"Yes. Are you?"

That was a good question. Was he OK? He didn't know. People in shock often didn't realise they'd been injured until someone pointed it out to them. There was no chance to check himself over though. He had more immediate concerns to deal with. He peeped from behind the mattress at the wreckage of the room. The smoke had cleared sufficiently for him to see that the lower half of the door was missing. The ragged, scorched upper section dangled from its hinge like a broken pub sign. The trolley bed had been thrown across the room and lay upside down. It and Craig had served to partly shield Jack from the blast. The constable was face down on the floor, limbs flung out at ominous angles. Somehow one of his shoes had been blown off. There was seared flesh and bone where his toes should have been.

Where were the brothers? Had they left, assuming the job was done? A figure kitted out in a balaclava and body armour ducked into the room. The brothers had assumed the job was done once before. They would not make *that* mistake again. A shotgun butt was pressed to the masked figure's shoulder. A second, identically dressed figure was close behind, handgun at the ready.

Jack jerked back out of sight. *Shit, shit! How the fuck was he supposed to tackle two armed men with his bare hands?* A strange sense of calm settled over him as he thought, *You're not getting out of this one, Jack.* Naomi's beautiful, worried face rose into his mind. With it came a piercing sadness. *I'm sorry, sweetheart. I'm so–*

A sound broke into his thoughts – a repulsively gurgling, incoherent yell. Jack risked another glance at the room. Craig was alive! He was clutching at the lead figure's ankles. The figure staggered and tried to shake him off, but the downed policeman clung on like a limpet.

This is your chance! Even as the thought rang out in Jack's mind, he was springing forwards. He propelled himself past Craig and the lead figure. The second figure just had time to get off a shot. Jack staggered as if he'd been punched in the shoulder. A numbness instantly paralysed his left arm, but it didn't stop him from thundering onwards. An *Oof!* whistled through the balaclava as Jack tackled his target to the floor. The handgun skittered away towards the doorway. Instead of trying to overpower the figure beneath him, Jack scrambled for the gun.

Behind him another deafening blast went off. He half-expected to feel shotgun pellets tearing into him, but nothing happened. Then his hand was on the pistol and he was rolling onto his back and taking aim. Smoke was curling out of the shotgun's muzzle, which was aimed point-blank at where Craig's head should have been. The blast had all but decapitated the armed officer, leaving behind a mess of shattered bone and mangled brain-matter. There was no time for anger or revulsion. The shotgun-wielding figure was raising the gun barrel in Jack's direction.

Jack squeezed the handgun's trigger. A round thudded into the bulletproof vest. The figure stumbled and tripped over Craig's corpse.

Jack swung the handgun towards the second figure who was advancing on him brandishing a combat knife.

"Don't," warned Jack.

The figure thrust the blade at him. Jack pulled the trigger and his attacker's head snapped back. The bullet hadn't come from a converted starter pistol. It didn't get lodged in its target's skull. It passed clean through and thunked into the wall behind. The figure swayed for an instant before toppling to one side.

"Gav!" cried out a winded voice.

Jack jerked his attention back to the other figure. The balaclava had been pulled up, revealing the flushed, sweat-sheened face of Ryan Mahon. Ryan's shotgun was once again aimed at Jack.

Jack flung himself sideways as the shotgun went off. A disc of pellet holes materialised in the wall behind where his head had been. He returned fire. Sparks flared as the bullet ricocheted off medical equipment.

Ryan ran for the doorway. Jack fired again, hitting the doorframe as Ryan disappeared from sight. Jack clambered to his feet and warily cast an eye into the corridor. Two nurses were frantically working on a figure on the floor.

They flinched aside as Ryan raced past them. Jack took aim, but there was no way he could risk a shot. He was trembling uncontrollably. Pain was washing over him in hot waves that gathered strength with every inrush. He lowered the gun and glanced at his shoulder. A bloodstain was flowering across his shirt. The bullet appeared to have struck him near his collarbone. A few centimetres lower and to the right and it would have hit his heart. He reluctantly accepted that he was in no condition to pursue Ryan. Besides, he had no intention of leaving Butterfly unprotected.

He pushed the Glock into his belt. Head swimming, he staggered to the mattress and moved it away from the wall. Butterfly stared up at him, her eyes wide with fear. The fear turned to relief, then concern. "You've been shot," she exclaimed.

"I'm OK."

Butterfly's gaze strayed to the gory remnants of Craig's head. "Oh Jesus," she gasped, clasping a hand to her mouth.

Jack grabbed a sheet and draped it over the upper part of the corpse. He checked the constable's radio. The handset was shattered. He took out his phone and awkwardly dialled Paul with one hand.

Paul picked up on the first ring and said anxiously, "Jack, we're receiving reports of a shooting at North Manchester General."

"The Mahons came after Butterfly." Jack stooped to pull up the gunman's balaclava, revealing Gavin Mahon's lifeless face. Tears of blood were haemorrhaging from Gavin's eyes. "Gavin's dead. Ryan fled the scene."

"Where are you now?"

"I'm with Butterfly."

"Stay there. We're on our way to you."

Jack grimaced as another tsunami of pain hit him. His phone clattered to the floor. He staggered, putting out a hand to steady himself. A stream of blood dripped from his other hand.

"Help!" Butterfly shouted. "We need help in here!"

Doctor Medland cautiously poked his head into the room. His keen grey eyes assessed the situation. He darted forwards to catch hold of Jack and guide him to the mattress. He took out scissors and cut open Jack's shirt. The bullet had ploughed a trough through Jack's shoulder.

"Did it go in and out?" Jack asked.

"Looks that way," Doctor Medland replied noncommittally. Bullets did all sorts of strange things when they hit people, fragmenting, ricocheting off bones, burrowing deep into places a long way from the entry wound.

Several nurses appeared at the doorway. Two of them hurried to Butterfly's aid. "I need a gunshot trauma kit," the doctor told a third.

As Doctor Medland pumped Jack full of painkillers and set to work on staunching the bleeding, the nurses manoeuvred Butterfly onto a trolley bed and wheeled her out the door. Jack made to stand up.

"I need you to stay still," said the doctor.

"I'm going with her."

"She's safe. The gunman's gone and you've lost a lot of blood."

"I'm going with her," Jack repeated in a tone of steely resolve.

His hand resting on the Glock, he followed the trolley bed to a nearby room. A bed was brought in for him. He lay looking at Butterfly as the nurses set up her monitoring equipment. She looked back at him in a way that only one other person had ever done. *Rebecca.* A sigh shuddered from him. He'd loved Rebecca so much. He still did. But she was the past. Butterfly was the present and, hopefully, the future.

Doctor Medland finished dressing the wound. "I'm ninety-nine percent sure it's just a surface wound," he told Jack. "But we need to do some x-rays to make certain. Your trapezius has been almost severed. It requires immediate surgery."

"I'm not going anywhere."

"It's your choice, but you need to remain as still as possible. If your trapezius detaches, you might never regain full movement in your arm and neck."

"Go," urged Butterfly.

Jack's gaze returned to her. "I'm staying right here until backup arrives."

A faint smile pulled at the corners of Butterfly's mouth. "Have you always been this stubborn?"

"I suppose I have been," said Jack, thinking about Rebecca. She'd called him stubborn too – stubborn for refusing to give up on their marriage through all the years of her depression. *I'm no good for you,* she would say. *I know it, your sister knows it, everyone knows it but you.* To which he would reply, *I couldn't care less if the rest of the world knows it. All I care about is what I know. And I know that I love you.* "Rebecca once accused me of always having to be right even when I know I'm wrong."

"Who is Rebecca?"

Who is Rebecca? Even with everything that had come to light since Rebecca's death, he couldn't fully answer that question. "Someone who's gone."

Perhaps sensing he wasn't comfortable with the subject, instead of pressing for information Butterfly said, "Well I like your stubbornness."

A smile touched Jack's lips too. Butterfly had a troubled past, but she wasn't Rebecca. She was someone who'd taken the worst life could throw at her and was still around to tell the tale. Stubborn like him. A survivor. She would never choose death over her family. She would fight until her last breath.

They lay silent, content simply to be close to each other. There was a thundering of feet in the corridor. Jack's hand darted to the Glock. He released it and held up his ID when an officer armed with a semi-automatic rifle appeared at the door.

Paul wasn't far behind. Concern spread over his features at the sight of Jack.

"It's not serious," said Jack.

"Not serious? They tell me you need surgery. So what the hell are you doing here?" Paul motioned briskly to someone in the corridor. "Get this man to where he needs to be right away."

Jack's gaze flicked to Butterfly. She smiled again, but there was fear in her eyes. She didn't want him to leave any more than he wanted to go. "I'll be back as soon as I can," he assured her.

"I know you will."

"For god's sake stop moving your head," reprimanded Doctor Medland, beckoning two porters into the room.

Jack kept his eyes exactly where they were until Butterfly was out of sight. The trolley bed passed through several large smears of blood on its way to the twisted remains of the ward's entrance door. The corridors beyond were a buzzing hive of police checking every corner, crevice and room. Armed constables were posted at the entrance to every ward and department.

Jack stated the obvious. "You haven't found Ryan."

"He was seen leaving the hospital," said Paul. "We're making sure he didn't double back. It would be suicide for him to do so, but..."

He trailed off meaningfully. Who knew what Ryan's mental state was? His dad and brother were dead. Maybe he was ready to join them just so long as he could take a few more coppers with him.

"Where's Steve?"

"Carrington. We had to call in the bomb squad. The warehouse is booby-trapped."

"We *have* to bring Ryan in alive."

Paul nodded understanding. A firearms officer now numbered amongst the victims. There would be some hair-triggers out there looking to take

Ryan down. But if he died, how would they find Butterfly's baby? "Don't you worry about that right now, Jack. Do you want me to contact Laura?"

"Yes, but tell her not to come rushing over here. I don't want her or Naomi anywhere near this place while that psycho's out there. Also, do me a favour, put a couple of officers on Laura's house. I killed Ryan's sibling. I wouldn't put it past him to try to do the same to mine. An eye for an eye. Blood for blood."

"Will do."

The porters wheeled Jack into a lift and pressed for Radiology. "Good luck, mate," said Paul.

Jack replied with the slightest of nods. *Mate.* He hadn't thought he would ever hear Paul call him that again. He still wasn't ready to respond in kind. Perhaps he never would be. But who knew? The older he got, the more he came to realise that nothing was ever certain. As the lift juddered into motion, he closed his eyes and pictured Rebecca's perfect pale face. He'd taken it for granted that they would be together forever. He wouldn't make that mistake with Butterfly. He would be grateful for every second they had together.

Chapter 32

Jack put the 24-hour news on and was greeted with Ryan Mahon's mugshot. Ryan's hard-bitten face had dominated the news for the past four days. Not that there was anything new to report. One of the largest manhunts in UK history had so far failed to turn up even a scent of him.

Jack's jaw muscles pulsed as he stared into the dark holes of Ryan's eyes. His knuckles whitened on the remote control. He quickly turned off the telly as Steve entered the room followed by Laura and Naomi. He somehow managed to simultaneously smile and frown at the sight of them. His smile turned to a laughing wince as Naomi ran to fling her arms around him and the stitches in his shoulder pulled. "Sorry," she said, drawing away worriedly.

"It's OK, sweetheart." Jack's shoulder had been throbbing like a hammered thumb all morning, but the love in Naomi's eyes did more to soothe the pain than any of the tablets he'd taken.

"How's it feeling?" asked Laura, surveying him from the opposite side of the bed to Naomi.

Jack gingerly rolled his shoulder. "Stiff and sore, but it's getting better. My arm feels stronger too."

"You'll be back to your normal self in no time," said Steve, grinning from the end of the bed. "Mind you, I've been enjoying the peace and quiet with you out of the office."

Naomi's forehead wrinkled at the mention of the office. Jack knew what she was thinking. She didn't want him to go back to the office. Not ever. He changed the subject. "Did you bring anything to eat? I'm starving. Breakfast this morning was two slices of rubber posing as toast."

Laura handed him a Tupperware container. "Salad, chicken and baked potato."

Smiling thanks, Jack peeled off the lid and tucked in.

"Are these new?" asked Laura, sniffing a bouquet of red roses and white lilies.

"Yes. You can have them if you want. Every time I give one bunch away another seems to arrive."

The entire window ledge and floor beneath were crammed with cards and vases of flowers. Some were from colleagues. Most were from strangers praising Jack for his heroics and wishing him a speedy recovery. In the aftermath of the attack, he'd become something of a minor celebrity. He'd switched off his phone to avoid unwanted calls from television and newspaper representatives. He'd been offered five figures for an exclusive interview, but he had no intention of doing anything that might provoke further retaliation from Ryan.

"Any idea when you'll be discharged?" asked Laura.

"They're talking about today or tomorrow."

"Today. Yay," exclaimed Naomi. "I could make your favourite pasta. Aunt Laura's been teaching me how."

"That sounds great, sweetie," said Jack. "Would you get me a coffee, please sis?" he asked Laura, flicking a meaningful glance at Naomi.

Laura took the hint. "Do you fancy a coffee, Steve?"

Smiling at her, Steve nodded. Jack spotted a gleam in his colleague's eyes that suggested he fancied a lot more than just a coffee. "Come and help me carry the drinks," Laura said to Naomi, ushering her from the room.

"What are you looking at me like that for?" Steve asked as Jack stared at him.

Bloody hell, I'm right, thought Jack. *There's something going on between the two of them.* The idea seemed absurd. Steve stood for everything Laura despised. And yet, who knew? In some messed up way, perhaps he was precisely the type she would go for. "You know I'm not comfortable with them coming here, Steve."

"Relax. I won't let any harm come to them. Besides, it's been days since that wanker went on the run. We've kicked in the doors of practically every scumbag in Manchester and found sod all."

"Doesn't mean he's not still in the area. We made the mistake once before of thinking he'd left the country."

"Yeah, but that was before his face was plastered over every TV channel and newspaper. On top of which, we've got the entire Mahon clan under round-the-clock surveillance. They can't fart without us knowing. I'm telling you, Ryan Mahon is long gone. And if he isn't, he won't be able to poke his head out of whatever hole he's hiding in without being recognised."

Jack chewed over Steve's words. They made sense – that is, if Ryan valued his life above revenge. In some ways, he hoped Ryan was unhinged enough to try something. Their chances of finding Butterfly's baby could well depend on catching him.

Heaving a sigh, he set aside his half-eaten food. Every second that the baby remained missing was a torment to Butterfly. Like him, she was regaining strength with each passing day. Doctor Medland's prognosis had shifted from overwhelmingly negative to cautiously optimistic. The bullet was still beyond reach, but daily scans showed no movement. At least for now, its position appeared to be stable. Of course, there was always the chance that it could suddenly move with fatal consequences. Butterfly's greatest fear was that she would die without being reunited with her baby. Even as her body recovered, this constant state of anxiety was mentally wearing her down.

Steve eyed Jack knowingly. "You've really fallen for her, haven't you?"

Jack nodded. They hadn't discussed his feelings for Butterfly, but Jack knew that Steve knew the score. It was obvious to anyone who saw Butterfly and him together. "You think I'm crazy."

"Who am I to judge anyone else's love life? All I'd say is be careful. Make sure she is who you think she is."

"And how am I supposed to do that?"

Steve shrugged. "You're asking the wrong person, mate. Women are life's biggest mystery to me. Oh that reminds me." He handed an iPhone to Jack. "I downloaded Find My Phone onto it so you can keep tabs on Butterfly."

Jack gave Steve a narrow look. They hadn't talked about what he wanted the phone for, but Steve was shrewd enough to guess. "I don't want to stalk her," said Jack. "I just want to make sure she's safe."

"Did I mention stalking? It hadn't crossed my mind for a second that you'd do something like that." Steve's impish grin contradicted his words.

"Oh fuck off, will you?"

Steve put on a mock-hurt expression. "That's lovely, that is. How about thanking me for bringing you the–"

He fell silent as Naomi and Laura reappeared with the drinks. For the next half-hour, the four of them chatted about lighter topics – Naomi and Laura's day, the weather, the upcoming Manchester derby. When it came time for them to leave, Naomi hugged her dad and said excitedly, "I'll make the pasta sauce as soon as I get home."

Jack laughed. "I should wait until we know for certain whether I'm getting out today." He kissed his sister and said, "Be good."

Her forehead creasing, Laura gave him a *What's that supposed to mean?* look. He lifted his eyebrows as if to say, *You know exactly what I mean.*

Jack watched them leave with sadness, but also relief. The entire time they'd been there, images of the Mahon brothers blasting their way into Butterfly's room had kept flashing into his mind. Every footstep in the corridor, every raised voice had made his heart skip and sweat gather on his palms. He'd felt that way a lot since the attack, especially in the dead of the night when he awoke gasping and disoriented with the stench of smoke and blood in his nostrils and the echoes of gunshots and screams in his ears.

Chapter 33

Taking care not to make any sudden movements, Jack got out of bed. The surgeon who'd operated on his shoulder was confident he would regain his full range of motion, but the rehabilitation process would take months. He stiffly put on his dressing-gown and headed into the corridor with the Tupperware container in one hand.

After a night on Intensive Care, he'd been transferred to a general ward. Butterfly was still on ICU. Despite advice to take it as easy as possible, several times a day he made the journey to her room. It wasn't far, but it always felt like miles. A temporary blank wooden door had been fitted at the entrance to ICU. The blast-damaged walls had already been re-plastered and painted. Soon there would be no scars left from the attack – at least no visible ones.

"Afternoon, sir," said an armed constable, opening the door for Jack.

The nurses greeted Jack with smiles, but he sensed their nervousness. As much as they admired him, his presence made them jittery. And who could blame them for feeling that way? Along with himself and AFO Craig Barton, the Mahons had injured a female nurse who'd been walking past the ward entrance when the first grenade detonated. Her horrifically long list of injuries included the loss of an eye, arm and leg. The only reason she'd survived was because of her proximity to emergency treatment. Several already critically ill patients had also required treatment for minor injuries and shock.

Amongst other things, the tabloids had branded the Mahon brothers 'Unspeakable Monsters' and 'Inhuman Psychopaths'. As dubious as he was of those kinds of labels, Jack found it difficult to disagree with the newspapers' assessment.

Workmen were fitting a new door to Butterfly's old room. Jack resisted the urge to glance into the room. He didn't want to see the spot where Craig's skull had been blasted apart by shotgun pellets. Not that it made any difference whether he looked. The image had seared his brain like a branding iron.

He entered Butterfly's room with the usual mixture of excitement and trepidation – excitement because looking into her eyes made him feel life's endless possibilities, trepidation because there was always the chance that the sword dangling on a thread over her head might have fallen.

Butterfly was sat up in bed, drinking coffee. In the past few days, she'd regained sufficient strength to feed herself. She'd even been allowed to make short walks around the ward. Most of the drips, wires and drains were gone. A square of gauze was all that remained of the bandages that had swathed her head. Jack had watched a nurse change Butterfly's dressing, exposing an ugly wound that looked like a stitched mouth. The bruises and superficial cuts on Butterfly's face were fading. Her skin looked tighter and firmer. The tattoo that flared away from her right eye somehow looked brighter, almost iridescent in certain lights. It rippled like a real wing as she smiled at Jack. He saw something else behind her smile too – a sadness as deeply embedded as the bullet.

Smiling back, he proffered the Tupperware container. "I brought you something to eat. It was made by my sister's own fair hand. Laura's not much of a cook, but it's a hell of a lot better than the stuff they serve around here."

During the hours they'd spent together, Jack had told Butterfly about Laura and Naomi. He'd also told her about how he'd moved up to Manchester after Rebecca's death. He hadn't mentioned *how* Rebecca died. It wasn't simply that he didn't want to. He didn't know where to begin. How do you tell someone that your wife jumped to her death from a clifftop? And how would Butterfly react to the revelation? Would it put her off him? What if she wondered whether he had driven Rebecca to suicide?

Jack carefully lowered himself into an armchair as Butterfly opened the container. He liked to watch her eat. Every mouthful was fuel for the healing process, bringing them closer to the moment when they would be together in the real world, not the netherworld of the hospital. After a few forkfuls, she set the container aside.

"It's not that bad is it?" joked Jack.

"I'm just not hungry." Butterfly's eyes strayed to the window as if she was on the lookout for someone.

Jack had seen that look in her eyes before. He knew what she was thinking. *We'll find your baby,* he wanted to assure her. But there were no guarantees and false hope could be more harmful than no hope at all.

"How many days has it been since they took my baby?" Butterfly wondered out loud.

"I'm not sure," said Jack, although he knew exactly how long the baby had been missing, right down to the hour and minute. It was 5:02 pm – eight days, seventeen hours and nineteen minutes since Butterfly had given birth. Long enough for her baby to have been smuggled to the far side of the planet or buried so deep that no one would ever find it.

"Baby," Butterfly repeated to herself. "It doesn't seem right to just keep saying 'baby'. My child should have a name. Charlie. That was my sister's name. That's what I'll call my child. That way it won't matter if it's a boy or a girl." As if testing out the feel of the name, she said again, "Charlie."

"It's a good name," said Jack, smiling through his own sadness.

"Is it?" Butterfly's eyebrows pinched together. "How would I know what's good or bad? Charlie. I know it's a name, just like when I look at my hand I know what it is. But it has no real meaning for me."

"Then give it a new meaning." Jack took Butterfly's hand. "After Rebecca died everything lost meaning for me." Shame lowered his voice. "Even Naomi. I thought I'd never be a real dad to her again. But I was wrong. I thought I'd never fall in love again. I was wrong about that too."

He faded off as if surprised by his own words. With Rebecca it had been months before he was confident enough to say, *I love you.* With Butterfly it was different. The nine days he'd known her were her entire life. It was like time had been compressed. The normal rules no longer applied.

She turned her gaze slowly towards him. His heart pounded as he waited for her to say something.

"Will you teach me how to be good?" she asked.

Teach you how to be good. Jack almost laughed. Was she having him on? Her expression was painfully serious. "I…" he hesitated, unsure what to say. He tried to teach Naomi to be a good person, but she was his child. Could he do the same for an adult? Even one whose mind was like an empty box? "I'm no angel myself. I've done things I'm not proud of."

"You're *my* guardian angel, Jack."

Leaning in, Butterfly kissed him as tentatively as if they were teenagers on a first date. The touch of her lips made him tremble. He resisted the impulse to throw his arms around her and crush her to him for fear that he might hurt them both. After a few seconds, they drew apart and she looked at him as if waiting to find out whether she'd done a good job of kissing him.

His words confirmed that she had. "I'm going to tell Naomi and Laura about us, if that's OK with you."

Butterfly smiled, and this time there was barely a hint of sadness. "It's more than OK with me."

Jack blinked as if he had something to feel guilty about. "They tell me I'm almost ready to be discharged."

"Oh. That's great." Butterfly's tone was less than convincing.

"Is it?"

"Obviously I'd rather you were here with me." Her eyes flicked towards the window again. Her voice hovered between fear and rage. "Especially while that murdering piece of fucking shit is–"

"Butterfly," Jack gently cautioned. The doctors had warned her that getting emotionally worked up could bring on another fit.

She took a couple of slow breaths. "You should be at home with your daughter. I'm happy for you."

Jack squeezed her hand. "Don't worry, I'll visit every day. You'll be sick of the sight of me by the time it's your turn to get out of here."

"No I won't."

The certainty in Butterfly's voice sent a tingle through Jack.

"The question is," she continued, her gaze dropping away from his, "even if I do get out of here, where will I go?"

"We've talked about this. You'll stay in a safe house until Ryan Mahon is dead or in custody."

"And what about after that?"

"After that you can come to live with me." Jack added quickly, "That is if you want to. I'll understand if you don't. But if you do, you'll be under no obligations. You can have the spare bedroom or..." he trailed off with the unfamiliar sensation of a blush spreading through his cheeks.

Butterfly lifted her eyes to his. "Or?"

"I..." Jack gave a little shake of his head. "Sorry, it's been a long time since I did anything like this."

"It's new to me too." Lines gathered between Butterfly's eyebrows once more. "Are you sure this is what you want, Jack? Neither of us knows who I really am. I could be just as bad as Ryan Mahon or Dennis Smith. And even if things work out between us, I could drop dead any second. Do you really want someone like me in your life?"

"I've asked myself that same question and one answer keeps repeating itself. I fell in love once before. I was starting to think it would never happen again. I told myself I could live with that, but now I realise I can't. Whether or not things work out, whether you live a month or until you're a hundred, it's worth the risk." Jack smiled. "Who knows, maybe we'll both live to a hundred. Then you really would be sick of the sight of me."

Even before Jack had finished speaking, Butterfly was leaning towards him again. This time she kissed him hard and deep. Pain lanced through his neck, but he hardly noticed it. For a moment it was like everything stopped around them. When Butterfly drew away, Jack stared at her dazedly.

"I can't remember the last time anyone kissed me like that," he said.

"Same here," Butterfly said, smiling at her statement of the obvious.

Jack was no longer listening. Rebecca had appeared in his mind like an uninvited guest. During the last few years of their marriage, depression had sucked the passion out of her – at least as far as he was concerned. She'd had enough passion for an affair with Paul. Unless he was confusing passion with the compulsion to self-destruct. He forced his thoughts back to Butterfly. It had been months since his mind had tumbled all the way down the Rebecca rabbit hole. He wasn't about to let it happen now.

"Where were you?" asked Butterfly. "You looked like you were miles away."

Jack feathered his fingers along her jaw. "I'm right where I want to be."

There was a knock at the door. Jack drew away from Butterfly as a nurse entered. The ward staff had clearly cottoned-on days ago that his interest in Butterfly was more than merely professional, hence they'd taken to knocking whenever he was in the room. Even so he wasn't comfortable with openly displaying his feelings for her. Somehow it didn't seem right when Naomi and Laura were in the dark about the relationship.

"Medication time," said the nurse.

Butterfly swilled down a rainbow of pills as the nurse checked her vitals.

"All good," said the nurse, turning to leave.

"I'm sorry," Jack said when they were alone again.

Butterfly gave him a look of understanding. "You've no need to be."

"I'll tell Naomi and Laura today. Then there'll be no more need for secrecy." Jack's stomach fluttered at the thought of that conversation. He could guess how Laura would react. At best, she would urge caution. More likely, she would outright disapprove. But how would Naomi take the news? Would she be upset? Or would she be happy for him? Whatever the case, the sooner she knew about Butterfly the better. Nothing good ever came from keeping secrets.

Jack glanced at the clock. "I've got to go. The doctors are assessing me at half-six." As an afterthought, he added, "Oh, I've got something else for you." He gave Butterfly the iPhone. "I programmed my number into it. There's also a tracking app on it just in case… well, just in case. You can track my phone with the app too. I thought while Ryan is still at large you'd feel more secure knowing we can locate each other, but if you're not comfortable with–"

"I'm fine with it, Jack," broke in Butterfly. She ran her fingers over the back of his hand. "Thank you."

With a slight shudder of pleasure, he wrenched himself away from her bedside. "I'll let you know as soon as the verdict's in." He pointed to the Tupperware container. "Make sure you eat something. That's an order."

Butterfly gave a mock salute. "Yes sir."

Jack darted her a final glance as he closed the door. She'd already resumed staring out of the window with that sad, searching look in her eyes.

Chapter 34

Jack slid the loose-fitting t-shirt over his head, awkwardly manoeuvring it past the thick gauze padding on his shoulder. He was packing his clothes and toiletries when Steve entered the room. "Congrats on your release," said Steve.

Jack responded with an unenthusiastic *mm*.

"Why have you got a face like a wet weekend? I thought you'd be over the moon."

"I am, but..." Jack's gaze strayed past Steve.

Steve glanced at the empty corridor. "Oh I get it," he said with a chuckle. "You don't want to leave *her* behind. She'll be fine. There's enough firepower guarding this hospital to blow away an army of Ryan Mahons."

"I know, it's just she's..." Jack tailed off again as if he couldn't put into words just what Butterfly was.

Steve laughed. "Jesus Christ, mate, you're doomed."

"I'd better go see her. Will you wait here?"

"Sure. Take as long as you need." As Jack headed for the door, Steve stretched out on the bed and reached for the TV remote.

For the third time that day, Jack made his pilgrimage to Butterfly's room. He opened the door but didn't enter. Butterfly's eyes were closed. The strands of her wavy auburn hair that hadn't been shaved off were fanned across the pillows. His heart gave a kick. She appeared to be asleep, but what if she was– He shook his head at the thought before it could fully form. She was still hooked up to the heart monitor, which was emitting a steady, low-level *bip... bip...*

Jack sighed. This was how it would always be. The anxiety would never go away while the bullet remained in Butterfly's head. Could he live with that? It wasn't even really a question, just another barely formed thought. He quietly closed the door. On his way out of the ward, he said to a nurse, "Could you let her know I've been discharged and I'll come to visit tomorrow morning?"

Steve was snoring when Jack got back. He prodded his colleague awake and pointed to his bag. "Carry that."

"What did your last slave die of?" grumbled Steve, getting up.

Jack smiled. Steve could be a pain in the arse, but it was hard to take things too seriously when he was around.

They made their way to Steve's car. Before ducking into the passenger seat, Jack stood breathing the crisp November air. "When Ryan and Gavin were coming at me, I really thought I was going to–" He fell silent as a choking lump formed in his throat.

"It's gonna take more than some tossers like the Mahons to kill a tough old bugger like you."

A faint smile found its way back onto Jack's lips. "Hey, less of the old. I'm not even forty."

"You will be before you know it. And it's all downhill from there. Trust me. First your stomach heads south. Then everything else follows. I used to be able to fuck all night long. Now I'm lucky if I can get it–"

"Alright, alright," broke in Jack, laughing. "I've heard enough. Just get in the car and drive."

As they negotiated Manchester's busy evening streets, Steve said, "I gave that tattooist, Viv, the heave ho."

"Are you sure it wasn't the other way around?" teased Jack.

"You're kidding. She was well into me. I just couldn't keep up. I tell you, mate, no more twenty-something-year-olds for me. Next time I'm going for a woman closer to my age."

Jack treated his colleague to a wry sidelong look. "You mean like Laura?"

Steve laughed. "I don't know. Yeah, maybe. Is that OK with you?"

"Go for it. She's always nagging me about meeting someone. She could do with taking her own advice. Just tread lightly. She acts tough, but that's all it is – an act. She's been badly hurt in the past."

"Don't you worry. I wouldn't dare mess around a woman like Laura."

As they turned onto the street of semi-detached houses where Jack lived, he drew in a long breath.

"You look as though you're getting ready to break some bad news," observed Steve.

"I'm going to tell them about Butterfly."

Steve compressed his mouth into an O. "Good luck with that."

"Thanks. I'll need it."

They pulled up behind Laura's little car. Jack eyed a Vauxhall with two men in it parked across the street. He nodded at the men. They replied in kind. He didn't know their names, but he'd seen them around HQ. Paul had assured him they were two of the best officers in GMP's Firearms Unit. The car was unmarked and the officers were plainclothes. If Ryan was foolish enough to try anything, they didn't want to alert him to their presence before he was close enough to takedown. Laura didn't like them being there, but she liked the thought of possibly being targeted by in her words 'some brainless psycho with a chip on his shoulder' even less.

Grimacing at the ache in his shoulder, Jack got out and approached the front door. It flew open and Naomi ran out to greet him with an excited flurry of words. "Dad! You're home. I've cooked the pasta and Auntie Laura's been cleaning and… and we've made everything nice for you."

Jack laughed, the tension draining from his face. "It's good to be home." His reply took him somewhat by surprise. It wasn't so long ago that he'd doubted whether he would ever look upon the house as his real home. He'd adored the Sussex cottage he'd shared with Rebecca, but the ghosts of memories had driven him to sell-up. He'd bought the Chorlton house because it was available and conveniently located. He'd never felt an emotional attachment to it – until now. The smell of cooking welcomed him as he stepped into the hallway.

Steve tousled Naomi's hair and set Jack's bag down. Laura appeared at the top of the stairs. "Hello you two," she called down. "Good timing, tea's just about ready."

"I can't stay," said Steve.

"Are you sure?" The disappointment in Laura's voice was unmistakable.

"I'd love to, but I have to be elsewhere."

"Oh OK. Well maybe another time."

"Definitely. I'll call you." Turning to Jack, Steve put on a bad cockney accent. "He who dares, Rodders. He who dares my son."

"Cheers, mate."

Steve closed the door on his way out.

"Ooooh, I think Auntie Laura's in love," said Naomi, her Mediterranean blue eyes sparkling with amusement.

"Don't be daft," retorted Laura, a tell-tale trace of colour rising into her cheeks.

"Auntie Laura and Steve sitting in a tree k-i-s-s-i-n-g," Naomi teased in a singsong voice.

"Right that's it." Pulling a mock-angry face, Laura rushed downstairs.

Naomi screamed and fled into the living-room. Laura caught up with her and set about tickling her into submission. The two of them collapsed onto the rug laughing. Jack looked on with a mixture of amusement and apprehension. They seemed so happy. He thought about Butterfly's sleeping face and a sigh welled up inside him. Why did life always have to be so fucking complicated?

Laura disentangled herself from Naomi and clambered to her feet. "Tickle me more," pleaded Naomi.

"Later. It's time to eat."

The kitchen table was laid with cutlery, bread and salad. Laura pulled out a seat for Jack while Naomi served up bowls of pasta. "Naomi did all this by herself," said Laura, glancing proudly at her niece. Naomi seated herself beside her dad. Jack looked at her. His gaze moved across the table to Laura. For the second time since being discharged from hospital, a lump formed in his throat. Tears threated to spill over. He blinked them back, not wanting to cry in front of Naomi.

Something lightly touched his hand. Glancing down, he saw Naomi's fingers curling into his. She gave him an *It's OK* smile. He should have known it was pointless trying to conceal his feelings from her. Her intuition would have put most of his colleagues to shame. He squeezed her hand back.

As they ate, she asked eagerly, "What do you think?"

"It's good," said Jack. "Not as good as when I make it, but still not–" He broke off as Naomi playfully poked him in the ribs. "OK, OK. It's the best I've ever tasted." He put another forkful in his mouth and rolled his eyes as if it was heavenly.

"What did Steve mean when he said, *he who dares*?" asked Laura.

The question wiped the grin off Jack's face. He'd planned to tell them about Butterfly after they'd had a chance to eat and settle down, but he saw that there was no putting it off. "There's something I need to speak to you both about," he began hesitantly. He'd recited what he wanted to say in his mind, but now that it came to it he wasn't sure how to best begin.

"Sounds ominous."

"No, no. It's… well I think it's…" He tailed off awkwardly. *Just bloody say it*! he ordered himself. "I've met someone."

"Oh." Laura's mouth hung open on the word.

"You've got a girlfriend," put in Naomi, wide-eyed.

Jack smiled. "I suppose you could call her that."

Naomi's forehead wrinkled as if she was trying to process the revelation. Then suddenly she was shooting questions at Jack, "Who is she? What's her name? Where did you meet her? How long have you–"

Jack put up his hands, palms out. "Whoa, easy officer. I'll tell you everything you want to know."

His attempt to make light of the situation met with an impatient, "So tell me then."

Jack answered the last question first. "It's only been going on a few days. Her name's Butterfly."

"Butterfly," echoed Naomi. "That's a funny name. I've never met anyone called Butterfly before."

"Neither have I," added Laura, eyeing her brother like a detective about to sweat a suspect. "Is this woman a nurse?"

"No."

"But if this has only been going on for the past few days, it's either got to be a nurse or…" Laura frowned as if uncomfortable mental gears were grinding into motion. "Or a patient." A meaningful little silence passed between her and Jack, before she continued, "It is, isn't it? It's a patient." The gears shifted rapidly from curiosity to concern to outright anxiety. "Hang on a minute, it's not… It's not *her* is it? It's not that woman those psychos tried to–" She broke off with a glance at Naomi. "Please, Jack, tell me I'm wrong."

Once again Jack made no reply.

"What psychos?" asked Naomi, her voice rising worriedly. "Does Aunt Laura mean those men who hurt you?"

"There's nothing to be scared of, sweetheart," Jack sought to reassure her. "One of those men is dead and the other is a long, long way away from here."

"How do you know that?"

"Because otherwise we'd have caught him."

"No you wouldn't. You couldn't catch him before. If you bring Butterfly here, he might come and try to kill her again."

"She won't come here right away. She'll go to a safe house until we're certain she's in no danger."

Naomi pulled her hand from Jack's. "I don't want her to come to this house at all. She can't come here. I won't let her!" she cried, her breath catching between words as panic took hold.

"It's OK, sweetheart. It's OK."

Naomi shook her head hard. As Jack reached for her hands, she sprang to her feet. Tears were rolling down her cheeks. "I don't want you to die."

"I'm not going to."

"Yes you are," Naomi exclaimed, turning to run into the hallway.

Jack made to pursue her, but Laura said, "Leave her, Jack. I'll speak to her."

Naomi's feet hammered up the stairs. Laura went after her. Jack stared at the table-top. His bowl was three-quarters full, but he had no appetite. After what felt like a long time, Laura returned. "Is she OK?" asked Jack.

"She's upset, but she'll be fine." With a sigh, Laura sat back down. "Are you sure about your feelings for this woman, Jack? You went through something incredibly traumatic with her. You could be confusing protectiveness with attraction."

"Love," corrected Jack. "What I feel for Butterfly goes beyond attraction."

"*Love*?" Laura repeated dubiously. "You barely know her."

"You're right, Laura. Everything you're thinking, I've already been through a thousand times in my head. I don't know who Tracy Ridley is."

"Who's Tracy Ridley?"

"That's who Butterfly used to be. Tracy's family was murdered. She got herself mixed up with bad people – thieves, drug dealers, murderers. Maybe she was a bad person herself. But Tracy died when the Mahons put a bullet in her head. The woman I'm in love with is Butterfly."

"But what if Tracy comes back and she's as bad as you think she might be?"

"Tracy's not coming back."

"You can't be certain of that. Even the experts struggle to predict long-term outcomes for brain injuries. Are you really willing to put Naomi at risk for the sake of this woman?"

"Of course not, but Butterfly wouldn't hurt anyone."

"You're going round in circles, Jack. We're talking about Tracy, not Butterfly. In fact, I'm not even sure Butterfly really exists. Oh I know there's a woman in North Manchester General that you call Butterfly. But I think maybe you're more in love with the idea of who she could be than who she actually is. She's a blank template. You can make her into whatever you want her to be. Who wouldn't fall in love with someone like that?"

Will you teach me how to be good? Butterfly's words echoed back to Jack. "You're wrong," he retorted, almost as if he was trying to convince himself. "Butterfly's mind is all her own."

"For now it is. Maybe it always will be, but you can't take that chance, Jack. You're a parent. That means you always come second."

"You don't need to tell me what it means," snapped Jack. "I know a hell of a lot better than you what it means."

Laura blinked as if he'd thrown a drink in her face. She'd always wanted children of her own, but for one reason or another – career, relationship breakdowns – it hadn't happened. Now she was in her early forties, single and resigned to the distinct possibility that motherhood had passed her by. But that didn't mean it didn't hurt. Jack read that hurt in her expression and hated himself for his insensitivity.

She rose to her feet. "I think I'd better go or you and I will fall out."

Jack followed her into the hallway. "Stay and finish your meal."

Laura shook her head. "I'll see you later." She glanced up the stairs, then her gaze returned to Jack. "I may not know what it's like to be a real mum, but I know I'd never do anything to endanger her."

"Neither would I."

"Perhaps you should tell her that."

Laura headed out the front door. Jack offered a forlorn wave as she got into her car. She drove away without waving back. He heaved a sigh, muttering, "Well that couldn't have gone much worse."

He knew things would soon get patched up between Laura and him. They'd fallen out more times than he could recall. She could be quick to take insult, but she was equally quick to forgive. As for her opinion on Butterfly, well, that was another matter entirely. Laura could also be stubborn. And in this instance she had every right to be. She was the closest thing Naomi had to a mum.

Jack glanced at the ceiling as incongruously upbeat pop music filtered through it. He headed upstairs. Naomi's bedroom door was closed. He knocked and said her name. When there was no reply, he entered the room. She was lying on her bed with her face to the wall. Music was blaring from her iPad docking station. He turned the volume down and perched himself on the bed. Her eyes were red and puffy, but she wasn't crying anymore. She kept her gaze fixed on the wall. He found himself uncomfortably reminded of the way Rebecca had lain staring at nothing for the last weeks of her life.

"I love you, Naomi," he began softly. "You're the most important thing in my life. You always will be."

Her eyes slid across to him. "Not if you're dead I won't be. Then I'll have no mum and no dad."

"I'm not going to die."

"Do you promise?"

Jack hesitated to reply. In his line of work there was always a chance you might not make it home, as had been starkly illustrated by the events of the past week, but the look of frightened appeal in Naomi's eyes was too much for him. "I promise."

The fear faded to a worried glimmer. Jack could see she wanted to believe him, but she wasn't naïve enough not to realise that his promise was made more to put her mind at rest than because it was something he could guarantee.

"There's something else I need you to know," he continued, "I love Butterfly. I don't know how things will turn out. No one ever does. I'd like for her to be part of this family, but as I said you come first. If you don't want me to be with her, I'll tell her we can't be together."

Naomi resumed staring at the wall. Jack could barely bring himself to breathe. He felt as if he was waiting for a verdict to be passed on his future. A chance at love or the torment of forever wondering what might have been? Which was it to be? "I…" Naomi began, her gaze meeting his once more. "I just want you to be happy, Dad."

Jack waited to see if anything else was forthcoming. The silence extended to thirty seconds. *I just want you to be happy.* Surely she was giving him the go ahead? He smiled and stroked her jet black hair. "That's all I want for you too, sweetheart."

"Does Butterfly look like Mum?"

"No. She's nothing like her. I'm not trying to find someone to replace your mum, Naomi. Nobody could ever replace her."

Naomi looked thoughtful for a moment, then nodded as if she was glad.

Jack rose to his feet. "Come on. It would be a shame to waste the pasta after all the effort you went to."

Naomi rose from the bed. She reached out and they left the room hand in hand. As they descended the stairs, Laura reappeared at the front door. "You weren't gone long," said Jack.

"Yeah well I'm hungry," she replied in her usual bluff way. "Besides, it's not as if I can have any privacy with your pals out there following me around."

"That won't be for much longer."

"It had better not be. They make me nervous."

"They're supposed to make you feel safe."

"Who are you talking about?" asked Naomi, the anxious glimmer returning to her eyes. They hadn't told her about the plainclothes officers.

"No one for you to worry about," said Jack.

Laura changed the subject. "Let's eat before the pasta gets cold."

I'm sorry, Jack mouthed at her as they went into the kitchen. She waved away his apology. They settled back down to their meal. The pasta was already cold, but it tasted infinitely better to Jack

Chapter 35

Over the next few days, Jack fell into a steady routine – drop Naomi off at school, head to the hospital, stay with Butterfly until it was time to pick up Naomi. When they got home, Laura would be bustling around the kitchen cooking tea. On the days when she had to work, they ordered a takeaway. Sometimes Steve came over and ate with them. He had a habit of telling Naomi inappropriate jokes, but Jack didn't mind. Naomi loved to see Steve. And although Laura did her best not to show it, he saw the gleam in her eyes whenever Steve called to say he was coming around. Besides, Jack wasn't the only one who'd been through a serious trauma. Occasionally he would catch Steve looking at Naomi with an uncharacteristic sadness and he knew the brash ex-para was thinking about Hawkshead Manor and the dead children.

Every hour, every minute, every second he spent with Butterfly, Jack could feel the two of them growing closer. He told her about his life in Sussex – falling in love with Rebecca, getting married, the cottage they'd shared, their love of walking on the coastal cliffs. Gradually he worked up the courage to tell her how Rebecca had died – the unfathomable depression that had ended with her jumping from the cliffs. He needn't have worried – there was no judgement in Butterfly's eyes, only sympathy. She drew him to her and held him silently.

It was three days after Jack had been discharged when Doctor Medland declared Butterfly fit enough to be moved to a general ward. "Your recovery rate has been nothing short of incredible," he informed her. "Keep this up and you'll be out of here in no time."

Butterfly smiled at the news, but always the shadow of her missing baby hung over her. In the same way that Jack felt himself growing closer to her, she felt herself growing more distant from her baby.

The following morning, at Butterfly's request, Jack bought her some clothes – tracksuit bottoms and a sweatshirt – and they went for a walk in the hospital grounds. She moved like someone learning a complicated dance. Jack held her elbow, steadying her. She inhaled deeply of the cold air. "Smells good, doesn't it?" he said, remembering how he'd felt after being discharged.

The walk put new colour in Butterfly's face, bringing out a depth of beauty that Jack hadn't seen in her before. They didn't go far, not because she was tired – walking renewed her strength – but because of concerns for her safety. Two armed officers shadowed them, but that wouldn't prevent someone with a long-range rifle from taking a pot-shot.

The next day and the day after that, they went on more walks, varying the time and route just to be on the safe side. Jack no longer needed to hold Butterfly's elbow. Her step was firm and sure. She eyed the city beyond the hospital grounds as if eager to go exploring. "It's funny," she said. "I don't remember any of it, yet when I look at it I get the strongest feeling of déjà vu."

"Maybe when you go out there you'll start remembering things," said Jack.

"Maybe," Butterfly echoed as if she wasn't sure whether that would be a good thing.

She remained silent for the rest of the walk, a knot tightening between her eyebrows. Jack sensed that something was brewing inside her. When they got back to her room, the storm broke. She clutched her belly – which had been slowly but surely deflating day by day – as if she was in agony and said, "It's gone!"

Jack tried to calm her down, but she kept crying out, "It's gone," until her voice was shrill with hysteria. When a doctor tried to sedate her for fear that she would injure herself, she fought him wildly, kicking and screaming. It took four nurses to hold her still enough to inject her safely.

After the medication dragged Butterfly down into sleep, Jack sat staring at her, his forehead furrowed. The lines remained even when the doctor informed him that her vital signs were stable, He couldn't stop thinking about her face as she'd lashed out. It had contorted into an unrecognisable mask of rage. Almost as if she was possessed by a malevolent entity.

Butterfly slept right through the day. Jack was about to leave when her eyelids fluttered apart. "Where are you going?" she asked, her voice hoarse but otherwise back to its normal self.

He looked at her intently, searching for signs of that other face. There were none. "To pick up Naomi."

"But you only just got here."

"It's almost three o'clock."

Butterfly's eyebrows lifted. "Did I fall asleep?"

Jack nodded. She clearly had no memory of what had happened. Her surprise turned to disappointment. "I'm sorry, Jack."

He gave her a strained smile. "I'll see you tomorrow."

Butterfly's tattoo came alive as creases spread from the corners of her eyes. "Are you OK?"

"I'm fine."

"Are *we* OK?"

Jack hesitated – only for a heartbeat – before replying, "Yes." He stooped to kiss Butterfly's forehead.

He could feel her eyes on him as he left the room. The raw need in them made him want to rush back to her side and reassure her that his feelings hadn't changed. But one question wouldn't allow him to do so – what if Butterfly had one of those episodes around Naomi?

He was still turning the question over in his mind as he pulled away from the hospital. He drove on automatic pilot, silently arguing with himself. *How can you risk exposing Naomi to that? It's just stress. Once the baby is back with her, she won't have any reason for those kinds of hysterics. But what if we don't find the baby? Or what if we do and the episodes continue?*

An extended *beeeep!* jerked Jack's full attention to the road. A car was pulling out of a side-street to his left. He slammed on the brakes, narrowly avoiding ploughing into it. The driver gesticulated angrily. Jack raised a hand in apology and the car accelerated away.

His phone rang. He took it out – 'Butterfly'. He heaved a breath as a pair of all too familiar questions came to mind – why couldn't life be simple just for once? Why did there always have to be anxiety and uncertainty? He put the receiver to his ear. "Hi there."

"Hi," Butterfly replied tentatively. "I just wanted to make sure that... Well it seemed like something was bothering you."

"Hang on a second, Butterfly. Let me pull into the side of the road and we can–" The roar of a vehicle fast approaching from the rear interrupted Jack. Twisting around, he saw a Range Rover bearing down on him like a charging rhino. Shiny steel bull bars enclosed the SUV's front end. Tinted windows masked the driver. He just had time to shout, "Shit!" before the vehicle slammed into his bumper. The back end of his car crumpled like a Coke can under the impact. His head whipped back against the seat, then forwards into an exploding airbag.

Blood dripped from his nose as he groggily lifted his head. The pain in his injured shoulder was almost as intense as when he'd first been shot. But it was nothing compared to the jolt that went through him as, in the wing mirror, he saw the face that had inhabited his nightmares for the past week-and-a-half. Ryan's dark stubble had thickened into a beard. He was advancing towards Jack with his usual dead-eyed calm, pistol in hand.

"Jack," Butterfly's worried voice came through the receiver. "Are you there?"

"It's Ryan," hissed Jack. There was no time to say anything else. Ryan was at the window and Jack found himself staring into the handgun's barrel.

Jack flung one hand up in front of his face as if he could deflect a bullet with it. With his other hand, he stuffed the phone down his trousers. Naomi's perfect little face flashed through his mind. He heard himself saying to her, *I promise.* It seemed he was about to break his promise. He braced himself for the flash of the muzzle, the explosion of noise and the impact of the bullet. At this range, he was sure he wouldn't feel much. It would all be over in a split second.

Instead of pulling the trigger, Ryan motioned for Jack to get out. Jack did so, his hands spread, his muscles coiled and ready. Ryan's eyes gleamed dully from their deep sockets, giving away nothing. His voice was equally emotionless as he said, "Get down on your face."

"Think about your children, Ryan. Give yourself up." Jack knew his words would have no effect, but every second that passed was a second in which a chance to fight or flee might present itself.

"Get down on your face," Ryan repeated in the same flat tone.

Taking his time, Jack did so. Ryan pressed the gun against the back of his head. Jack fought against a rising tide of panic, telling himself, *He won't shoot you – at least not here – otherwise you'd already be dead.* Ryan's next words confirmed the thought, "Put your hands together."

Jack grimaced as a plastic zip-tie was slipped over his wrists and yanked tight. It felt like his injured shoulder was being twisted out of joint. The grimace turned into a yelp as Ryan hauled him upright. "You can still stop this, Ryan," gasped Jack. "You can still live to see your children grow up."

Ryan thrust him towards the Range Rover. A hundred or so metres further on a van pulled out of an industrial unit. *This is your chance!* Jack's mind yelled. *Run for the van.*

Steely fingers closed around Jack's arm. "Don't try anything," Ryan warned as if reading his mind.

The van drove away in the opposite direction. The chance passed as quickly as it had come.

The Range Rover's boot was open. Ryan shoved Jack into it. He looped a zip-tie around Jack's ankles and pulled it tight.

"It doesn't have to be this way," said Jack as Ryan picked up a roll of Duct tape and tore off a strip.

"Yes it does," stated Ryan, slapping the tape over Jack's mouth. He closed the boot, confining Jack in darkness. The engine came alive and they accelerated away as casually as if Ryan had stopped for groceries.

Chapter 36

Jack tried in vain to work his wrists and ankles free. The zip-ties cut into his flesh. He felt warm blood running over his skin, but even with that lubrication the ties were too tight to escape from. He squirmed around, feeling for anything that might be of help – a sharp edge to saw through the ties, a latch to open the boot. There was nothing. Scrunching himself up, he kicked at the tailgate until he was breathless and soaked with sweat. He rubbed his face against the boot's carpeted base, peeling away the Duct tape.

"Help!" he yelled over and over until he was hoarse.

Finally, he lay motionless and concentrated on breathing slowly and conserving his strength. He could feel the phone pressing into his groin. While it remained there he had a chance. *Butterfly heard what happened,* he told himself. *She's called the police. Wherever this bastard's taking you, they won't be far behind. Just do as he says. Don't give him any excuse to kill you too quickly.*

"If you're still there, Butterfly, I'm tied up in the boot of a black Range Rover with tinted windows and bull-bars," Jack said as loudly as he dared. He strained his ears for a reply. Nothing. "I was on Waterloo Road in Cheetwood when Ryan got me. He has a handgun." Again, only silence in reply.

After maybe ten or fifteen minutes, the Range Rover came to a stop. There was a muffled metallic rattling. The SUV pulled forwards a short distance. "We're stopping," Jack said on the off-chance that the call hadn't been cut off. "I think we're in a building." There was more rattling. "Sounds like it has a roller door." A breathless moment passed, then the boot swung open.

Jack blinked as what seemed like blindingly bright light streamed into his eyes. Pain lanced through his shoulder as Ryan pulled him feet-first out of the boot. The breath whooshed from his lungs as he dropped onto an oil-stained concrete floor. He squinted at his surrounds as he was dragged along the floor. They were in some sort of industrial building. High overhead strip-lights dangled from cobwebby wooden beams that supported a corrugated roof. Hulking machinery clogged with grease and rust inhabited the shadows to either side. Alongside the machines was a collection of high-end vehicles – SUVs, BMWs, Mercedes, Audis. Ryan had clearly taken him to a storage unit similar to those at Hawkshead Manor. But they hadn't been driving long enough for this one to be located outside the city.

"Where are we? Is this another of your stolen car warehouses?" Jack said more for the benefit of Butterfly or anyone else who might be listening in than because he expected an answer.

In reply, Ryan got hold of Jack's arms and lifted him into a wooden chair. Next to the chair was a scratched old Formica table. Panic welled up inside Jack again at what was on the table – pliers, a hacksaw, bolt-cutters, knives, what looked to be a blow torch, bundles of zip-ties. *Keep it together!* he commanded himself. *Say something to delay this fucker. But what? Anything!*

"What do you want from me?" Jack asked, fear threatening to snatch away his voice. "I'll tell you anything you want to know."

Ryan wordlessly set to work on securing Jack to the chair with zip-ties.

"I can help you," continued Jack, "I can tell you how many constables are at the hospital and where they're posted."

Ryan took off his jacket and laid it on the table, exposing his 'LOVE::. ALICE::' tattoo. There were two freshly inked dots. Ryan's unreadable eyes roamed over the table's contents. He selected the bolt-cutters.

"Don't do this, Ryan," pleaded Jack. His mind scrambled for something else to say that would give Ryan pause for thought. "I… I…"

Ryan raised a finger to his lips. He tapped his tattoo. "You know what this means, don't you?"

"Yes."

He traced a finger almost tenderly over the new dots. "PC Tim Jones. PC Craig Barton." His finger came to rest on an unadorned patch of skin. "This is where you're going."

Jack looked at the blank space as bleakly as someone surveying a graveyard plot reserved for them.

Ryan's finger moved towards Jack's feet. "I'm going to cut off your toes," he said matter-of-factly. "Then I'm going to cut off your fingers, your ears, your nose, your tongue, your arms and legs. And when there's nothing else left, I'm going to cut off your head. And then I'm going to do the same to your sister."

In an instant, Jack's expression transformed from fear to fury. He bucked in the chair, straining against his bonds, not caring about the pain in his shoulder. The chair tipped over but didn't break apart. Ryan looked on impassively until Jack lapsed into gasping stillness. Then he bent to lift the chair upright.

Jack bit down on his anger, telling himself, *Don't give this psycho the satisfaction*. Somehow, from somewhere deep inside, he found sufficient calm to say, "We both chose this life. We accepted the risks. But Laura didn't choose this. Don't involve her."

"It's a bit late for that."

Ryan put down the bolt-cutters and moved into the shadows behind Jack. There was the sound of something heavy being dragged across the floor. Ryan retreated into view, pulling a chair with a gagged figure zip-tied to it. Jack's eyes swelled at the sight. Laura's hair was glued to her face by sweat, her cheeks were as white as his knuckles, her eyes were swollen and bloodshot. The collar of her nurses' uniform was torn as if she'd fought with Ryan, but she appeared to be unharmed.

"Motherfucker!" exploded Jack, straining so hard that the veins on his neck swelled like overinflated inner-tubes.

Ryan positioned Laura so that she had an unobstructed view of her brother.

Jack's voice echoed from the rafters as he raged, "Hurt her and I'll kill you! I swear to fucking god!"

Ryan stared at him as if to say, *Is that it? Are you finished?*

Jack subsided into trembling silence. Ryan squatted to undo Jack's shoelaces. He drew back as Jack kicked at him. "Do that again and I'll start with her," warned Ryan, glancing at Laura.

Jack hauled in a shuddering breath. *The AFOs are on their way,* he told himself. *They could be creeping up on this place right now. Even if Butterfly somehow doesn't realise what's going on, the officers assigned to protect Laura will be searching for her. The longer you can keep your head, the better her odds of getting out of this alive.*

Ryan reached for Jack's laces again. Jack remained motionless as Ryan removed his shoes and socks. Laura gave out a muffled cry, squirming against her bonds as Ryan retrieved the bolt-cutters. *It's alright, sis,* Jack tried to tell her with his eyes. *Everything will be alright.*

He held her gaze as Ryan positioned the cold steel jaw of the bolt-cutters against one of his small toes. Ryan brought the handles together in a single effortless movement. There was a crunch of bone. Jack expelled his breath in a spittle-flecked rush. Little convulsions shook him. Laura sobbed and writhed as if it was her toe that had been severed. Ryan picked up the toe and examined it with clinical detachment. Blood was rapidly pooling around Jack's foot.

Ryan tossed the toe aside, sparked a lighter and lit the blowtorch. He adjusted the yellow flame to a fierce blue hiss and aimed it at the bloody stump. There was a sizzle of burning flesh. The pain was worse than anything Jack had ever experienced. He would rather have been shot again. Somehow he held himself still so that Ryan could get the job done, but he couldn't stop a scream from tearing out of him.

Ryan stepped back and surveyed his handiwork with that same detachment. "One down, nine more to go."

"Fuck you!" Jack spat.

He stiffened as Ryan opened the bolt-cutter's jaw and placed it against the next toe in line. Jack glared defiantly at his torturer. His head jerked backwards as if he'd been punched as the handles snapped together again.

"Oh you bastard," gasped Jack, wrenching his gaze back to Ryan. "You sick bastard. I hope they put a bullet in your head like you did to Butterfly."

"You'd like that wouldn't you. You fucking murderer," said Ryan.

Jack let out a semi-hysterical laugh. "You're off your head!"

Ryan reached for the blowtorch. Jack hyperventilated as the flame moved towards the fresh stump. That same sizzle. That same bitter, roast pork stink of burning flesh. His scream echoed to the furthest reaches of the cavernous building. His head lolled, eyes rolling. He felt himself losing his grip on consciousness. Ryan tapped his cheek like a parent rousing a child from a deep sleep. "Jack. Jack."

Through a sea of pain, Jack's vision swam back into focus. His heart was playing a rapid, irregular beat that made him feel as if he couldn't catch his breath. *You can't take much more of this,* said part of his reeling mind. *Yes you can!* retorted another part. *You'll take it because Laura has to survive. Naomi needs her.* He wondered how long it had been since he was kidnapped. Half-an-hour? An hour? Surely the police couldn't be far away.

"That's it, Jack," said Ryan. "Show me how strong you are."

Jack gave no sign of having heard. Ryan wanted him to suffer for as long as possible. Jack was willing to oblige, but he was done giving the bastard the satisfaction of any response. His eyes lifted to Laura. She was shaking all over. The shaking subsided as she returned his gaze. A sense of stillness swept over Jack too. It was as if they were drawing strength from each other.

"Shall we go for number three?" Ryan suggested as if Jack had a choice.

This time Jack really didn't hear him. His heart was banging out that crazy beat again. Something was moving in the shadows behind Laura. Or were his eyes playing tricks on him? He blinked to clear the tears from them. No. There it was again. The AFOs were here!

A figure emerged from the shadows. It wasn't an armed officer.

Chapter 37

It was all Jack could do to stop his jaw from falling slack. Butterfly! She was wearing the tracksuit he'd bought her. Her face was pale, but her eyes were gleaming with resolve. She was gripping an iron bar. As Ryan positioned the bolt-cutters against the next toe, she padded towards him.

What the hell was she doing? Why hadn't she called the police?

There was no time to ponder the questions. Jack had to make enough noise to cover her footfalls. "Please don't!" he cried. "Please, I can't take anymore! Just finish me off. Put a bullet in my head."

A frown pulled at Ryan's forehead. He gave Jack a reassessing look as if wondering whether he'd misjudged him.

Butterfly was only a few steps away. She raised the bar over her head. It was steady in her hands.

"Kill me," continued Jack, "Just kill me."

Ryan shook his head, seemingly more in disappointment than in response to Jack's plea. His gaze returned to Jack's toe. Laura flinched but didn't make a sound as Butterfly glided past her. Butterfly was close enough now that Jack could see wiry threads of muscle standing out on her neck. He tensed as the steel jaws closed against his toe. At the same instant, Butterfly brought the bar down swiftly and surely. There was a crunch as it connected with the crown of Ryan's head. He dropped the bolt-cutters and staggered sideways, but managed to stay upright. Butterfly hit him again. This time he keeled over, blood streaming down his face. He crawled forwards, reaching for the table to pull himself up. Butterfly aimed a third blow at the centre of his back. He collapsed onto his face, straining to suck air into his winded lungs.

"Don't move or I'll split your skull wide open!" warned Butterfly. Her eyes darted around as if looking for something and came to rest on the table. She grabbed the zip-ties and set about securing Ryan's wrists and ankles with them.

"Cut me loose," urged Jack.

Ignoring him, Butterfly moved away into the shadows.

"What are you doing?" he called after her. "Talk to me, Butterfly."

She returned with a third chair. Jack had a queasy feeling that he knew the answer to his question as she struggled to lift Ryan into the chair. Head lolling, Ryan slipped through her grip like melted cheese. She gave up and plonked herself down on the chair, breathing heavily.

"If you're doing what I think you're doing, please don't," pleaded Jack, trying to catch her eyes.

Butterfly stared at her lap as if she couldn't bring herself to meet his gaze. "Why shouldn't I?" she asked quietly.

"He's going to prison for the rest of his life. He'll never hurt anyone again."

"What about Charlie?"

"He'll tell us where Charlie is. I'll make him. But it has to be done the right way."

A knot formed between Butterfly's eyebrows. Her gaze slid across to Ryan. He stared back at her with a blank challenge in his eyes. She shook her head. "You can't make him talk, Jack, but I can."

Sucking in a breath like someone about to dive into deep water, she moved to untie Ryan's shoelaces. He didn't struggle.

"Please, Butterfly," said Jack. "This isn't you."

"How do you know?" she asked without looking at him.

"Because I… I…" Jack stumbled over his words, realising he had no answer.

"But *you* know who I really am, don't you?" Butterfly said to Ryan. "I can see it in your eyes. You know what I'm capable of."

Ryan blinked, just once, but it was all the answer she needed. She set aside his shoes and reached for the bolt-cutters.

"You asked me to teach you to be good," Jack said in desperation as she opened the steel jaws and slid them into place. "So let me show you there's another way to do this."

Butterfly stared at Ryan. He returned her stare stonily as if to say, *Go on then. Do it.*

"Where's my baby?" she asked with only the faintest tremor in her voice.

Ryan remained silent.

"Where's my baby?" repeated Butterfly. "I won't ask again."

Silence.

"Don't," implored Jack.

"I'm sorry, Jack," Butterfly replied and she brought the handles together.

Ryan's little toe popped off like a cork. He arched his back, letting out a high-pitched scream.

"Oh Christ, Butterfly," groaned Jack. He jerked his gaze to Laura as if she might be able to help him convince Butterfly to stop this madness. Seemingly reading the appeal in his eyes, Laura gave a sad little shake of her head.

Butterfly didn't bother with the blowtorch. She simply moved on to the adjacent toe. "Where's my baby?" There wasn't even the faintest tremor in her voice now. There was only the promise of more pain.

Clawing back his composure, Ryan fixed his eyes on her again. His face was a mass of agonised twitches, but there was still a challenge in his eyes. Butterfly's thin arms flexed against the handles. Another scream raked the air as the jaws sliced through bone. A dark urine stain spread down Ryan's trouser legs.

"Stop!" shouted Jack. "Stop or we'll never be together."

She met his gaze, her eyes deep wells of sadness. "I love you, Jack. But Charlie has to come first. You understand, don't you?"

"Yes but…" Jack trailed off resignedly. If it was Naomi missing, he'd have torn apart the world to find her.

Butterfly returned her attention to Ryan. "Where's my baby?"

The question drew a whimper from him. Stifling it, he stared at the roof, his eyes glazed with tears. Butterfly reversed the bolt-cutters so that they rested against his big toe. She pushed the handles together, her arms trembling as the blades struggled to bite through the thicker bone. Ryan screamed and writhed, trying to pull his toe free. Butterfly held on with grim determination.

The screaming seemed to go on and on without pause for breath, rising to an ever more excruciating pitch. If Jack's hands had been free, he would have jammed his fingers into his ears. Butterfly's tattoo was distorted into a meaningless shape. Her lips were compressed so tightly as to be almost invisible. But her eyes looked to have swollen to twice their normal size. He saw nothing of the woman he wanted to spend his life with.

The scream formed itself into a just barely comprehensible word. "Kavanagh!"

Butterfly released Ryan's toe. It dangled by a few shreds of tendon and skin. "What did you say?"

"Kavanagh," Ryan repeated, spittle flecking his lips. "He… he's the man we sold your baby to."

For a moment, Butterfly stood in stunned silence. "Who is he?" Now there was fear in her voice. Such fear that Jack could feel it radiating from her. "Is he… Is he a…" She couldn't bear to say what was in her mind, but the words were etched into her eyes, *Is he some sort of pervert?*

"He's some bigshot businessman from London." Ryan hauled in a ragged breath and went on, "He wanted a red-haired baby. That's all I know."

Butterfly thrust the bolt-cutters at him menacingly. "You must know more. Where does he live? What's his first name? Is my baby alive or, or…" She trailed off again into agonised silence.

"The only other thing I can tell you is your baby's a boy."

"A boy," Butterfly murmured to herself. In the space of a breath, her expression shifted from savage to tender and back. She put down the bolt-cutters and picked up a knife. "Tell me why I shouldn't stick this in you?"

"Because we've got a name," put in Jack. "That's all we need to find your son."

"In which case I don't need this piece of shit alive any longer."

"But what if Kavanagh isn't this businessman's real name?" Jack jerked his chin at Ryan. "Or what if he's lying?"

"I'm not lying," Ryan protested. "I swear on the lives of my kids."

Butterfly's eyes flitted uncertainly between Ryan and Jack. She took out her iPhone and tapped at its screen. She showed a page of photos to Ryan. A Google search box read 'Kavanagh + London businessman'. There were several photos of a thirty-something, trendily dressed man drinking champagne and stepping out of nightclubs with different women on his arm. "Is that him?"

"No."

Butterfly scrolled down to an older, more conservatively dressed man outside a modern business premises. "What about him?" Another no. The next few photos were of a clean cut forty-something man, tall, slim and always smiling. He looked about as unlikely a criminal as was imaginable. In one photo he was perched on the bonnet of a flashy car. In another he was piloting a helicopter over a sprawling city. In a third he was wearing a dinner suit and bow tie. His arm was wrapped around the waist of a beautiful woman with long auburn hair who looked to be about a decade younger than him.

"That's him," said Ryan.

"Are you sure?"

"Yeah."

Butterfly slumped onto the chair again as if she'd reached the end of her strength. She followed a link to an article in a business e-zine and read aloud, "Say hello to Mark Kavanagh. The most successful entrepreneur you've never heard of. Mark, the owner of Kavanagh Limited, an international building materials company operating out of Guildford, admits he has always shied away from the public eye. But that all changed last week when he became a new entrant in our annual rich list with an estimated wealth of one hundred and eight million pounds."

"We've got him," said Jack.

Butterfly glanced at Ryan's Range Rover. "Where are the keys?"

"In the–" Ryan started to answer.

Guessing her intention, Jack interjected, "There's no need for you to do anything else, Butterfly. We'll get your son back for you."

"Don't trust them," slurred Ryan, his eyes rolling as he floundered on the edge of consciousness. "They're murderers."

"You know you can trust me," said Jack.

Butterfly turned to him with those heart-breaking eyes he'd been falling in love with since the first time he looked into them. "I do trust you, Jack, but what if Kavanagh has sold Charlie to someone else?"

"Kavanagh sells bricks not babies. Look at that woman in the photo with him. Her hair is almost identical to yours. I bet she's infertile. Or he is. Either way, they wanted a baby they could pass off as their own."

Butterfly's eyes returned to Ryan. "Is that why he wanted my baby?"

"I told you, I don't know," he said. "He paid up and we went our separate ways."

Her eyes glittered as if she was reconsidering whether to stick the knife into Ryan. "That's all that matters to you, isn't it? Money. How much was my son's life worth?"

"Fifty grand."

"Fifty grand," murmured Butterfly. "All this for fifty grand."

"It was just business. No one would have got hurt if you hadn't done what you did."

Butterfly winced as if the words were knives slicing into her. "You're saying I knew what you planned to do with Charlie. What type of person would sell their own baby?" The question was dripping with self-loathing.

"But Tracy didn't go through with it," put in Jack.

"*Tracy*," Butterfly spat out the name as if it was too bitter to swallow. "Don't ever say that name to me again. Tracy Ridley is dead. She wasn't capable of love. *I* am and *I* will get Charlie back." Her eyes jerked to Ryan. "Keys?"

"In the ignition." Ryan's voice was faint. There was so much blood around him it was hard to believe he had any left in his body.

"Gun?"

"Glove compartment."

"Wait," exclaimed Jack as Butterfly headed for the Range Rover. "You're not strong enough to drive down to London."

"I made it here," Butterfly replied over her shoulder. She ducked into the vehicle and emerged with the keys and Glock.

"Do you even know how to drive?" asked Jack.

"I guess we'll find out." She took out the gun's magazine, checked it was loaded, pulled back the slide. A round popped out. She slid it into the magazine, reinserted the magazine and released the slide. "Seems like I know how to use one of these." She gave a contemptuous laugh. "You find out something new about yourself every day."

"You don't know where Kavanagh lives. People like him don't put their address online."

"Which is why you're going to find it out for me."

"Why would I do that?"

Butterfly pointed the Glock at Ryan. "Because otherwise I'll kill him."

Jack stared into her eyes. There was no bluff in them. "You'll spend the rest of your life in prison."

"I'll take that if it means Charlie's safe. Please, Jack, every second we stand here arguing my Charlie could be..." Her voice snagged on the thought of what Charlie might be going through. "I'm going to count to three. One... Two..."

Whimpering, Ryan curled into a tight ball.

"Alright, alright," exclaimed Jack. He heaved a sigh. "I need a phone."

Butterfly swiftly moved behind Jack and cut his hands free. Groaning with relief at the release of pressure on his shoulder, he rubbed the feeling back into his wrists. Butterfly proffered her phone. "Just find out the address. Don't say *anything* about anything else," she warned.

Jack dialled Steve. It was nearly four o'clock. Only an hour had passed since he left the hospital. He'd been through a lifetime of pain in that short time. His thoughts suddenly turned to Naomi. Was she still waiting for him in the schoolyard? She wouldn't have been allowed to leave on her own. Wherever she was, she would be worried.

Steve's gruff voice came on the line. "Hello?"

Jack forced himself to focus on the task at hand. "It's me."

"Jack. What's up?"

"Are you at HQ?"

"Yeah, but not for much longer, thank fuck. I'm gasping for a–"

"Listen, Steve, I need a favour."

Steve's voice took on a note of concerned curiosity. "You alright? You sound stressed."

That's because I'm in fucking agony, Jack felt like retorting. He was soaked through with sweat from the pain in his foot. "Yeah, I'm good. I need you to run a name for me. Mark Kavanagh."

"Who the hell is Mark Kavanagh?"

"I'll explain later."

"Does this have anything to do with–"

"Just do it will you, Steve," Jack interrupted sharply.

"OK, keep your hair on. Bloody hell." There was the sound of tapping keys. "There are one, two, three… Forty six Mark Kavanagh's in the system."

"This one's in his forties, Caucasian, brown hair, medium height, slim build. He might have previous."

There was another pause, then Steve came back on the line. "How about this? Mark Kavanagh. Forty-two. Lives in Carlisle?"

"No. This Mark probably lives down near London. Possibly in Guildford."

"Erm… Ah, here we go, I think we've got a winner. Mark Kavanagh. Warwick's Bench Road, Guildford. Forty-seven. He's clean except for a couple of points on his licence. Spouse: Suzanne Kavanagh, thirty-one and drop dead gorgeous. I'd say Mark's batting well above his average."

"Thanks, Steve."

Jack hung-up before Steve could ask any awkward questions. Butterfly was looking at him expectantly. He told her the address. "Now what?" he asked. "Are you just going to leave us here?"

"No. You're coming with me. You and Laura." Butterfly looked at Laura for the first time. She carefully peeled the tape off Laura's mouth. "Hello Laura. Jack's told me all about you. I would say it's nice to meet you, but…" Her voice faded almost apologetically.

"I get why you're doing this," Laura said in a dry-throated rasp, "but Jack has about twelve hours to get his foot sorted out. After that they won't be able to reattach his toes."

"How long does it take to get to Guildford?"

"About four hours," said Jack.

"Then there's enough time."

"The sooner he gets into surgery the better the chance of success," said Laura.

Butterfly gave Jack a pained look. "I'm sorry, Jack. I wish I could take you to hospital."

"I wouldn't go even if you offered. If I can't persuade you not to do this, then I *want* to come with you."

The two of them stared at each other, their eyes mirrors of sadness and need.

"I hate to interrupt this moment," said Laura. Jack was glad to hear the sardonic edge to her voice. Even after what she'd just been through, her bone-dry sense of humour was intact. She glanced at Ryan who appeared to have lost his battle with unconsciousness. "But what about him? I can probably stop the bleeding, but even so he could die if we leave him here."

Butterfly looked darkly at Ryan. "We'll dump him somewhere where he'll be found. That's the best he's going to get and it's a lot more than he deserves."

She cut the remaining zip-ties securing him to the chair, before turning to do the same for Laura. Grimacing, Laura rose unsteadily to her feet. Jack limped forwards to help her, but she raised a hand to stop him. "I'm fine, just a bit dizzy. The sneaky sod clobbered me from behind."

"How did he snatch you from under the noses of the officers watching you?"

She cast him a sheepish glance. "I gave them the slip. Sorry Jack. I was sick of the sight of them."

Jack wasn't surprised – Laura had been moaning about the officers for days. He was more relieved than annoyed by her recklessness. He'd been steeling himself to hear that Ryan had two more dots to add to the tally of victims inked on his forearm.

Laura bent to check Ryan's pulse. "He's alive. Just about." She unbuckled her belt, made a noose and pulled it tight around the thigh of Ryan's injured leg. The bleeding from his foot slowed to a trickle. She checked his head. "There's a big dent. You may well have fractured his skull."

"Excuse me if I'm not sympathetic," said Butterfly. She glanced at Jack who was on his hands and knees examining a selection of severed toes.

"I think these two are mine," he said.

"You don't sound very certain," said Laura.

"They're covered in blood."

"Take them all."

Jack gathered up the gory digits and put them in his pocket.

"We need ice for them, but first..." Laura hooked her arms under Ryan's knees. Jack stooped to get hold of his arms.

"I'll do it," offered Butterfly.

"It's OK."

"What about your shoulder?"

"My shoulder won't kill me. That bullet might kill you if you strain too much and it moves."

Teeth gritted against the pain, Jack lifted Ryan. The unconscious man hung as limp as a sack of spuds as they carried him to the Range Rover. With a grunt of effort, they heaved him into the boot. Jack furtively retrieved his iPhone from his trousers and slipped it into Ryan's jacket pocket. If things went bad down in Guildford, someone would need to know where they were.

"I'll drive," said Laura. "You two are in no fit state."

Butterfly accepted the offer with a weary nod. She looked as if she had nothing left in the tank – eyes like black holes, sunken cheeks. She clambered onto the backseat. Jack retrieved his shoes and gingerly got into the front passenger seat. He exhaled as he took the weight off his injured foot.

Laura lifted a rust-mottled roller door and fading daylight slunk into the warehouse. Jack saw that they were in what appeared to be a car chop-shop. At far end of the building, a pair of semi-dismantled luxury cars were elevated on ramps. Tracy's car had most likely been stripped down here too. Bumpers, alloys, wing-mirrors, windscreens and the like were stacked ready to be shipped out. Laura climbed behind the wheel, started the engine and accelerated out of the building.

Chapter 38

A pot-holed driveway led to a cobbled street flanked by sooty redbrick terraced houses and a graveyard. The sight of the gravestones seemed grimly appropriate. Jack wondered whether any of the Mahon brothers' victims were double-buried in the graves. At the end of the street was a busy road lined with terraced houses and local businesses.

"I think this is Moston," said Laura.

Jack switched on the in-built sat nav. She was right. They were only a mile away from North Manchester General.

He inputted their destination and a tinny voice instructed them to turn left. They headed west through a hotchpotch of Victorian terraces, post-war semis and modern houses. Butterfly rested her head back, her eyelids heavy with fatigue. Grimacing, Jack tried to put on his shoes.

"Leave them off," said Laura. "Let the air get to the burns. How are you feeling?"

"Like I've been tortured half-to-death," said Jack. "Next daft question."

"Do you feel cold, sweaty, shaky, dizzy?"

Jack displayed a trembling hand. "All of the above."

"You're going into shock. Keep your breathing slow and steady. If you feel like you're going to faint, put your head between your knees. Have a look in the glove compartment. There might be a first aid kit."

Jack flipped open the glove compartment. "No first-aid kit, but there is this." He took out a wad of twenty-pound notes.

Laura swerved off the road into the carpark of a McDonald's. "What are you doing?" asked Butterfly, her eyes popping wide.

"I told you, we need ice." Laura headed for the drive-through.

"Don't do anything–"

"Yeah, yeah, don't worry, I won't make any secret signals or anything like that."

Laura ordered bottled water, coffee, fries and burgers. "Can I get two cups of ice," she said to the girl in the pay booth. "Oh and some extra sugars and cling-film if you've got any."

The girl obligingly handed over everything Laura asked for. As they pulled away from the booth, Laura thumbed towards the boot. "This might be a good place to drop off you know who."

"I've been thinking," said Butterfly. "What if he warns Kavanagh?"

"He's in no fit state to warn anyone about anything."

"Just keep driving. I'll tell you when to stop."

"If we don't do this soon, we might as well not bother at all."

"If he dies, he dies." Butterfly's voice was devoid of emotion.

"If he dies, it's murder," said Jack.

Butterfly's forehead furrowed as she mulled over his words. She nodded as if to say, *I can live with that.*

"Wrap those toes in cling-film and put them in the ice," said Laura.

Jack fished the severed digits out of his pocket, wrapped them up and buried them in the ice. He placed the cups in the cup-holders.

"Now pour water over your burns," instructed Laura.

Jack opened a bottle and did so. He groaned. "God, that feels good."

"Pour it over the rest of the cling-film too, make sure it's clean. Now cover the burns with cling-film. Not too tight."

Jack gingerly did so. His foot was throbbing as if it was ready to explode. "I could really do with some painkillers."

"I'm sorry, Jack," said Butterfly. "There's no time to stop."

"You're all heart," muttered Laura.

Butterfly jerked forwards as if Laura had slammed on the brakes. "My son's out there!" Her voice was frightened and angry. "They could be hurting him!"

"Calm down," said Jack, looking at her worriedly. "Remember what Doctor Medland said. You need to avoid extreme emotions and sudden movements."

Butterfly flopped back against the seat, her breath coming in rapid little pants.

"Breathe with me." Jack drew in a slow breath. "That's it. Good."

"Give her something to eat," said Laura.

Butterfly shook her head as Jack proffered a burger. "I'm not hungry."

"Eat it," Laura said firmly. "You need to keep up your strength. For Charlie's sake."

At that, Butterfly accepted the burger. "You need to eat too," Laura said to Jack. "Start with the fries. And put all the sugars in your tea. You have to replace the salt you've sweated out and up your blood-sugar level."

Jack ate the fries and sipped the tea. The icy sensation in his stomach gradually thawed out and his trembling eased off. Laura kept glancing at him. "You're looking better."

"I feel it, thanks."

"How about you?" Laura asked Butterfly. "How are you feeling?"

"How am I feeling?" Butterfly murmured as if she didn't fully understand the question. She touched the gauze pad on head. "I can feel it in there, you know. The bullet. It feels heavy. Sometimes it's so heavy I can hardly keep my head upright."

"Well if you feel nauseous or your vison goes blurry or whatever, let me know straight away."

Butterfly gazed out the window. They were on the M60, working their way south through heavy traffic. "What does it matter how I feel?"

"It matters to me," said Jack.

"Why? We're not going to be together. Not after what I've done. Why would you want someone like me around Naomi?"

"Naomi!" Jack and Laura exclaimed simultaneously.

"Give me your phone," Jack said to Butterfly.

She handed it over and he dialled Naomi. A small, worried voice answered, "Hello? Who's this?"

Jack's heart squeezed. "It's me, sweetheart."

"Dad! Are you OK?"

"I... I'm fine," he said with a guilty stumble. Naomi always put others' feelings before her own. That was another way in which she was different to her mum. "Where are you?"

"I'm still at school. Mrs Wright wants to talk to you."

Mrs Wright came on the line, "Hello, Mr Anderson, we've been trying to contact you."

"I'm sorry, an emergency came up. I can't come for Naomi. Nor can her aunt. I'll give you the number of someone who should be able to pick her up." Jack gave the teacher Steve's number. Steve would know for sure that something serious was going down, but there was no one else Jack could turn to. Except perhaps Paul. Despite the recent shift in their relationship, Jack couldn't stomach the thought of Naomi being looked after by a man who'd had an affair with her mum.

Mrs Wright put Naomi back on the phone. "Don't worry, sweetie, Steve will pick you up," Jack told her.

"Why can't you?"

"I'm on a job."

"But you're off work."

Even the pain in Jack's foot couldn't stop him from smiling faintly. When would he learn that it was almost impossible to pull the wool over Naomi's eyes? "I'll tell you all about it later. Right now I've got to go. See you soon, sweetheart. I love you."

"Bye, Dad. I love you too."

Jack hung up with a sigh and gave the phone back to Butterfly.

"I'm sorry for making you lie to her," she said.

Jack held up a hand as if to say, *There's no need.* They drove on in silence. Every so often, Jack glanced at Butterfly in the rear-view mirror – partly to check she was OK, but mostly because he needed to see her face. His own face was riddled with uncertainty. Butterfly's question swirled round his mind – *Why would you want someone like me around Naomi?* He kept coming back to the same simple answer: *Because I love you.* But was that enough? Did love justify the risk? And what about what Butterfly had done to Ryan? Did love justify that too?

The phone rang. Butterfly showed the number on the screen to Jack. "It's Steve," he said. "Don't answer it."

The ringing stopped. There was the buzz of a text message. Butterfly read aloud, "On my way to pick up Naomi. The DCI's in a right old lather. Your girlfriend's gone AWOL. Don't suppose you know where she is."

Jack could almost hear the sarcasm in the message. He took the phone again and messaged Steve, 'No idea.'

There was the buzz of a reply: 'Why do I find that hard to believe? I hope you're not doing anything silly.'

'Would I? Naomi likes pizza. Don't know what time I'll be round to pick her up. It'll be late. Thanks for this.'

'You'd better have a good explanation ready.' responded Steve, refusing to be distracted. 'And not just for me. The DCI's kicking off because he can't contact you. Don't worry. I won't give him this number.'

Jack didn't message him back. The explanation would have to wait. As he returned the phone to Butterfly, he told Laura what was going on.

She arched an eyebrow as if she wasn't sure whether she approved. "He'll probably take Naomi down the pub. I'll kick his arse if he does."

They were south of Manchester now, passing between flat fields on the M6. The traffic had eased off and they were speeding along in the fast-lane. Ryan hadn't made a noise the entire time he'd been in the boot. The silence emanating from him was growing more ominous by the minute.

"What about here?" Laura suggested when they passed a sign for 'Crewe Sandbach Services'.

"OK," agreed Butterfly.

Laura pulled onto the slip road and into a busy carpark. She headed for the trucker's area and stopped alongside an HGV. They got out and warily opened the boot. Their caution was needless. Ryan was out cold. The boot exhaled an acrid stench. Ryan's lips were ringed with vomit. Laura expertly cleared his mouth out and checked his breathing. "He's alive," she said, puffing her cheeks. "Frankly I'm amazed."

Butterfly made a *hmpf* as if unsure whether to be relieved or disappointed.

Jack only felt relief. If Ryan lived, there was still a chance – not matter how slim – for Butterfly and him. But if he died…

They lugged Ryan out of the boot and put him in the recovery position below the driver-side door of the HGV. Butterfly stared at him for a moment as if committing every detail of his face to memory. Then they got back into the Range Rover and sped away.

Jack and Laura exchanged a furtive glance. He saw she was thinking the same as him. With Ryan out of the way, what was to stop them from refusing to go through with Butterfly's plan?

Seemingly reading their minds, Butterfly said, "I love you Jack. Honestly I do. I know we've only just met, Laura, but I like you a lot. But make no mistake, I will do whatever it takes to get Charlie back. Do you understand?"

Jack looked into Butterfly's eyes. His gaze fell to the Glock. Her finger was hooked through the trigger guard. He nodded.

The traffic ebbed and flowed as they passed through the industrial outskirts of Birmingham and negotiated Spaghetti Junction's concrete jungle of slip roads and flyovers. Then they were south of the city. It was a clear night. The moon dimly illuminated the rolling countryside of Warwickshire and Oxfordshire.

Butterfly was scouring the internet for anything she could find about Mark Kavanagh. There wasn't much beyond what they already knew. She scrutinised the photos of Mark as if they might contain a clue as to Charlie's whereabouts. She showed the photos to Jack. "What do you see when you look at him?"

Like a hawk studying its prey, Jack's gaze moved over Mark perching on the sports car's bonnet, Mark piloting the helicopter, Mark with his arm around the beautiful redhead. He noted how proprietorially Mark was holding the woman. As if she was a trophy he'd won. Throughout the photos, Mark's smile never wavered. There was something fixed about it – not necessarily false, but not entirely convincing either. In the car and helicopter photos Mark's hair was uniformly brown. In the other it was grey at the roots. Was he letting the grey grow out?

"I see a man who likes to spend his money on flash cars and beautiful women, but who has reached a time in his life when he's ready for something else. Something more meaningful."

"What makes you say that?"

Jack pointed to the photo of Mark and the redhead. "His hair's been recently dyed in the other photos, but in this one his grey is showing. He's not trying to hide his age from the woman. He's comfortable being himself with her and he wants everyone to know it. He loves her."

Butterfly scowled. "And that's why he stole my son, is it? To show her how much he loves her?"

"I don't know. Let's hope so."

"Shall I tell you what I see? An arrogant bastard who thinks his money can buy him whatever he wants, no matter what the price to others. Well I'm going to show him he's wrong."

Jack fixed her with a hard stare. "If you're going to hurt Kavanagh, we can stop the car right now and you can put a bullet in me. I'm here to help you get Charlie back, not to help you commit murder."

"Don't worry, Jack, I won't hurt him." Butterfly added ominously, "Unless he's hurt Charlie."

"In everything you've read about Kavanagh, has there been any mention of him having children?"

"No."

Jack nodded as if that backed up his earlier suspicion. "I think he left it too late to start a family – at least naturally."

"I guess we'll find out if you're right soon enough, won't we?"

Butterfly glanced at a road sign that read 'London Orbital M25. Guildford 15'. Jack's gut instinct told him he was right, but he had to be ready for the other possibility. "I'm warning you, Butterfly. I won't stand by while you hurt someone."

"I know you won't. That's why I love you." She turned away as if it hurt too much to look at him.

The iPhone rang again. "It's Steve," said Butterfly. She let the call go through to the answering service. 'Voicemail. Slide to listen' flashed up. She swiped and put the phone on loudspeaker. "Jack, pick up the sodding phone will you?" said Steve. "A man fitting Ryan Mahon's description has been found at Sandbach Services on the M6. The guy's in hospital. Sounds like someone's done a real number on him. Jesus Jack, please tell me it wasn't you. *And* I've just spoken to the guys assigned to Laura. The daft bloody mare's gone and snuck off on them. At least I hope she's only snuck off. She's not answering her phone. Tell me she's with you, Jack. I'm starting to wonder if I should tell the DCI about Mark Kavanagh. Naomi's fine, by the way. She's scoffing pizza in my living-room. She wants to know where you and Laura are too. Call me."

"Ryan's alive." Jack's words came out in a long breath. "Let me call Steve," he implored Butterfly. "Half-an-hour from now Guildford police could have Kavanagh in custody."

In response, she returned the phone to her pocket and said, "Drive faster."

"I'm already doing the speed limit," said Laura.

"I don't give a shit. Put your foot down."

Laura floored the accelerator, swerving into the middle lane to undertake several cars. They left the motorway behind for the equally busy A3. Laura weaved in and out of traffic, using the hard shoulder, prompting irate beeps and gestures from fellow motorists. "If we carry on like this, we'll get pulled over," said Jack.

"Ryan might have already contacted Kavanagh," Butterfly shot back.

Jack shook his head. "Right this minute Ryan's under armed guard. From now until the day he dies, he won't be able to take a piss without asking permission."

From the expression on Butterfly's face, he might as well have been talking to a brick wall.

"Daft bloody mare," Laura repeated Steve's words with a *hmpf.*

"He likes you," said Jack. "A lot."

"Should I be flattered or worried?"

"Both."

As they neared their destination, Butterfly's eyes grew feverishly bright with anticipation. Despite her obvious exhaustion, her feet tapped out a rapid rhythm. Jack watched her, half-fearing, half-hoping that her agitation would bring on another one of her 'events'. The thought of her potentially suffering further brain damage was agonising, but so was the possibility that she would do something to Kavanagh from which there would be no coming back.

It wasn't long before they were speeding through the leafy outskirts of Guildford – big, mock-Tudor detached and semi-detached houses, privet hedges, parkland, oh-so-English Surrey. The sat nav directed them along the western outskirts of the town centre through streets of Georgian and Victorian terraces. On the south side of town, they found themselves amongst detached houses that grew more ostentatious with every passing mile. Many of the houses could only be glimpsed set well back from the road behind tall walls, hedges and gates. In the near distance a wooded hillside basked in the moonlight.

"You've reached your destination," announced the sat nav.

They pulled over at the end of a broad driveway that led to wooden double-gates flanked by brick gateposts and a wall. A sandstone plaque set into the wall was engraved with 'Kavanagh House'. A galaxy of solar lights cast a soft glow over a sprawling garden. The house was set on a slight rise. Four huge bay-windows with sandstone architraves overlooked the garden from either side of a first-floor balcony reached via French windows. The house was topped off by arched attic windows recessed into a slate roof that sported three towering red-brick chimneys. At the left-hand side of the house, welcoming orange light emanated from a suitably big conservatory.

"Not bad," Laura commentated with typical dry understatement.

Breath whistling through his teeth, Jack pulled on his shoes. The pain made fresh sweat pop out on his forehead. He examined himself in the mirror. There was a crust of blood on his upper lip from head-butting his car's airbag. He cleaned it off with bottled water and dampened down his hair. He still looked like baked shit, but it would have to do.

"Get in the back," he said to Laura. "And both of you get down behind the seats."

Laura clambered into the back and he shifted across into the driver's seat. "OK, so here's how we're going to play this. I'm going in there alone. You two stay hidden in here. If I pick up on anything suspicious, I'll come out and let you know."

"I want to come in with you," protested Butterfly.

"That's not going to happen." Jack pointed to a Victorian-style cast-iron lamppost outside the gates. "You see that odd-looking lightbulb. It's a CCTV camera. I guarantee you the entire grounds are covered by cameras. The chances of someone sneaking in there are zero. But if you want to give it a go, be my guest."

Butterfly stared at him uncertainly for a second, then hunkered down into the foot-well. Jack turned to Laura. "You don't have to come with us."

"Just try and stop me."

He smiled thinly. He would have been surprised if she'd said different. "Have you got your phone?"

"Ryan took it."

"Give her the phone," Jack said to Butterfly. Again she hesitated and Jack continued, "Look, we either do this my way or not at all."

"I won't call anyone," Laura assured her.

"Unless things go to shit," said Jack. "Then you get the hell out of here and call 999. Do you hear me?"

"What if you're still in the house?"

"Leave me behind." Seeing his sister's reluctant frown, he added, "I'm serious, Laura. I can't protect you in there."

Laura arched an eyebrow. "I seem to remember it's me who's done most of the protecting in the past few years."

"You know what I mean. This is different."

With sudden urgency, Butterfly pressed the iPhone into Laura's hand saying, "OK, Jack. We'll do it your way."

He eyed the gates uneasily. "Let's just hope Kavanagh doesn't recognise Ryan's car."

Chapter 39

Jack pulled the Range Rover forwards, lowered the window and leant out to press the intercom button. A well-spoken female voice came through the speaker, sounding surprised that someone had come calling at this time of day. "Hello. Who is this?"

"My name's Detective Inspector Jack Anderson." Jack displayed his warrant card to the camera. "Apologies for disturbing your evening, but I'm here to speak to a Mr Mark Kavanagh. May I ask who you are?"

"Oh... erm..." The voice sounded flustered now. "I'm his wife, Suzanne Kavanagh. What's this about?"

"I urgently need to talk to your husband. Is he in?"

"I'm not sure. Hang on, I'll erm... I'll just have a look."

He's in, thought Jack. Whatever else she might be, Suzanne wasn't a very good liar. Several seconds passed. The seconds extended to a minute. "Something's wrong," Butterfly whispered from the backseat.

"Shh," retorted Jack as the intercom crackled back into life.

This time a gravelly male voice with a thick East London accent said, "Hold your identification out of the window." There was no deference to authority in the voice. It belonged to a man used to giving orders.

Jack did so. "Am I speaking to Mark Kavanagh?"

"Greater Manchester Police. You're a long way off your beat, aren't you?"

"Is this Mark Kavanagh?"

"What could Greater Manchester Police possibly want to speak to me about?"

The reply confirmed that it was Mark. He didn't sound like someone who'd been born into wealth. He sounded more like an East

End barrow boy done good. Maybe that was how Kavanagh had heard about what the Mahons had to offer. Perhaps he had some dodgy pals back in Kray country. "It would be best if we spoke face to face, Mr Kavanagh."

"I'll decide what's best. Now let's hear what you have to say. Unless you have a search warrant that is."

This isn't the first time this guy's had dealings with the police, thought Jack. *Either he's not fazed or he's a fucking good actor.* "I don't have a search warrant, Mr Kavanagh. There's no need for anything like that. I'm here in regards to a case involving stolen building materials."

"I don't deal in stolen materials. My company's record is above reproach."

Mark's tone was indignant, but Jack thought he caught a trace of relief. "I'm aware of that, Mr Kavanagh. You're not under suspicion. We have reason to believe someone has been stealing from you and using–"

"Stealing from me?" Mark broke in with disbelief. "No one's steals from me. I can tell you that with one hundred percent certainty."

"Unfortunately we have different information."

"What bloody information?"

"Let me in and I'll show you. I assure you this won't take long. And it would be very much to your benefit, Mr Kavanagh."

The intercom lapsed into silence. Jack waited tensely. He was banking on being right about Kavanagh's background. A man who'd worked his way up from the East End to millionaire's row Surrey was not the type to tolerate someone stealing from them, be it one pound or thousands. And even if Kavanagh suspected the stolen building materials story was bullshit – which someone as savvy as him surely did – he wouldn't want to appear suspect by turning the police away from his door.

"Come up to the house," Mark said at last and the electronic gates swung inwards.

"Here goes," said Jack, accelerating along a driveway that curved upwards between ornamental pine trees. "Keep your heads down."

"Shouldn't you have a weapon?" said Laura.

"No. I'm going to talk to the guy and have a look around. That's all. Now zip it."

At the top of the slope the driveway widened into a floodlit circle with an oversized SUV and a sleek sports car in it. To the front of the house an immaculate lawn descended towards colourful flowerbeds and shrubberies. Jack gave Laura the car keys and, gritting his teeth, got out of the Range Rover. He limped to the front door. Through the tall conservatory windows a grand piano and a selection of expensive-looking furniture was visible.

Mark was waiting within an arched brick porch. Jack recognised him from the e-zine article – swept back, silvery brown hair; same height as Jack, but slimmer build; smooth, tanned face; sharp features and even sharper dark eyes. He was casually dressed in jeans and a jumper. He looked like a man at ease with the world and his place in it. There was no sign of Suzanne. He held his hand out, but not to shake Jack's.

"ID."

Jack showed his warrant card. Mark took another long look at it before gesturing for Jack to follow him inside. The house's interior was as pristine as its exterior – polished parquet floors, plush carpets, chandeliers, elaborate cornices, tasteful paintings. A perfect marriage of period features and modern comfort. There was a sideboard overflowing with flowers and gilt-framed wedding photos of Mark and Suzanne. The happy couple were kissing outside a picture-perfect chapel. The photos didn't look to have been taken long ago. If anything, even with the silver hairs, Mark looked younger now than then, as if someone had been taking good care of him.

"How long have you been married?" asked Jack.

Mark gave him a look that was more annoyed than suspicious. He clearly wasn't one for small-talk. "Why?"

"I was looking at your wedding photos."

"Two years." For the first time, the brusque edge was absent from Mark's voice. "Are you married?"

Jack's mind went back to the Sussex church where Rebecca and he had tied the knot. It was similar to the one in the photos – lichen-scarred stone, ancient stained-glass, faded gravestones. Thinking about it now, it seemed like another lifetime. "No."

"I used to say I'd never get married. Now I wish I'd done it ten years earlier."

"Why's that?"

"Suzanne's a godsend. She looks after me better than my old mum did."

Jack wondered whether there was more to it. Perhaps ten years ago Mark wouldn't have had to buy an heir to his fortune – if that was indeed why he'd paid fifty grand for Charlie. Glancing around, Jack saw no baby paraphernalia. After Naomi's birth, the cottage had degenerated into a chaotic jumble of bibs, nappies, baby bouncers, dummies, rusks and the like. But then again, they hadn't been able to afford a cleaner. It must have taken a small army of cleaners to keep this place in tip-top shape. If nothing came of this visit, it would be worth tracking them down for a chat. Cleaners often knew as much about the goings on in a house as their employers.

Mark led him to a large dining-kitchen fitted with glossy white units, integrated chrome appliances and black marble work surfaces. Half the kitchen was given over to deep sofas and armchairs. The other half was dominated by a central island surrounded by chrome and leather stools. A wall of glass doors overlooked a patio furnished with rattan furniture and exotic potted plants. If Butterfly's baby was here, Suzanne obviously wouldn't be breastfeeding him. There would be bottles, formula milk and sterilisers. But the work surfaces were free from any such clutter. Everything was spotless. As if it had never been used.

A bolt of pain crackled up Jack's leg. He leant against a work surface. "You don't look well," observed Mark, his tone more curious than concerned.

"I've got a bad foot."

"How did you do that?"

Jack shrugged. His brain was too fogged with pain to come up with anything.

"That's what happens when you hit middle-age," said Mark. "Your body goes to pot. Things stop working as they should do."

What things? Jack resisted the urge to ask.

Mark perched himself on a stool. He didn't offer Jack a cup of tea. *You don't get rich by giving things away,* Jack mused cynically. He sat down too, puffing his cheeks as he took the weight off his injured foot.

"So what have you got to show–" Mark started to ask, but broke off, his eyes widening at something over Jack's shoulder.

Jack jerked around. "Shit," he hissed.

Butterfly was advancing along the hallway. Laura wasn't far behind her. "I'm sorry, Jack," said Laura. "I tried to stop her."

Mark sprang to his feet, exclaiming, "What is this? Who are you?"

"You know who the fuck I am," Butterfly retorted.

"Why would I know who you are?"

Mark flinched backwards against the fridge as Butterfly levelled the handgun at his face. "Where's my son?"

"Butterfly," snapped Jack. "You agreed to do this my way."

Ignoring him, Butterfly demanded again, "Where's my son?" Her voice was hard and tremulous.

"What son? I don't know what–"

"Bullshit!" exploded Butterfly. "I'm going to ask one last time and if you don't answer me I'll start putting bullets in you."

"No," said Jack, half-rising.

Butterfly turned the gun on him. "Don't move, Jack." She motioned at the stool. Spreading his hands, Jack sat back down. The gun returned to Mark. "Where is my son?"

Mark's eyes darted from her to Jack.

"Don't look at him," said Butterfly. "He won't help you."

Mark looked at her narrowly. There was fear in his eyes, but not the kind of paralysing fear you would expect from someone staring down the barrel of a gun. It was more the calculating wariness of a fox. "You won't shoot me in front of a copper."

"Won't I?" Butterfly pulled a McDonald's cup from inside her sweatshirt. She slid it across the work surface towards Mark. "Look in that."

As if the cup might explode in his face, Mark hesitantly peeled off its plastic lid. His face grew pale under its tan when he saw what was floating in the cup.

"Those belonged to Ryan Mahon," Butterfly told him. "Now they belong to me."

Mark's tongue darted nervously between his lips. His eyes were full of that other kind of fear now. Sweat filmed his upper lip. "I... I'll give you money. However much you want. One million, two–"

"One more word and I swear..." Butterfly let the threat hang between them.

"I'd do as she says," put in Jack. "She made Ryan Mahon piss himself and I'm guessing he's a lot tougher than you."

Mark's lizard-like tongue flickered out again. Suddenly his shoulders slumped and he seemed to shrink several centimetres. "I knew this was coming," he said to Butterfly, his voice as heavy as his features. "Ever since I saw on the news what those morons did to you. They told me you'd agreed to the sale."

"Yeah well I changed my mind," said Butterfly. "Take me to my son. Slowly," she warned as Mark started towards the hallway.

"Go back to the car," Jack told Laura.

With a nod, she turned to hurry towards the front door. Mark ascended a broad staircase. Jack came next, then Butterfly. The gun was visibly shaking in her hand. Her complexion would have made milk seem colourful. She stopped halfway up, clutching the bannister. She shook her head when Jack made as if to hold her up. "I'm OK," she said hoarsely, motioning with the gun for him to continue. Her hand remained affixed to the bannister as they completed the climb. The landing was a large rectangular area furnished with deep armchairs arranged to take in the view from glass doors leading onto the balcony.

Mark approached one of six interior doors. "Suzanne." His voice was as soft as a summer breeze. He sounded like a different man.

"Has he gone?" asked a muffled female voice – the voice from the intercom.

"Open the door, darling."

There was the click of a key turning. The door swung inwards. A pair of almond-shaped eyes peered out anxiously from between curtains of auburn hair. Suzanne sucked in a sharp breath at the sight of Jack and Butterfly. Her eyes returned to Mark, hurt and bewildered.

"I'm sorry," he said. "I had no choice." He reached for her hand, but she pushed him away.

"They shouldn't be up here," Suzanne said in a hushed voice as if afraid of waking someone. "Tell them to leave."

"They know everything, Suzanne." Mark glanced at Butterfly. "This is her."

"Her," Suzanne echoed in a way that made it clear she knew who Butterfly was. Her perfectly made-up features trembled. Tears threatened to ruin her mascara. "Tell them to leave," she repeated hollowly.

Jack couldn't help but feel a twinge of sympathy. The desperation in Suzanne's voice made him wonder whether it was her not Mark who had fertility problems.

"Move out of the way," Butterfly demanded, unable to contain herself any longer. There wasn't the faintest trace of sympathy in her voice.

Mark took hold of his wife's shoulders. She tried to shrug him off, but he firmly guided her to one side. Butterfly strode past them, her footfalls deadened by a thick sheepskin rug. The room's pastel blue walls were stencilled with fluffy clouds. In one corner there was an armchair. In another there was a baby changing table. Soft light glowed from a cloud shaped lamp. On the walls hung several conspicuously large photos of Suzanne apparently in various stages of pregnancy. Had she previously got pregnant and miscarried? wondered Jack. The air was subtly perfumed by talc, nappy cream and something else, something that Jack recognised from when Naomi was a baby – the intoxicatingly sweet milky scent of a newborn.

In the darkest part of the room a white wicker Moses Basket rested on a rocking-stand. The basket's hood was drawn up, shadowing a tiny form swaddled in a blue blanket.

Butterfly stopped as if she'd walked smack into a glass wall. The trembling of her hands was so severe that Jack found himself worrying whether the Glock might go off accidentally. Butterfly frowned at the gun as if the same thought had occurred to her. Turning to Jack with an almost ashamed look in her eyes, she held out the gun to him handle first. He gladly took it, glancing at Mark to make sure the handover didn't give him any funny ideas. Mark was staring at the floor as if a heavy hand was pressing on the back of his head.

Slowly, ever so slowly, Butterfly padded closer to the basket.

"Don't," pleaded Suzanne. "You'll wake Lucas."

Butterfly flashed her a razor-sharp glance. "His name's Charlie." Her eyes softened as she peered into the basket. A tiny sob escaped her throat. She tentatively reached out, but drew her hand back as if realising Suzanne was right. She turned and gestured towards the landing. "Out."

Suzanne's eyes never left the basket as Mark pulled her from the nursery. Jack followed, taking care not to get close enough for Mark to snatch for the gun. Butterfly stepped out of the room too, gently closing the door.

"Where's a phone?" asked Jack.

Mark pointed to a cordless handset on a sideboard. "Are you sure there's no arrangement we can come to?"

Butterfly scowled. "You think money can buy anything. Well it can't."

He looked at her imploringly. "Don't you think I know that? We paid for the best doctors. Had every fertility treatment available. But none of it made any difference." His eyes swept over his surrounds. "All this means nothing to me. I'd give the lot away for a child of my own."

A conflicted frown replaced Butterfly's scowl. "So why not adopt?"

"A child of *my own*," repeated Mark.

Jack suddenly understood. The photos in the nursery were fakes. Suzanne had pretended to be pregnant. Coming up with false birth documents wouldn't be a problem for someone with Mark's money and contacts. Butterfly nodded as if she too understood. "Vanity," she muttered, contempt curling her lips.

"No," put in Suzanne, shaking her head hard. "Mark did this for me. I was adopted and everyone knew it. Shall I tell you what the children at school used to sing?" She put on a spiteful, childish voice. "'Your real mum's a prozzie, your real mum's a prozzie.'" Tears choked off her words. Mark took her hand and she managed to continue, "I didn't want that for Lucas."

"Charlie," corrected Butterfly, her tone swaying between anger and something closer to sympathy.

"We're so sorry," said Mark.

"Sorry isn't going to cut it," said Jack. "People are dead."

Mark hung his head again as Jack dialled. Paul picked up straight away. "This is DCI Paul Gunn." He sounded stressed.

"Hello Paul."

"Jack! I've been trying to call your for hours. Where are you?"

"Guildford."

"Guildford? What the hell are you doing there?"

"I'm with Butterfly. We've found the baby."

"What? How–"

"I'll explain later." Jack told Paul the address, adding, "Have Guildford Police send someone over here. And send an ambulance too."

"Is someone hurt?"

"Yeah, me."

"How bad is it?"

"Let's just say I'm going to need extra time off work."

"OK, Jack, I'll get on it. Hang tight."

Jack got off the phone and said, "Let's wait downstairs."

"Hang on," said Butterfly, turning to re-enter the nursery. She reappeared carrying the Moses Basket as if it was made of glass. Jack glimpsed wispy red hair, soft round cheeks, a button nose and rosebud lips. The baby stirred in the brighter light, but didn't wake up.

They went down to the kitchen. Even carrying the extra weight, Butterfly didn't need the bannister. She seemed to have found a new well of strength. She put the basket on the central island. Charlie stirred again. His eyelids drifted open revealing bleary blue eyes. He let out a mewl like a hungry kitten.

"He always wakes around this time for a feed," said Suzanne. Springing into action, she fetched formula milk, a bib and bottle from a cupboard. She prepared a bottle of warm milk, then started towards the basket. Butterfly blocked her way. A spasm of anger pulled at Suzanne's features. "He's hungry." She said it like an accusation.

Butterfly took hold of the bottle. Suzanne didn't let go of it. The women eyeballed each other, competing in a silent tug-o-war.

"Give it to her, Suzanne," said Mark. It was a plea not a demand.

She blinked, but kept held of the bottle.

"For Christ's sake, Suzanne," snapped Mark. "You're not his mother. She is. Now let go!"

Suzanne's hand flinched away from the bottle. She looked on with a strange mixture of hope and fear as Butterfly awkwardly scooped Charlie up in her arms. Charlie's mewling grew more distressed as his head lolled backwards.

Suzanne moved towards him again, but this time Jack blocked her path. "Support his head," he instructed Butterfly, his mind flashing back to the countless hours he'd spent bottle-feeding Naomi. For months after giving birth, postnatal depression had rendered Rebecca barely able to feed herself, never mind Naomi. She'd seemed to make a full recovery, but that had been the first real warning sign of what lay ahead.

Butterfly adjusted Charlie's position so that he was nestled in the crook of her arm, cushioning him against her breasts. She slid the teat into Charlie's mouth. As Charlie eagerly sucked on it, Jack reached to raise the angle of the bottle, explaining, "You don't want him swallowing air."

Charlie contentedly settled down to his milk. Butterfly glanced at Jack with a kind of wonder as if she couldn't quite believe what she was doing. The sight was too much for Suzanne. She collapsed to the floor, sobbing. Mark stooped to console her. She shrugged him off, clutching her stomach as if she'd drunk acid.

Distressed by the noise, Charlie spat out the teat and gave a warbling wail. "Shh," soothed Butterfly, moving into the hallway. He took the teat back into his mouth, closing his eyes. When the bottle was empty, Butterfly rested him against her shoulder, patting his back and kissing his head.

"That's right. Go to sleep," she murmured as the faint sound of sirens came from outside. "Mummy's here. Mummy will always be here."

Chapter 40

"Jack... Jack."

For the second time in the space of a fortnight, Jack felt himself surfacing from a general anaesthetic. A nurse smiled down at him. "How are you feeling? Any pain?"

"No," Jack said woozily. He felt as if he was floating on a bed of warm air. "How did it go?"

"The consultant will be in to see you shortly. He'll discuss the operation with you. There's someone else here to see you."

The nurse left the room. Jack expected Laura or Steve to take her place, but Paul approached the bed. Jack realised with astonishment that he was glad to see his oldest colleague. They'd been through so much together over the years – good and bad. As much as Jack hated what Paul and Rebecca had done, he couldn't deny that there was no one – besides perhaps Laura – who knew him better. It came to him suddenly that the shift in his feelings had nothing to do with the passage of time, his capacity for forgiveness or even simple common sense. It had everything to do with one thing, and one thing only – Butterfly.

Paul surveyed Jack's foot, which was elevated in a sling and heavily bandaged. "Bloody hell, Jack."

"Is that all you've got to say?"

"What do you want me to say? Good job?" Paul looked at Jack with the sort of exasperation a teacher might reserve for a gifted but unruly pupil. "What in god's name were you thinking?"

"I love her," Jack replied simply.

Paul heaved a sigh, repeating, "Bloody hell, Jack."

"Stop sounding like a broken record and get me a glass of water."

Paul poured water from a jug into a plastic cup and gave it to Jack. He seated himself at the bedside. "Tracy and the–"

"Butterfly," broke in Jack. "Her name's Butterfly."

"Well whatever you want to call her, she and the baby are fine. So is Laura. Mark and Suzanne Kavanagh are cooperating."

"What about Ryan?"

"He's conscious."

"Are we charging Butterfly?"

Paul spread his hands. "With what? Ryan won't talk to us. Laura says she didn't see anything."

Jack's eyebrows lifted. Laura was usually scrupulous about telling the truth. Why had she lied for Butterfly?

"What about you, Jack? Do you know how Ryan lost his toes?"

Jack shook his head. "When Ryan cut off my toes, I passed out." He didn't elaborate. He needed to talk to Laura and Butterfly, make sure their stories were in sync.

Paul nodded as if that was the answer he'd expected.

"Where are Butterfly and my sister?"

"Laura's around here somewhere. She only left your side to get a coffee. Butterfly's here too with the baby. He's perfectly healthy. The Kavanaghs looked after him like... well like he was their own. They're keeping him under observation as a precaution. And there's also the matter of establishing maternity. There's no real doubt who his mother is. You only have to look at him to see that. But you know how it is."

Jack nodded. Proper procedure had to be observed.

Paul looked at Jack for a moment, then gave another shake of his head. "You're a pain in the arse, Jack. You always have been." He sighed. "But I can't imagine where we'd be without you on the team."

"I'm not the only pain in the arse around here," said Jack, cocking an eyebrow at Paul.

"Yeah well maybe that's why we've always got on so well."

Even as Jack smiled at the sarcastic comment, he was drifting back off into dreamless medicated sleep. Some time later, he had no sense of how long, a murmur of voices broke into his consciousness. He opened his eyes and saw Laura talking to a bespectacled middle-aged man. Noticing that Jack was awake, she smiled at him and said, "Welcome back." There was a strained edge in her voice. As if she'd just received some bad news, but was putting on a brave face.

"Hello, Jack," said the bespectacled man, extending a hand. "I'm Doctor Will Byers."

Jack shook the doctor's hand. "So tell me about the operation."

"It didn't go well, I'm afraid. We were unable to reattach your toes. The tissue damage was too severe."

"Oh. Well thanks for trying." Jack's indifference wasn't a pretence. If someone had asked him to give up two toes in return for Butterfly's baby, he would have gladly agreed. Toes he could live without, but she would have been lost without Charlie.

Doctor Byers spoke about recovery times and the prospect of skin graft surgery once the burns had healed. When he left, Laura said, "Well you don't seem too upset. I'm not sure I'd be so calm if I were you."

"I'm just glad everyone's alive." Jack looked at his sister remorsefully. "I'm sorry you got caught up in this, Laura."

"There's no need to be sorry." She crooked up one side of her mouth. "My life's been about as much fun as a rainy day in Blackpool recently. I was ready for some excitement."

Jack squeezed Laura's hand. "There's something I need to ask you."

"You want to know why I lied to Paul."

"Yes."

"Because I was wrong about Butterfly. You two are perfect for each other."

Wrinkles of surprise crowded Jack's forehead. "You really think that after what she did to Ryan?"

"Especially after what she did to that arsehole. I'd like to think I'd do the same in her position, but I'd probably just lie down and die. She's…" Laura sought the appropriate word, "unusual. And I mean that in a good way. And besides, she saved my life. I can hardly send her to prison after that."

"But what about Naomi? Do you think I can trust Butterfly with Naomi?"

"It depends what you mean by trust. Do you want someone who'll fight for Naomi? Or someone who takes the easy way out when the going gets tough?"

Jack winced inwardly at his sister's not-so-subtle reference to Rebecca. He made no reply. The question didn't need answering.

"Smile," said Laura. "You've got the royal seal of approval. What more do you want?"

That was a good question. What more *did* he want? Rebecca's painfully beautiful face materialised in his mind as vividly as if she was in the room. He'd loved her so much. Never mind a couple of toes, he would have given his life for her. She hadn't given him that chance though. Had suicide been the easy way out of her depression? Or had she been taking back control the only way she could? He imagined himself standing on the edge of Fairlight Cliffs. The wind whipping around him. The sea chewing up the rocks hundreds of feet below. Nothing to stop him from stepping into the abyss. Ending the whole crazy ride. Life distilled to a single choice – jump or don't jump. That was true freedom. It had nothing to do with anyone but yourself.

Laura was right about one thing. Butterfly was as different from Rebecca as day was from night. But there was one parallel – Rebecca had lived and Butterfly was living in the shadow of death. What if Naomi came to love

Butterfly only for some slight wrong movement to fatally dislodge the bullet? Could he put her through that?

"Jack," Laura interrupted his thoughts in a cautioning tone. "You've got *that* look in your eyes." She'd nursed him through his grief after Rebecca's death. She'd come to know only too well when he was dwelling on the past. "Stop over-thinking things. What does this tell you?" She pointed at his heart.

The lines fled Jack's forehead. He looked around himself with sudden urgency. "Where are my clothes?"

"A policeman took them. Whoa," exclaimed Laura as Jack removed his foot from the sling. "What do you think you're doing?"

"I have to see her."

"Hang on." Laura left the room. She reappeared with a wheelchair. She helped Jack into it and pushed him through the corridors to a room kitted out with a bed and cot.

Mother and baby were both asleep, but Butterfly's eyes opened as Jack wheeled himself into the room. She offered him a tired smile. "Hi."

"Hi," Jack whispered back. He peered into the cot and smiled at Charlie's scrunched red face. "He looks like you."

"Everyone keeps telling me that, but I don't see it."

"You will do. Give it time."

"I'm sorry I haven't come to see you, Jack. I didn't want to leave Charlie alone."

"You did right. He needs you more than I do."

"Does he?" There was doubt in Butterfly's voice. "I keep thinking about the Kavanaghs, about everything they had to give him. I have nothing. No money. Nowhere to live. Maybe he would have been better off with them."

Jack looked her in the eyes. "You're his mother. No one can give him what you can. Believe me, I know."

She blinked guiltily away from his gaze. "Laura told me they can't fix your foot."

"It doesn't matter."

"It does. This is my fault. All of it. I agreed to sell my baby. I ran away and let those children die. You and Laura were almost killed because of me. I don't blame you for not wanting me anywhere near your–" Butterfly broke off in surprise as Jack lurched to his feet and planted a kiss on her lips. They stayed like that for a long moment, their lips softening into each other.

When they drew apart, Jack murmured, "I want you…" he glanced at Charlie, "both of you to come and live with us."

Butterfly's eyes were awash with stunned uncertainty. "Are you sure?"

Jack nodded, tenderly holding her gaze.

"OK," she said, her lips spreading into a full smile.

"OK," echoed Jack, almost incredulous laughter welling up in him. It was actually going to happen! They would be a family. "I'm going to have to sit down before I fall down."

He dropped back into the wheelchair. A tiny mewl came from the cot. Charlie's misty blue eyes were open and fixed on Jack. Butterfly reached for a pre-prepared bottle of milk. "Do you mind if I do the honours?" asked Jack.

She hesitated, caught off guard for the second time in minutes.

"It's OK if you want to do it," said Jack.

She handed him the bottle. "If we're going to live together, there has to be trust. Right?"

Trust. Such a vast word. Without it nothing else would work. Both of them were going to have to work on relearning its true meaning. "Right."

Jack lifted Charlie, cushioning him against his chest. He touched the teat to Charlie's lips. When Charlie opened his mouth, Jack put the teat into it.

"You make that look easy," said Butterfly.

"I've had plenty of practice." Jack smiled at Charlie. "Good boy," he cooed as Charlie suckled on the teat. "You and I are going to be best mates."

When Charlie had drunk his fill, Jack burped him, checked to see if his nappy needed changing, then returned him to the cot. Butterfly took Jack's hand and together they watched Charlie sleep.

Chapter 41

Naomi rocked the Moses Basket, singing softly, "Rock-a-bye baby in the treetop..."

She insisted on singing to Charlie every evening when he was put down to sleep. Not that he stayed asleep for long. He usually woke five or six times in the night for a feed. His mewl had strengthened into a warbling cry. He'd grown chubbier in the weeks since coming home from the hospital. Jack could only carry him for a few minutes before his shoulder started throbbing.

When she finished her song, Naomi ever so gently kissed Charlie's forehead. "Night, night, Charlie."

Jack looked on smiling. He never tired of watching Naomi with Charlie. She seemed to have fallen in love with him at first sight. She'd become a proper little mum to him too, changing his nappies, feeding him, playing with him.

"It's your bedtime too," said Jack.

"Can I say goodnight to Butterfly?"

Jack nodded. Naomi ran lightly downstairs. He followed slowly, carefully placing his injured foot on each step. The burns were healing well, but were still sore. Added to which he was struggling to find his new centre of gravity. At first he'd walked like a drunk. A few times – particularly when bending to pick things up – he'd lost his balance and toppled over. Day by day, his stride was adjusting itself to compensate. He no longer needed a walking stick to make it to the shops for a resupply of wet wipes or nappies. The physios were confident he would be back to full mobility within a few months.

He went into the living-room, taking care not to trip over rattles, building blocks and soft toys. They'd been inundated with gifts from Jack's colleagues. He'd never seen so many hardened detectives turn to mush as when he'd taken Charlie into the office. He'd tactfully requested that no more presents be given. Steve had taken no notice. Almost daily he turned up at the house with some new toy that he'd 'just happened to see' on his way over.

The mantelpiece was cluttered with get-well-soon and Christmas cards. In one corner stood a Christmas tree that Naomi and Butterfly had decorated with baubles, tinsel and chocolates. This would be the third Christmas since Rebecca's death, but the first that he'd bought a tree or even put up decorations. Rebecca had always struggled with the long nights and forced jollity of the festive season. Jack wondered with a mixture of excitement and trepidation what that time of year would be like with the new additions to the family.

Naomi was leaning in to kiss Butterfly's cheek. Butterfly had grown too over the past few weeks. Her face and frame had filled out healthily. Her lustrous autumnal hair was now long enough to conceal the puckered scar. She still looked tired, but only in the way all new mothers do. Her headaches and bouts of nausea and dizziness were also becoming increasingly infrequent.

She kissed Naomi back, saying, "Sleep tight."

The two of them had hit it off immediately. It filled Jack with relief and pride – mostly pride – that, despite everything, Naomi remained open and trusting. She hadn't inherited her willingness to see only the best in people from Rebecca or him. That facet of her personality was all her own. It helped that the first time they'd met, Butterfly had broken the ice by telling Naomi, "I'm not looking to replace your mum. All I want is for us to be friends. If that's OK with you."

To which Naomi had nodded and said, "I really like your tattoo. Butterflies are my favourite."

"Then we're definitely going to be good friends," Butterfly had laughingly replied.

As he did every day, Jack reminded himself that he would never take this second chance for granted. He would fully appreciate every single second they had together. "I'll be up in a minute to tuck you in," he said as Naomi headed back upstairs to brush her teeth and change into her pyjamas.

He flopped onto the sofa beside Butterfly. "Little man's spark out. I reckon we might get an hour or two to ourselves."

Butterfly snuggled up. "That sounds like bliss. I've been waiting for a chance to get my hands on you." She twisted to kiss him, but pulled away putting a hand over her mouth to stifle a yawn.

Jack chuckled. "The only thing you'll be getting your hands on is a pillow."

Butterfly kissed him, murmuring, "I promise I'll make it up to you."

As they rose to leave the room, his gaze strayed to the photo of Rebecca. The old pain was still there, but it was different. Less deep than before. Like the ache in his shoulder. He'd offered to take down the photo, but Butterfly had said, "Don't. It's important to keep her memory alive."

Memories. If anyone knew just how important they were it was her.

They made their way upstairs, holding hands, parting as Butterfly went into the bedroom and Jack checked on Naomi. She was stretched out on her bed, staring into an iPad. "Hey, you know that's not allowed at bedtime," Jack quietly remonstrated, holding his hand out.

Naomi handed over the iPad. Jack tucked her in, kissed her and left the room. He found himself infected by Butterfly's yawn. He'd intended to go over the testimony he was due to give at the Kavanaghs upcoming court hearing, but his mind was too foggy. Mark and Suzanne had been denied bail and remanded into custody. The Crown Court agreed with GMP that they posed a significant flight risk. Mark had immediately started pouring money into making sure the case was brought to trial as quickly as possible.

Ryan Mahon on the other hand seemed intent on mutely rotting in prison. He'd refused to speak to both the police and the Public Defender who'd been appointed him. His silence would doubtless have done his dad proud. Not that it would make any difference to his sentencing if he opened his mouth – he was facing a 'life-means-life' sentence regardless – but Jack's colleagues had dug up half-a-dozen murders that bore the hallmark of the Mahon brothers. Ryan could have given some sort of closure to the victims' grieving families. He wasn't about to do that though. He was keeping those cards close to his chest. They were the only power he had left.

Jack crept into the bedroom, careful not to disturb Butterfly and Charlie. Butterfly was lying on her side, facing the Moses Basket. Judging from her soft snoring, she was already asleep. Jack undressed, slid beneath the duvet and curled up against her silky skin. At first it had felt awkward getting into bed with her. He'd lain awake all night riddled with a strange guilt, almost as if he was betraying Rebecca. The following night Butterfly had pulled him to her and they'd made love, exploring every part of each other's body, lingering tenderly on old and new scars. Afterwards he'd felt only contentment.

With a long exhalation, Jack closed his eyes. When he next opened them, a deep silence hung over the room. He'd rolled away from Butterfly. The alarm clock read '1:47 am'. His heart was suddenly beating fast. He'd been asleep for hours. Why hadn't Charlie woken him crying for a feed? He turned to Butterfly. She was lying motionless in the same position. Too motionless.

Fearfully, he sat up. Butterfly's pallor was deathly in the glow of lamplight filtering through the curtains. He touched her shoulder. She stirred and opened her eyes. A faint frown touched her forehead. "What is it, Jack? Are you OK?"

Her voice prompted a soft gurgle from the Moses Basket. "I'm fine," he whispered, bending to kiss her frown away. "Go back to sleep. I'll sort out Charlie."

Smiling gratefully, Butterfly closed her eyes.

After feeding Charlie and rocking him into silence, Jack lay staring at Butterfly as if watching for signs of distress. He thought about the way he'd used to feel in bed with Rebecca before depression sank its claws into her. It had seemed like nothing in the world could touch them. That had turned out to be a blissful illusion. What he felt with Butterfly was real and that was good enough.

OTHER BOOKS BY THE AUTHOR

Now She's Dead

(Jack Anderson Book 1)

What happens when the watcher becomes the watched?

Jack has it all – a beautiful wife and daughter, a home, a career. Then his wife, Rebecca, plunges to her death from the Sussex coast cliffs. Was it an accident or did she jump? He moves to Manchester with his daughter, Naomi, to start afresh, but things don't go as planned. He didn't think life could get any worse...

Jack sees a woman in a window who is the image of Rebecca. Attraction turns into obsession as he returns to the window night after night. But he isn't the only one watching her...

Jack is about to be drawn into a deadly game. The woman lies dead. The latest victim in a series of savage murders. Someone is going to go down for the crimes. If Jack doesn't find out who the killer is, that 'someone' may well be him.

* * *

Don't Look Back

What really haunts Fenton House?

Adam's eyes swelled in horror at the sight that confronted him. Henry was standing with his back against the front door, pale and rigid, his left hand pressed to his neck. Blood was seeping between his fingers, running down his wrist and dripping from his elbow onto the back of Jacob's head. Jacob was facedown on the tiled floor, arms outstretched to either side with blood pooling around his wrists. There was a faintly metallic butcher's shop smell in the air...

After the tragic death of their eleven-year-old son, Adam and Ella are fighting to keep their family from falling apart. Then comes an opportunity that seems too good to be true. They win a competition to live for free in a breathtakingly beautiful mansion on the Cornish Lizard Peninsula. There's just one catch – the house is supposedly haunted.

Mystery has always swirled around Fenton House. In 1920 the house's original owner, reclusive industrialist Walter Lewarne, hanged himself from its highest turret. In 1996, the then inhabitants, George Trehearne, his wife Sofia and their young daughter Heloise disappeared without a trace. Neither mystery was ever solved.

Adam is not the type to believe in ghosts. As far as he's concerned, ghosts are simply memories. Everywhere he looks in their cramped London home he sees his dead son. Despite misgivings, the chance to start afresh is too tempting to pass up. Adam, Ella and their surviving son Henry move into Fenton House. At first, the change of scenery gives them all a new lease of life. But as the house starts to reveal its secrets, they come to suspect that they may not be alone after all…

* * *

Blood Guilt

Is it ever truly possible to atone for killing someone?

After the death of his son in a freak accident, DI Harlan Miller's life is spiralling out of control. He's drinking too much. His marriage and career are on the rocks. But things are about to get even worse. A booze-soaked night out and a single wild punch leave a man dead and Harlan facing a manslaughter charge.

Fast-forward four years. Harlan's prison term is up, but life on the outside holds little promise. Divorced, alone, consumed by guilt, he thinks of nothing beyond atoning for the death he caused. But how do you make up for depriving a wife of her husband and two young boys of their father? Then something happens, something terrible, yet something that holds out a twisted kind of hope for Harlan – the dead man's youngest son is abducted.

From that moment Harlan's life has only one purpose – finding the boy. So begins a frantic race against time that leads him to a place darker than anything he experienced as a policeman and a stark moral choice that compels him to question the law he once enforced.

* * *

Angel Of Death (aka *Lost Angel* in the US)

Murderer? Or heroine? You decide...

Fifteen-year-old Grace Kirby kisses her mum and heads off to school. It's a day like any other day, except that Grace will never return home.

Fifteen years have passed since Grace went missing. In that time, Stephen Baxley has made millions. And now he's lost millions. Suicide seems like the only option. But Stephen has no intention of leaving behind his wife, son and daughter. He wants them all to be together forever, in this world or the next.

Angel is on the brink of suicide too. Then she hears a name on the news that transports her back to a windowless basement. Something terrible happened in that basement. Something Angel has been running from most of her life. But the time for running is over. Now is the time to start fighting back.

At the scene of a fatal shooting, DI Jim Monahan finds evidence of a sickening crime linked to a missing girl. Then more people start turning up dead. Who is the killer? Are the victims also linked to the girl? Who will be next to die? The answers will test to breaking-point Jim's faith in the law he's spent his life upholding.

* * *

Justice For The Damned
(aka *Lost Girls* in the US)

When is a life worth less than the truth?

Melinda has been missing for weeks. The police would normally be all over it, but Melinda is a prostitute. Women in that line of work change addresses like they change lipstick. She probably just moved on.

Staci is determined not to let Melinda become just another statistic added to the long list of girls who've gone missing over the years. Staci is also a prostitute – although not for much longer if DI Reece Geary has anything to do with it. Reece will do anything to win Staci's love. If that means putting his job on the line by launching an unofficial investigation, then so be it.

DI Jim Monahan is driven by his own dangerous obsession. He's on the trail of a psychopath hiding behind a facade of respectability. Jim's investigation has already taken him down a rabbit hole of corruption and depravity. He's about to discover that the hole goes deeper still. Much, much deeper...

* * *

Spider's Web
(aka *Lost Sister* in the US)

'So he wove a subtle web, in a little corner sly...
And merrily did sing, "Come hither, hither, pretty fly..."'

A trip to the cinema turns into a nightmare for Anna and her little sister Jessica, when two men throw thirteen-year-old Jessica into the back of a van and speed away.

The years tick by... Tick, tick... The police fail to find Jessica and her name fades from the public consciousness... Tick, tick... But every time Anna closes her eyes she's back in that terrible moment, lurching towards Jessica, grabbing for her. So close. So agonisingly close... Tick, tick... Now in her thirties, Anna has no career, no relationship, no children. She's consumed by one purpose – finding Jessica, dead or alive.

DI Jim Monahan has a little black book with forty-two names in it. Jim's determined to put every one of those names behind bars, but his investigation is going nowhere fast. Then a twenty-year-old clue brings Jim and Anna together in search of a shadowy figure known as Spider. Who is Spider? Where is Spider? Does Spider have the answers they want? The only thing Jim and Anna know is that the victims Spider entices into his web have a habit of ending up missing or dead.

* * *

The Lost Ones

The truth can be more dangerous than lies...

July 1972

The Ingham household. Upstairs, sisters Rachel and Mary are sleeping peacefully. Downstairs, blood is pooling around the shattered skull of their mother, Joanna, and a figure is creeping up behind their father, Elijah. A hammer comes crashing down again and again...

July 2016

The Jackson household. This is going to be the day when Tom Jackson's hard work finally pays off. He kisses his wife Amanda and their children, Jake and Erin, goodbye and heads out dreaming of a better life for them all. But just hours later he finds himself plunged into a nightmare...

Erin is missing. She was hiking with her mum in Harwood Forest. Amanda turned her back for a moment. That was all it took for Erin to vanish. Has she simply wandered off? Or does the blood-stained rock found where she was last seen point to something sinister? The police and volunteers who set out to search the sprawling forest are determined to find out. Meanwhile, Jake launches an investigation of his own – one that will expose past secrets and present betrayals.

Is Erin's disappearance somehow connected to the unsolved murders of Elijah and Joanna Ingham? Does it have something to do with the ragtag army of eco-warriors besieging Tom's controversial quarry development? Or is it related to the fraught phone call that distracted Amanda at the time of Erin's disappearance?

So many questions. No one seems to have the answers and time is running out. Tom, Amanda and Jake must get to the truth to save Erin, though in doing so they may well end up destroying themselves.

ABOUT THE AUTHOR

Ben is an award winning writer and Pushcart Prize nominee with a passion for gritty crime fiction. His short stories have been widely published in the UK, US and Australia. In 2011 he self-published *Blood Guilt*. The novel went on to reach no.2 in the national e-book download chart, selling well over 150000 copies. In 2012 it was picked up for publication by Head of Zeus. Since then, Head of Zeus has published three more of Ben's novels – *Angel of Death, Justice for the Damned and Spider's Web*. In 2016 his novel *The Lost Ones* was published by Thomas & Mercer.

Ben lives in Sheffield, England, where – when he's not chasing around after his son, Alex – he spends most of his time shut away in his study racking his brain for the next paragraph, the next sentence, the next word...

If you'd like to learn more about Ben or get in touch, you can do so at *bencheetham.com*

38898350R00167

Printed in Poland
by Amazon Fulfillment
Poland Sp. z o.o., Wrocław